UP SHE GOES

and

THE BREIGHTON TWINS

by

Joan Vass

First published in 2004

Published by
Paul Mould Publishing UK
in association with
Empire Publishing Services USA

Library of Congress C-I-P data can be obtained from
the British Library, Boston Spa

ISBN 1-904959-15-6

Printed in Great Britain by
CLE Print Limited

Dedication

I dedicate this book to all my family both past and present.

Acknowledgements

I would particularly like to mention the following people who have helped and supported me during the many years I have been waiting to have my books published:

My daughter Mandy, my sister Rose Turner, Peggy Wight from Canada, Vicky and Bill Andrews, Chris & Sue Vass and of course Paul Mould!

To you all a huge thank you!

An extra thank you to Chris Vass for my wonderful website www.jvass-author.co.uk

Love Joan x

UP SHE GOES!

CHAPTER 1

The raw wind whistled around the large hanger and the snow some three days old had frozen into dark dirty patches. In contrast the surrounding countryside resembled a scene from the arctic. But this was England in 1942.

A batch of recruits sat restlessly in the hanger of the Air Force camp at Innsworth Gloucestershire this was their first introduction to life in the armed forces. They had been kited out with uniforms and learned to clean brass buttons until they gleamed like gold. The endless polishing of black flat shoes that refused to shine made arms feel like lead. The skill of laying out kit for inspection was a frustration that relentlessly dogged them. Then these shivering rookies emerged from the camp hairdresser with hands plunged deep into pockets with coat collars turned up against the biting wind that now whipped around exposed ears.

A row of neat trestle tables were set out in the vast hanger. W.A.A.F. Officers thumbed through papers as they interviewed the new recruits in preparation for their chosen trade.

Muriel's stomach turned over as she studied the stern faces of the officers. Blimey they look more like prison warders, she thought despondently, I'll never get through this lot.

It had been relatively easy in the London recruiting office some two days previous when she blurted out her story in a moment of blind panic to the recruiting officer as to why she wanted to join the Air Force under age. Stumbling over her words and praying the officer understood she was stopped in her tracks when the officer put up her hand. There was a brief pregnant silence before the officer explained how much she admired her courage to be truthful albeit at the eleventh hour, before going on to make it clear that she would not stand in her way. Her steely blue eyes met Muriel's as she added. "You must understand that I cannot help you further. It will be entirely up to your own initiative as to how you break through the rest of the red tape!"

That morning in the Acton recruiting office had seemed to be the longest she had ever known. A dozen girls were waiting to be interviewed but her ordeal was over. And so with hands clasped tightly in her lap in an attempt to hide her anxiety about the problem that now lay before her she introduced herself to the two girls sitting nearest.

The slim attractive young woman she discovered was Edie. A mischievous bubbly personality with an obvious cockney sense of humour. By contrast Phyllis was quiet and reserved. A tall shapeless figure of a woman whose hair was scraped back severely in a bun and whose head seemed rarely out of a book. It had taken Edie the best part of the morning to establish that Phyllis came from Hertfordshire.

The three young women from very different

backgrounds had been accepted into the Air Force by the time coffee was served and had bonded as mates.

Now feeling more relaxed having poured out her confession to the W.A.A.F. officer, Muriel explained to her new found friends... "You see my Dad gave his permission with no problem but my Mum went berserk. She would have moved heaven and earth to have stopped me from joining up. So there was no way I intended hanging around until I was of age that would have given her time to get to work on my Dad... so here I am!"

"How old are you then?" Edie asked.

"Seventeen and one month exactly."

Edie's eyebrows shot up in surprise because Muriel looked older than her years.

She was a well built girl with some residue of puppy fat, apart from that she was relatively attractive. But her strong personality was often misunderstood, She had been accused of being arrogant, but the reality was she was shielding many fears and insecurities for her young life had been cloistered amongst a strict Salvation Army background. She had never seen the inside of a cinema, and dance halls were dens of iniquity according to her mother and grandparents. It had been instilled into her since a child that these worldly pursuits were the works and places of the devil. If the truth be known, her mothers fear of joining the armed forces at such a vulnerable age was that she would be exposed to all of these temptations, and worse, enjoy them!

Throwing her hands in the air Edie exclaimed' "Christ, is this the extent of yer problems joining up under age? The solution is easy mate, all yer 'ave ter do is change the year of yer birth on all yer documents. Make yerself a year older... easy!"

Muriel looked puzzled but deeply interested in this new world of deceit and intrigue. Turning to her new found friend she asked... "But how?"

Phyllis was listening her face pinched in disapproval. Edie moved closer and dropped her voice to a whisper. "When we get to camp, buy a bottle of Milton, they sell it in the NAFFI, then I'll show yer 'ow it's done."

The delicate operation of fraudulently changing documents had now taken place in the toilets. With the wicked deed completed no one would have known the difference... no one that is, except Muriel who now sat with teeth chattering as her turn came nearer.

"Fer Christ's sake smile girl!" Edie remarked, seemingly amused by the intrigue and drama about to unfold. "Anyone would fink you'd robbed a bleedin' bank to see the look on yer face... it's a dead give-away... so lighten up."

"It's all right for you, you haven't got to face this little lot." hissed Muriel.

Edie sighed and with eyes flaying up into her head she snatched the document saying; "For Christ's sake give 'em 'ere. Lets 'ave another look."

Edie glanced over the paperwork with the eye of an expert. "Naa... never in a million years will they guess." she whispered confidently, "You'll get through this don't worry. You've got this bloody far and we're all sticking togever aint we?" she added looking directly at Phyllis who smiled a faint half hearted smile that screamed of doubt.

Edie began powdering her nose with one eye on the officer who was about to call another batch of names.

"What's all the glamour for? There aren't any blokes in here" Muriel commented but before Edie could reply her name was called.

"I hope we all get this Balloon Operating Muriel remarked to Phyllis in an attempt to forget her fears, but Phyllis looked pained. "I'm beginning to wonder what it involves?"

"We shall know soon enough" Then a new wave of anxiety swept over Muriel as she burst out, "Do you reckon these papers will be all right? Only I'm worried sick about them."

Phyllis looked down her nose before remarking. "It's certainly not the sort of thing that I normally approve of. I could hardly teach my children in Sunday School such devious tricks, but it's entirely up to you. I thought you came from a Christian background." she remarked icily before dismissing the subject.

Just as Muriel was considering what a blooming comforter she turned out to be she heard... 2020942 Airwoman Berry, come here please."

The WAAF Officer was now searching the faces of the remaining new recruits Muriel lurched forward, the faces before her a complete blur.

Just at the point when she thought she would throw up the familiar voice of Edie was heard in passing; "Go on mate, give it all yer got!"

Muriel sat down grateful for the seat that had been offered. She found herself within inches of the searching glare of the officer who began to scrutinise every document slowly and thoroughly. The sweat began to trickle down Muriel's spine. She wiped her wet hands on to her skirt that thankfully was well hidden beneath the table. The face of the officer swam before her as her heart pounded in her head. Then with the final document placed to one side the officer said "So... you want to become a Balloon Operator do you?"

"Yes Ma'am" came the relieved response.

"Lets have no illusions about this trade Berry, it's tough and dangerous, very technical, exciting and rewarding. You will be trained for a period of twelve weeks at one of our training camps. We cannot at this stage say where that will be. There are eight subjects to study and pass by examination. You will then be posted to either an industrial city or maybe a remote site in the country."

Muriel shuffled in her seat listening intently to this account of her future trade, but the officer hadn't finished. "All balloon sites are self contained which means each operator has to take her share of cooking and domestic duties. There are twelve girls to a crew with a sergeant and corporal in charge. Night duties are not an option, they work on a rota system of two hours on duty and four off, this applies from six in the evening until six the following morning. However it does not entitle you to a day of rest the following day." Muriel straightened her back to ease the tension whilst the officer continued. "You should get a day off once a week but again a lot depends on the compliment of the crew at the time. You will be required to take a self defence course for your own safety during night duties. Finally a word of warning. The

6

enormous amount of physical strength that is required for this work plus the open air life does tend to develop the body. I note with respect, that you are on the big side, so if you don't mind the possibility of getting somewhat larger and think you can cope with this tough life then I will recommend you for this trade,"

Muriel burst out enthusiastically "It certainly does appeal to me Ma'am, and I'm sure I can cope."

"Very well then, that is all." she said dismissing Muriel abruptly.

The babble of conversation was deafening as Muriel entered the barrack room. Girls were chatting excitedly about the their chosen trade. Muriel searched for Edie through the sea of faces. Suddenly Edie was pushing her way through the crowd shouting... "Bash Bash... how did yer get on?"

Muriel turned around to see who she was addressing, but then got caught up in the excitement of what had just transpired and then jumping up and down she yelled "I'm in... she passed me... papers and all!"

"Good old Basher... see... I told yer so!" Edie yelled as she turned her back to search for someone in the crowd.

Muriel gave Edie a good poke in the back and asked... "Er... excuse me... but who is this Basher person you keep referring to?"

Edie threw back her head and laughed uproariously; "You are me old mate, no offence, it's just... well... yer looks like a Basher, yer build yer personality... yer know..." she added rather cautiously as she flung a reassuring arm around the shoulder of her mate. Then swiftly changing the subject asked "What trade did yer get after all?"

Basher paused while she considered her newly acquired name, then smiled at the sheer cheek before replying. "Balloon Operator why?"

"Oh boy, 'ope we all train togever Bash and get some gorgeous blokes to teach us" she said smiling.

"Men! That's all you ever think about" Basher replied but amused by her friends frankness.

"What else?" Edie said her eyes twinkling.

It was Basher's turn to scan the crowded room." Seen anything of Phyll?"

"Aven't seen 'er all morning" Edie replied flatly.

Both girls spotted Phyllis at the same moment. She was sitting on her bed reading, totally oblivious to the noise going on around her. "Hey, there she is Bash, go and asked 'er 'ow she got on"

Basher pushed her way through the excited group of girls "How did you get on then Phyl?" she asked.

Phyllis lifted her head momentarily from her book. "Fine, I got the Balloon Operating job. It sounds hard if you ask Me." she remarked her face creasing in pain.

"But it sounds challenging. Edie's got it too you know, so far so good. Hope we all get the same training course. Mind you, the blokes had better stand by their beds once Edie gets loose!"

Phyllis gave a weak smile but made no comment instead returned to her book dismissing Basher at the same time. Basher sat on the edge of her bed watching Edie chatting first to one then the other. How attractive she is Basher considered. Her bright blue eyes sparkled and her full sensuous mouth showed a set of brilliant white even teeth when she smiled. Raven black hair with curls that clung to edge of her cap and her slim well proportioned body left no doubt in Basher's mind that heads would turn once she was in the company of a mixed camp.

"All right you lot calm down," roared the sergeant from the doorway. The din suddenly ceased, for one of the first things they had learned in a short space of time was the application of discipline. "Collect your feeding irons then line up outside this door," she crisply ordered. The babble of conversation started up again as the girls scrambled into their lockers to grab their knives, forks, spoons and mugs. "Shut it! ...Now we are going to march quickly and quietly to the cook house for lunch. I want you back here in good time to prepare for your kit inspection this afternoon. Do I make myself quite clear?"

There were moans groans and grunts at this spectacular news, but all reluctantly agreed. The tall slim sergeant with her short cropped hair, thin lips and rosy cheeks that were devoid of any make up eyed her new recruits with some contempt, but obviously enjoying the power she had over them. When they were lined up in some resemblance of order she bellowed with great authority...

"Squad.........atten....tion. Forw.......ard...... march. left right left right, no talking in the ranks. Come on pick'em up, left right. Christ you lot need some lessons in marching... left right... don't know yer left from yer bloody right?"

The massive cookhouse had two entrances both north and south of the building, and queues had formed at both ends. Basher was near the front of the queue so was able to see the set up. The cooks stood in the serving area their white uniforms crisp and clean with ladles at the ready. Tea urns stood on separate tables adjacent to the serving bay and were billowing steam. The duty officer arrived and paused whilst his eyes swept around the rows of spotlessly clean wooden tables. All eyes were riveted on him as he painstakingly inspected every pan of food, tasting each dish in turn. Anticipation was now reaching its climax as a chorus of 'Why Are We Waiting' rippled through the queues. He moved to the tea urns pouring some into a cup he tasted it with the panache of a professional wine taster. When satisfied that all was in order he nodded to the Flight Sergeant Chef to begin the service.

Those in front of Basher could see what was on offer and passed the word back with lightening rapidity. The murmur rose to a crescendo with the clanking ladles and cutlery being slung on to tables then the hissing of the tea urns added to the pandemonium.

Basher collected her meal then realised that Edie was only about six behind her.

"I'll save a place Ede" she promised, "And hey... bring some bread will you?"

"Not a problem mate, save a place for Phyll, she's right at the back. She'd be too bloody late for her own funeral that one.

The girls who stood nearby tittered at Edie's comments. Basher rushed to find a table with three empty seats and stood chairs against the table to reserve them. Edie quickly arrived and slung the bread in the middle of the table saying,

"Ere get this lot down yer."

Basher cut into her pie and began to examine the contents. "Blimey what's in these pies Ede? ...It looks horrible."

"Minced up aircrew!" came the quick response.

Basher pulled a face. "Do you mind? For gawd sake what yet trying to do put me off me grub?"

"All contributions gratefully received, I'm starving, could eat a 'orse never mind the aircrew" Edie remarked as she spotted Phyllis nearer to the front of the queue. She stood up waving her arms madly and bawled. "Oye...Phyll...we're over 'ere, come on, 'urry up."

Phyllis smiled her usual weak smile that often indicated embarrassment. Finally she ambled toward her two friends in her usual dream world, seemingly oblivious as to what was going on around her.

Basher took a swig of her tea and spat it out. "God love me... what the hell's in this tea it's bitter?" she said shuddering.

Edie looked first at Basher then at Phyllis, her mouth dropping open.

"Come off it... didn't you know they lace the tea with bromide?"

"What for?" Basher asked naively.

"Oh gawd blimey we've a right one 'ere. Don't tell me you didn't know?"

Edie yelled making certain that all in the immediate vicinity heard her. Then suddenly noting Basher's blank look she continued... "You really don't know do yer? Clearly not wanting to embarrass her friend further she turned her attention to Phyllis "They wouldn't 'ave to bovver wiv 'er drinks because she obviously finks it's just to pee fru!"

A titter of laughter went around at this remark whilst Phyllis glared at Edie as if wishing she would drop dead, whilst Basher felt her cheeks burning for she dare not admit how little she knew about this subject. Her sketchy knowledge had been picked up from working colleagues in the past. She smiled as she recalled the time in her childhood when her younger sister had dared to approach their mother to ask where babies came from. Poor Mum had hidden her face with acute embarrassment and resentment at being asked such a question.

Mum had muttered that they would be told when they were fourteen. It then occurred to Basher that at seventeen she was out in the big bad world a war raging and *still* none the wiser, as poor old mum had never summoned up the courage to explain the facts of life to her two daughters. But school of life was about to begin and Basher was to learn a great deal more other than Balloon Operating!

CHAPTER 2

"Come on everybody.... up you get.... rise and shine!" the voice of the flight sergeant jarred on the nerves of the new airwomen first thing in the morning. As the barrack room lights blazed heads appeared from under blankets and eyes had to be shielded from the brilliant glare of the light. Whilst fingers clutched at the meagre bedding and quickly went numb from the cold air of the unheated room. Basher lay rubbing her thighs to relieve the cold that had almost paralysed her from the waist down during the night. She had never slept in such uncomfortable conditions in her life. Edie's bed was next to Bashers. Her blanket was pulled tightly under her chin and with teeth chattering as her body convulsed into bouts of sever shivering. Her usual cheerful self temporarily lost in the misery of the moment.

"This is worse than Stalag bleedin' two" she moaned.

"You can say that again! My mattresses came apart during the night and the cold air went right through to my bones" Basher complained as she bent to pull on her large dark blue bloomers.

"And yer arse is tattooed wiv the bed springs!" Edie noted. The flight sergeant reappeared just then to check her charges. She crashed a rolled up newspaper against the barrack room door yelling... "Wakey! Wakey! ...Come on... get a move on... your hot baths await you!" she teased.

Edie's eyes narrowed, she sat on the edge of her bed pulling on her thick grey lisle stockings. "I'll swing for that bleedin' cow before long," she threatened, "She's a bloody sadist she is!"

The ablutions were situated some yards from the barrack room and could easily have been mistaken for cattle sheds. The only protection from the bitter weather was a corrugated sheet of tin that was placed either end of a line of ten stone sinks, a cold tap to each sink that had overflowed during the night leaving massive icicles hanging from them. The ground was frozen solid with dark puddles of ice scattered randomly between the barrack room and the sinks. It was essential to hurry or the sinks would be quickly occupied causing further waiting in the arctic conditions. Edie and Basher tried to walk as quickly as they could but Basher suddenly went down with a thud, her rear end so cold it obliterated any pain. Edie giggled momentarily and offered her mate her hand.

"Up yer get Bash, not quite time for the winter Olympics yet!" Her laughter quickly diminished when she had to break the thick icicles from her tap and bowl.

"Blimey it's enough to freeze the balls off of everything, never mind the brass monkeys" she moaned.

"I'll never complain about our cold bathroom at home again, not after this lot" remarked Basher as she splashed the icy water over her face.

The new batch of recruits was lined up on the parade ground immediately after breakfast for their first inspection. The crown of their caps stood up like cottage loaves, with thick overcoats making them look like oversized teddy bears. Neatly folded gas capes strapped across their shoulders and weighty khaki bags carrying gas masks slung across their chests. Heavy flat shoes crippled every one of them.

The duty sergeant was clearly enjoying the power that this parade in excess of one hundred young women, afforded her. Standing erect in front of them with an air of superiority she bawled...

"Squad...... atten...tion!" What little training had so far taught them was that they smartly clicked their clumsy shoes together at this command.

"Stand.... at... ease!" Her voice echoed over the Gloucestershire countryside.

"What man would fancy that?" Basher remarked through the side of her mouth.

Edie giggled, "She ain't interested in men mate" Basher looked puzzled which made Edie giggle all the more. They stood for what appeared to be hours not daring to move an inch whilst the biting wind penetrated their thick layers of clothing and feet and fingers feeling as if they no longer belonged to their owners.

At long last the duty officer arrived to carry out her inspection. She strode up and down each line carefully scrutinizing each woman. The wind occasionally caught her voice as she could be heard saying. "Get that hair off of your collar" and then... "Don't appear on this parade again until those buttons shine properly"

Basher stood motionless her body rigid her eyes riveted directly ahead of her. The officer passed without comment. Phew! Basher thought, thank God for that. With the inspection over each squadron was marched from the parade ground into different directions. Basher's squad was halted outside one of the gas chambers. The corporal in charge issued full gas equipment and instructed them to put them on. Shrieks of laughter erupted when Basher appeared looking like the original Bessie Bunter. The baggy oilskin trousers and massive jacket covered her entire body when the helmet was pulled over her head her face appeared like a full moon. The corporal explained the details of the exercise. They were to enter the chamber in threes, take off their gas mask get a good whiff of the gas before coming out. Bashers group went in first and within a few moments emerged coughing and spluttering with tears steaming down their faces. "Blimey it's to be hoped gerry never drops any of that stuff it's enough to bloodywell kill yer" Edie remarked having now sufficiently recovered from her bout of coughing.

Basher was still coughing as if her lungs were about to explode. "You can say that again" Basher said trying to control the spasm.

It was then that Edie began to giggle uncontrollably. "Bash you should just see yerself in that get up. If I 'adn't already named yer Basher this would certainly 'ave been the moment ter do it. But a word ter the wise, if we 'ave to wear this gear on our balloon site fer Christ's sake don't go near the bleedin' fing, or yer might find yerself 'undreds of feet in the air at the end of a cable!"

Basher was not amused but hurt by her mate's cruel suggestion. Swinging round on her and near to tears she retorted "Very funny... have you quite finished? Frankly I would rather have puppy fat than risk a bad name for dropping my drawers for anything in trousers." Edie pulled a face as she always did when she knew she had over-stepped the mark.

Phyllis who had been listening was not going to allow her to get away so lightly. She turned on Edie and in her sternest voice said. "I think you can be diabolically cruel... unnecessarily so," then directing her comments to Basher added "It has puzzled me for ages why you suddenly had a name change, now I realize it was *her* who gave it to you. It's not very complimentary, but still that's up to you" she said shrugging her shoulders.

Edie realising the tide was turning against her did what she always did, changed the subject dramatically. "Crumbs look at this little lot Bash.... that girl has nearly passed out. It makes me feel bad to watch 'em" she remarked as she turned her head dramatising the entire situation.

Basher shook her head. "You've missed your vacation mate, you should have gone on the stage."

The corporal appeared and instructed those who had been through the chamber to change and fold their gear neatly away. "Off you go to the NAFFI for your tea break, I've no doubt you could do with a cup after this ordeal" she remarked sympathetically.

The day dragged on endlessly with lectures followed by more marching and drilling around the barrack square. The comparative laziness of the evening was a welcome break. Some girls attempted to light a fire in the belly stove that was situated in the centre of the hut. Others wrote letters blowing into their hands every now and again to keep their circulation going.

The flight sergeant could be seen disappearing into the

sergeants' room that adjoined the entrance to the hut.

"Can't leave us alone for five bloody minutes." Edie moaned as she huddled around the stove with the fond hope it might eventually ignite.

Basher began taunting her mate knowing it would wind her up. She considered it poetic for her cruel remarks earlier on. "Go on... you know you like her really... the sound of that melodious voice sends you in ecstasy. Come on own up"

"Like a bleedin' 'ole in the 'ead" Edie said now rising to the bait.

The teasing exchange was about to turn when the flight sergeant appeared with some notes in her hand.

"Quiet" she commanded as she stomped to the centre of the room pulling a chair with her as she went. She clambered up and stood above the rest. Silence fell like a stone. They all knew this was serious stuff.

"I've some news that most of you have been waiting for. Gather round so that you all can hear me" she ordered.

A murmur rose as they all crowded around closely.

"Berry?"

"Yes flight" Basher bawled.

"You have been accepted as a Balloon Operator as has Smith and Bourne."

Basher and Edie yelled for joy jumping up and down hugging each other, whilst Phyllis stood like a statue smiling wistfully.

"Quiet! Now listen. You three will be going to a Balloon Training School, but first you have a month of hard disciplinary training at Morecambe... and not before time! ...This does apply to you all by the way."

Edie pulled one of her faces but the flight sergeant hadn't finished.

"You will all report to the cookhouse tomorrow morning at 04.00 hours complete with full kit. After breakfast you will be issued with a packed lunch and taken to the local railway station. Is this clear to you all and do we have any questions so far?"

"Yes flight" Basher spoke up

"Where is the Balloon Training camp?"

"I haven't the foggiest idea" the flight sergeant answered curtly.

A girl from the back asked. "What about the rest of us, have we got the trades we applied for?"

"Oh yes. Now be quiet while I read out the rest of the names and trades."

The list was quickly gone through before the flight sergeant advised them all. "I would get into bed sharpish if I were you, you've only a few hours sleep left.

The hub-bub of excitement mounted the moment the flight sergeant left the room. Edie did somersaults in the middle of the floor before hugging Basher as she cried "To fink we'll be out of this lot by morning Bash... yippeeeeeee"

The inmates of the barrack room stood around in groups chatting about their own particular chosen trade. Future cooks, telephonist and wireless operators all talking at once. Someone turned on the radio and Jo Loss was playing 'In The Mood' Edie grabbed Basher's hand and attempted to jive, but Basher had no idea where to begin.

The moment Edie realised she broke away and danced solo around the hut finally flinging herself on her bed with exhaustion.

Phyllis in the mean time had begun to lay out her kit, meticulously checking each item before packing it neatly away in her kit bag. When Edie spotted the intense look on the face of her colleague she called "Come on Phyll, get out yer silk stockings there's bound to be bags of blokes where we're going." Edie was now raving euphorically about the proposed move, but Phyllis simply glared in disgust.

"I haven't got any silk stockings and I'm not particularly interested in men either!" It seemed that for the first time since they had met Edie appeared slightly sensitive to the icy response of Phyllis, but in her usual manner attempted to get away with it by counting on her special brand of humour.

"Get 'er, camp as a row of tents... I reckon yer 'iding yer light under a bleedin' bushel if the truth be known. Yer probably raring ter go... the quiet one's are always the worst."

Phyllis went taut her face lighting up like a beacon as she glared at Edie, if looks could have killed Edie would have dropped there and then. But without a further word Phyllis returned to her packing. Edie's eyes met Bashers, she pulled a face and shrugged her shoulders, but then realising as usual, she had gone too far, she appealed to Phyllis. "Aw come on gal, snap out of it, let yer 'air down, I'm only kiddin'."

CHAPTER 3

Dark clouds hung heavily over the vast expanse of ocean whilst the biting wind whipped up rough waves across the Morecambe promenade jostling the three girls as they dragged their feet wearily along uneven pavements. They were forced to change their kit bags at intervals from shoulder to shoulder because pain seared down their arms from the weight.

Just twelve hours previously they had left Gloucester station full of anticipation of this moment. Morecambe a holiday town in peace time, on the north east coast of Britain had the girls imagining to be buzzing with activity. On their arrival they had been met and given instructions to proceed to their billets. This was to be their home for the next few weeks. Their landlady would give further information on arrival they were advised.

Having now followed the directions for about a mile with no sign of the road they were trying to locate, with intermittent rain soaking the paper that Basher was clutching, making the ink run words into each other made the information almost impossible to read.

"At least we're together" Phyllis remarked hoping it would raise the spirits of her colleagues.

"Yes but look at the poxy plac! Hotels boarded up, bleedin' barbed wire on the beach, sandbags everywhere. Charming I'm sure!" Edie moaned.

"What do you expect? There *is* a war on you know".

Basher peered at the next road sign trying to read it in the half light. Then against yet another gust of wind she yelled. "I think this might be it".

"You need fucking glasses mate. That's Windermere Avenue not Western." Edie retorted irritably. Then slinging her kit bag to the ground in an act of defiance she began dragging it behind her.

"You'll wear a hole in that" warned Basher.

"Don't give a stuff." Edie replied now gathering pace.

Basher and Phyllis let their mate trundle ahead of them she was in a foul mood and best out of the way.

"Here we are at last!" Phyllis announced relieved. "Look this *really* is it... Western Avenue.

"Thank God for that. Oye Ede... come on back. We've found it" Basher yelled.

Finally the three girls stood outside number seventy-six. So this was to be their home for the next month Basher considered. It was a large rambling Victorian townhouse with steps leading down to a basement. They peered through the lace curtains and could see a huge fire flickering in the half light with two girls huddled around it with outstretched hands.

"Looks cosy" Phyllis remarked.

"Never mind bleedin' cosy, lets get in before I die of pneumonia" moaned Edie.

A rotund middle aged woman answered the door. "Ah you've arrived at last. Come on in you look frozen just sit yourselves by that fire and I'll bring you a nice cup of tea. You must be exhausted after such a long journey."

They all stood like stuffed pigs until the landlady left

the room, Then glad to off load their kit and remove their heavy overcoats they pulled up armchairs around the fireplace and began to rub the life back into their frozen hands.

The landlady returned with a tray of piping hot tea and thick slices of toast dripping with fresh butter. "Come on now girls, I'm sure you must be ready for this it's been a heavy day for you. When you've finished I'll show you to your room" she said, before disappearing back into the kitchen.

In silence they gulped down the hot tea that tasted like nectar in comparison to the bromide laced tea they had endured for their breakfast. The toast was a treat they had long forgotten. The warmth of the fire and their refreshment began to spread through their bodies until their faces radiated like beacons.

"She seems a nice lady" Phyllis remarked to her two friends.

Edie's eyes rolled in her head. "I prefer to reserve me judgment."

The landlady was back again announcing cheerfully "Now allow me to introduce myself properly. I'm Mrs Williams. My sister and I run this establishment; of course before the war we were more commonly known as seaside landladies. But it's nice to be able to help the war effort no matter how small. Now then if you all collect your things I'll show you to your room."

Then having climbed what seemed like a hundred stairs the girls found themselves puffing and blowing on the threshold of an attic bedroom.

Two single beds were side by side with a small table

dividing them. The third was situated under the sloping roof.

The window was situated into the sloping roof, which let in some light, but alas the scenery was the roof tops of adjoining houses. The room had a chinzy look about it. The wallpaper had small red roses hanging in bunches with a few green leaves. The bedroom furniture was brown, a single bedside table each and one single wardrobe between the three of them. Alongside was a chest of drawers, which gave them a drawer each for their smalls. Mrs Williams bounced into the room exclaiming; "Here we are then. You must familiarise yourselves with the fire drill that's attached to the back of the door. I'll leave you to unpack. When you are ready please return downstairs and I'll explain the rules of the house, as well as your daily instructions." With that she left the room and quietly closed the door.

"I reckon we've a right one 'ere" Edie announced as soon as the woman was out of earshot.

"Don't be so awful Edie, she seems a perfectly kind respectable lady to me."

Phyllis said defensively as she began unpacking her kit. Edie looked at Basher her eyes flaying in her head. The two of them then quickly began pulling their kit from the bag and ramming it in the drawers out of the way. The bedroom was so cold their main concern was to get back to that fire as quickly as possible.

Once downstairs they grabbed two empty chairs and resumed warming their hands. It was then Mrs Williams shuffled back and looked surprised to see only two of them. "Is your friend not ready yet?" she enquired.

"You'll soon get used to 'er, she'll be too bloody late for 'er own funeral" Edie announced as she held up her legs to get them warm.

Mrs Williams mouth went into a thin line and it was clear she was not amused. The once beaming smile turned into a dark scowl. "I don't like to hear bad language from my girls. It's not nice coming from young ladies." she said as she left the room.

Edie's face coloured slightly but as soon as Mrs Williams had left Edie pulled one of her faces and remarked. "Stupid old cow."

"Perhaps she's religious." Basher suggested.

"Gawd preserve us 'ope not. No wonder sister Phyllis likes 'er, but I'll tell yer this Bash she 'adn't better start treating us as if we are at Finishing School, I am as I am and that's it! She can like it or lump it."

Phyllis bustled in followed by the landlady. "Sorry to have kept you waiting. I do like to do things thoroughly" she said addressing Mrs Williams.

Mrs Williams smiled her approval before sitting down. Her rather oversized breasts rested on the table and her bottom seemed to overspill each side of the chair. Her rough hands were clasped before her and wisps of grey hair clung to her sweaty brow.

"There are twelve of you in this house and a very nice bunch of girls they are too. So I hope you are all going to get on well together" she began as she looked at Edie. "Breakfast is served at seven fifteen, this gives you plenty of time to be ready for your parade which takes place at eight fifteen.

Your parade takes place right outside the front door.

Your sergeant will be here in the morning to give you further instructions. A light lunch is served at twelve thirty sharp you cannot afford to dawdle for you have to be back on duty again at one thirty. The evening meal begins at six and you will attend meals in full dress. I don't allow slovenly behaviour. You are then free to do as you please, but if you go out you must be back by ten sharp, the door is locked at this hour."

Edies eyes rolled in her head at this announcement, but Mrs Williams hadn't finished.

"We do expect you to make your own beds before you leave in the morning. One further thing, I provide cocoa and biscuits at nine in the evening for those of you who are in. I count heads at eight forty five, if you are not in at that hour then I'm afraid you miss out. One piece of motherly advice, I would forget all ideas of 'painting the town red' you will quickly discover you have little energy for such pleasures after all the marching you are required to do. In any event there is little left in this town for a social life. But I hope your stay is a pleasant one. If you have any questions then fire away."

"What about our laundry. How does that get done?" Phyllis enquired,

"You must have it parcelled up ready on Monday morning making certain it is clearly marked with your name. It will be returned to you on Fridays" Mrs Williams rose at this point and announced "I now have to attend to the evening meal, it will be served in a quarter of an hour."

The three girls sat in contemplative silence for a few moments then Phyllis said "I'm going to freshen up before the meal, anyone coming?"

Basher could feel Edie's agitation so readily agreed. Once in the bedroom Phyllis smiled to herself as she gathered her toilet bag and towel. "I'm going to be quite happy here, it's a lovely comfortable home and the landlady is so nice." she said simply.

"Trust you... yer really 'avn't live 'ave yer?" Edie exploded.

Phyllis looked shocked at Edie's outburst, but she was now in full flow.

"I've met 'er type before. All sweetness and light providing you obey *her* rules. She's worse than the bleedin' Gestapo. We 'ad more freedom back in camp. Fancy trying to bribe us wiv a poxy cup of cocoa... get real! We didn't 'ave to be in till midnight 'eiver... Yer don't fink she does this fer the love of it do yer? No mate she'll be on a nice little earner from this lot I can tell yer. The likes of you won't 'ave any problems" She said looking directly at Phyllis, "But just watch the 'over side of 'er when I start" she threatened as she swept out of the room banging the door behind her.

"Oh dear I do hope we aren't going to have any unpleasantness" Phyllis whined.

"Don't take any notice of her PhyLl. She's wild because Mrs Williams had a go at her about her swearing."

The dining room was filled with the babble of conversation as all twelve girls sat around the long table waiting to be served with their evening meal. Introductions had been made and exchanges of experiences and previous postings were the main topic of conversation.

The clatter of knives and forks made a din as everyone

27

delved into a hearty home made Lancashire hot pot.

"What's *she* like?" Edie enquired as soon as Mrs Williams disappeared into the kitchen. "Strict... but the secret is not getting caught" the girl advised smiling.

"How long' ave you been 'ere then?" Edie asked of her neighbour.

"Two weeks, and its hard slog. I warn you."

"What have you done so far then?" Basher pressed.

"Marching, marching and more marching. Lectures and physical training. You'll discover muscles you never thought you had!"

"Hey don't forget the injections!" someone piped up from the other end of the table.

Edie looked horrified and momentarily lost her colour. "What bleediin' injections are yer on about naaaaa?" she almost screamed.

The girl at the end of the table was enjoying this rather sadistic scenario as she watched the newcomers' horrified expressions. She continued with all the gory details. "This coming Friday you are in for a treat when you receive a cocktail of injections. They do it on Fridays so that you have the weekend to get over it. They aren't silly. You on the other hand get a week-end of shivers and the most abominable pain you'll ever had to endure."

Edie looked flushed and upset by the forthcoming prospect as she burst out with "It sounds fuckin' charming, I must 'ave been mad to join this lot!"

The following morning at eight fifteen sharp a sergeant stood on the threshold of their doorway and hollered "Come on you lot... look sharp... everyone out!"

"What charm school did she go to?" Basher asked as all twelve girls crowded the doorway trying to push through at once. They automatically formed two lines in the roadway outside of their digs. Basher craned her neck for as far as she could see were groups of WAAF's lined up intermittently right to the end of Western Avenue with their sergeant in front of them.

"I've never seen so many WAAF's at the same time" Basher remarked to Edie as they stood at ease waiting for their command.

"Stop talking in the ranks" the sergeant bellowed.

Edie sniffed. The sergeant glanced down the road checking that everyone was ready to move off.

"Squad..... atten....tion. Stand at.....ease. Now, if nobody minds we'll do it together this time and a bit more smartly. Squad....... atten....tion. That's better. Ri...ght dress." The parade shuffled their feet holding their left arm level with the shoulder of their neighbour and eyes firmly fixed to the left. They shuffled some more until the line was dead straight. The when the sergeant was satisfied she continued her instruction. "Ri....ght turn and qu.....ick....march. One two, one two, come on swing those arms.

A series of similar commands could be heard echoing down the entire street as their squadron marched off. Their thick overcoats were limiting their arm movements and gas mask straps rubbing against their breasts as they went.

Leaving Western Avenue they were marched directly to the promenade. The sea lashed against the wall sending a spray of water over them and the biting wind whipped around their faces deadening their features.

"Left right...... left right...... come on....... pick 'em up" yelled he sergeant clearly showing off as a squadron of airmen passed.

Wolf whistles filled he air as they came level and Edie nearly tripped up as she glared at the passing boys.

The sergeant spotted her and bellowed "Keep your eyes to the front... it's only men... you've seen them before..." she screamed sarcastically.

"Not since I joined this lot I 'aven't" Edie mumbled, determined to have the last word.

For the next two hours they were marched and drilled constantly until perfected. The wind gusted at times to such a pitch it almost knocked them from their ranks, which caused the sergeant to have a near nervous breakdown. Finally they were halted outside a cinema that clearly had been closed down for the duration of the war.

The aroma of coffee permeated the air as two mobile NAFFI canteens were seen waiting on the corner of the street. The sergeant instructed them to get their coffee break and then file into the cinema for their first lecture.

Basher and Edie sat side by side waiting for the arrival of the officers, their sergeant walked up and down the aisle checking her own charges.

"What a butch cow she is" Edie said, clearly still smarting from her earlier remarks about the airmen.

Phyllis turned around from the row in front having heard Edie's remarks. "She's only doing her job." Edie and Basher exchanged looks.

"And who rattled your bleedin' cage? Doing her job be buggered, she's a sadist, she loves the power of yelling 'er orders. Come to fink of it, it's probably all she's got if the truf be known for no bloke would give 'er a second glance, ugly git" Edie said with some passion.

"It could be possible that she's not in the least interested in men anyway" Phyllis retorted with some fervour.

Edie nudged Basher. "I'm beginning to seriously wonder about 'er". It was at that point that several officers filed on to the stage.

The cinema rose as one, the flight sergeant signalled the audience to be seated the moment the officers bums touched their seats. A young medical officer was on her feet beginning her lecture on hygiene explaining the importance of keeping ones self clean and free from infections, pointing out that living in close proximity to so may people had its dangers as so much could be passed on. She then developed the theme to the unsavoury subject of venereal disease, crabs, head lice and scabies; this had her audience fidgeting uncomfortably. In conclusion she went on to explain precaution is always better than cure, therefore they would all be subjected to what was commonly known as F.F.I. (Free From Infection). Their heads, armpits and pubic parts would be regularly examined by trained medical staff. A gasp went around at this news, the murmur rising to a crescendo of disapproval until the flight sergeant called order.

Two lectures on world affairs and how the war was progressing was explained in great detail with no opportunity for questions.

Edie whispered to Basher. "What a bleedin' turn up. Why do they always assume we 'ave no minds of our own or any brain to work fings out. Talk about being brain washed"

The sergeant was by their side in a flash. "Stop talking along there, try listening you might just hear something to your advantage" she hissed.

Edie put two finger up which certainly were not meant as the victory salute.

The last lecture of the morning was taken by yet another medical officer. "On Friday those of you who have just arrived will be taken to the medical centre and given three injections of typhoid, yellow fever and smallpox. You can expect to feel unwell, maybe even have a rise in temperature. We therefore advise you to stay in bed. However we do assure you that you will be fit and ready again by Monday morning." Then having delivered her final announcement the officer took her seat. The flight sergeant gave instructions for the afternoon activities. The entourage of officers then rose. The clanging and banging of cinema seats seemed louder than usual as the entire audience stood whilst their superiors filed out The feet of the new recruits were sore by lunch time that Friday, they had marched the length and breadth of the promenade several times that morning.

After lunch with shoes still pinching they marched once again but this time to the medical centre. The three girls stood in a single queue with their left arm out of their shirts, and as modestly as they could they draped the remaining shirt over their bosoms, which was just as well for a group of airmen had joined them making another queue beside them, they were striped to the waist.

The medical officer smiled sadistically with a long needle poised ready to puncture several arms. Edie preened and smiled at the airmen having allowed her shirt to fall provocatively, revealing a peep of her firm rounded breasts. She deliberately smiled one of her come hither smiles before remarking to Basher, "He's a bit of a hunk eh?" Before Basher could respond several thuds could be heard as some of the airmen fell to the floor like flies. Basher did wonder whether it was the sight of Edie's breast or the doctors needle that had caused such a number of grown men to go down in a dead faint. Medical orderlies hauled them out of the way for nothing would stop this conveyor belt of human flesh as they whipped needles in and out of arm upon arm.

CHAPTER 4

The moans and groans echoed throughout number seventy six Western Avenue as if it were inhabited by ghosts that night. The three girls tossed and turned in a feverish sleep with beads of sweat saturating their nightclothes as the fever swept over them. Feeling too ill to care, and not daring to move as pain seared through their arms at the lightest touch, they lay for twenty four hours sipping water intermittently for this was all their nauseated bodies could handle until the crisis was reached.

"I wish my Mum was here" wailed Basher. Phyllis began to sob, whilst Edie let out moan after moan intermingled with her particular brand of foul language.

Monday morning soon dawned. The three had reasonably recovered but looked white and drawn from the unpleasant experience. A post mortem was held during breakfast, and an exchange of red angry mounds of flesh were exposed looking like boils ready to burst, each girl claiming hers to be the worst. An orchestration of further moans as they each attempted to put on their overcoats for the tightness of the sleeve sent a sear of pain throughout their bodies.

The sergeant bellowing from the doorway did little to soothe their frayed nervous system. The routine of drill was yelled with monotonous repetition, except on this particular morning the sergeant seemed to take more than her usual sadistic delight in making them swing their arms just that little bit higher!

Edie happened to be marching in front of Basher on this occasion when suddenly she turned her head around and yelled "I 'adn't better meet this cow on me night off for I swear I'll swing for 'er."

"Quiet! No talking in the ranks, come on now, left right, swing those arms... and swing them much higher!"

After a brisk if not painful twenty-minute walk on this cold February morning found them outside what could be described as a disused factory. Two enormous corrugated doors were thrown back at both ends allowing the wind to whip through at an immense rate. The drill sergeant smiled to herself as she instructed her charges to join the physical training lesson that was in full swing. She then dismissed them.

The newcomers pulled their coat collars around their ears, and with hands plunged deeply into pockets they huddled together hoping not to be noticed. They gazed around them in disbelief for the vast arena was filled with at least four hundred women dressed in navy blue shorts, white shirts, ankle socks and black plimsoles. The instructor was bouncing up and down on the spot overflowing with excess energy. A whistle dangled from a piece of ribbon around her neck and her full firm breasts bounced up and down with the rhythm of her movement. This petite fitness freak who stood no more than five feet in her plimsoles was clearly enjoying her role. Her bright fresh complexion was devoid of make-up her fair hair a mass of natural waves and curls, and her very being screaming of good health.

Edie's eyes narrowed as she surveyed the scene around her. "Oh no! ...not in our state of 'ealf, she's *got* to be joking. What does she fink she's doing anyway training for the fuckin' Gestapo!?" Basher's hand flew to her mouth on hearing Edie's remarks in an attempt to hide her mirth at her perception of what lay before them.

The instructor now changed the routine jumping with feet together then apart. "Come on girls... one two...one two.... swing those arms... cone on right over your head!" Suddenly she spotted the new comers huddled in the corner. She blew her whistle to halt the class. Then picking up a megaphone she yelled. "Er... excuse me... yes you lot over there... come on get yourselves changed and join in with the rest... look lively now."

"Do you know what Bash, I reckon they've conscripted some of these cows from the Nazi prison camps, for they couldn't be crueller if they soddinwell tried."

The instructor held up the lesson for as long as it took for the small group to join in. A crescendo of yells and moans were heard as they peeled off their clothing and put on their sports kit. On hearing their cries of pain the instructor bellowed down the megaphone "Come on girls... don't be babies... you aren't dying so lets have you running on the spot... come on.... one two... one two."

Basher tapped Edie on the shoulder to draw her attention to Phyllis who had tears of pain streaming down her face. "Poor cow she 'aint used to the 'ard life. Mind yer if it comes ter that, neither am I. I didn't offer to serve me king and country to be tortured like some bleedin' criminal" Edie said through clenched teeth.

The instructor was now getting into her stride and fully

aware of the suffering of some of the girls. "Right" she bellowed down the megaphone." I want those left arms swung round in a big circle. Think of your arm as a windmill. We'll do it to music this time and quicken the pace as we get into it. And... one two... one two... come on right round... big circles."

As arms were swung painfully around, cries could be heard and then a series of thuds as girls passed out. Nobody came to their aid. Suddenly Edie exploded and yelled indignantly. "Oye... Corp... we've some casualties 'ere."

"Leave them alone they'll come round... eventually" the instructor yelled with seemingly little concern.

"You sadistic bastard! Edie yelled, now out of control. Basher held her breath. The fact that there was no response indicated it hadn't been heard which was just as well because Edie could have found herself on a serious charge and Basher gathered *they* always win!

Some few nights later over the evening meal Edie announced her intention of sussing out the town, asking her mates if they were game enough to join her.

With pain subsiding substantially and feeling much better from their latest ordeal they agreed that the change could do nothing but benefit.

The cold grey sea ebbed and flowed with monotonous regularity. Shops were closed and hotels boarded up. They wandered the deserted streets and glared at the Fun Fair that was now covered in tarpaulin their fancy lights dead. At this point their spirits had taken a dive.

Then Edie suddenly spotted the familiar sign of the

Red Shield Club. "Thank gawd for small mercies. Come on lets get in!" Then just as they were going through the doors Basher dramatically grabbed Edie's arm saying "You *do* know this lot is run by the Sally Army and they might try to save you?"

"As long as they save me a bleedin' bloke I couldn't care less" Edie retorted as she marched straight in.

"You are awful" Phyllis remarked speaking for the first time since they had left their digs.

The club was warm and inviting. Small tables were laid with brightly coloured table clothes and Service personnel sat around in groups. Some enjoying a cigarette with a mug of tea whilst others enjoyed a hot cooked meal.

A small queue had formed at the counter, which the three girls had now joined. Edie wasted no time. Her eyes traversed around the room weighing up the talent.

"Oh shit... look at that gorgeous hunk over there Bash" she remarked excitedly and consequently not too softly.

"Dear God, don't start in here *please,*" Basher pleaded, as she began to treat the place as if it were sacred. Feeling Bashers concern and seeing the look of dismay in her eyes Phyllis rounded on Edie and said sharply; "Do try and have some sense of decorum." But Edie wasn't listening instead her eyelashes had began to flutter like butterflies and her full sensuous smile was fully into play. They each had a tray with coffee and buns and were negotiating where to sit.

Suddenly one of he soldiers yelled "Here you are girls, plenty of room over here."

Edie didn't need a second bidding she was off like a shot. Basher and Phyllis declined the offer and sat at a separate table. Now with overcoat and gloves off the two girls sipped their coffee. Basher watched intrigued as Edie gazed first at one then another answering questions being put to her. She then remarked to Phyllis "I'll be honest I thought all her talk about blokes was just showing off. But it's not. The way she throws herself at guys is embarrassing. I've never met anyone quite like her in my life."

Phyllis kept her eyes averted and cut daintily into her bun. "Each to his own" was the only remark she would allow.

But Basher couldn't take her eyes off of her best mate. She was engulfed with mixed feelings of envy and outrage. What must it feel like to be so attractive that guys fall over themselves to get to know you? But her outrage took hold of her as she burst out "She's going to find herself in more hot water than she can handle one of these days!" Then picking up her cap, gloves and coat she turned to Phyllis and announced "Are you ready then? I'm leaving her to it."

The following morning Basher discovered that Edie was not in her bed. Panic swept over her. As Phyllis returned from the bathroom Basher blurted out "My God she's in for it now. She's been out all night!"

Phyllis remained silent whilst Basher began putting on her uniform.

It was then that the bedroom door slowly opened and Edie crept in. Basher's mouth opened ready to explode, but Edie put her finger quickly to her mouth saying;

"Shshsshsh... don't forget Bash, I've been 'ere all

night... right?"

"How the hell did you get in? All the doors are locked." commented Basher.

The old lady opens the door dead on seven I discovered. I sat on the basement steps and waited for her to go to the kitchen, then crash bang wallop here I am! Told yer it would be easy, nobody's any the wiser, that is... unless yer open yer great gate."

The day arrived for them to leave Morecambe. The morning was spent as usual with hour after exhausting hour, marching and drilling up and down the promenade. The girls complained that they knew every flagstone off by heart. At lunch time they were told to report to the cinema at two sharp.

The hub-bub of excited conversation was deafening as the cinema filled to capacity. Officers filed on to the stage, and the first of the lectures began.

The girls shrunk down in their seats and prepared to get comfortable for a bit of a kip until they heard..." You will no doubt be relieved to know that your general training is now at an end."

A deafening cheer went up. The officer had to hold up her hand to silence her audience. She continued "As you know you all go to your various training units and undergo severe technical training. I would like to wish you good luck in all that you endeavour to do for the war effort.

Each and everyone has a vital part to play. Be proud to know you helping to defend this great Island of ours. Good luck to you all," As she took her seat another rousing cheer broke out that shook the rafters.

The flight sergeant was now on her feet and began her instructions. "You will now return to your digs and pack your kit. We suggest you all have an early night." A hiss went around at this suggestion, so lifting her hand to get order the flight sergeant continued "If you don't I warn you, you will die on your feet before reaching your destination tomorrow. You will be transported to the railway station at 04.00 hours sharp. You will then be issued with packed lunches and railway warrants that will take you to your destinations. Should you be late without doubt you will miss your train, and we may then have to detain you for a further months training."

A massive groan of "Oh no!" rippled throughout the cinema.

CHAPTER 5

The train rumbled into the quiet rural station at four fifteen. Edie wound down the window of the carriage and leaned out. The sight of a station platform swarming with sailors threw her into ecstasy.

"Sod me Bash the bleedin' fleets in! Take a gander at this lot!

But before Basher could blink the train screeched to a halt. She pushed Edie out of the way and reached for the handle, then flinging open the carriage door she said "Never mind them lets get out."

Both Basher and Phyllis emerged tired and grubby after their long tiresome journey, whilst Edie gazed around her in disbelief. Her eyes danced, as she excitedly exclaimed "I'll have a bloody ball 'ere.' "

Sailors jostled to get on to the train as Phyllis pushed her way through to get to Edie her face red with anger and her jaw in motion as she gritted her teeth. She gave Edie a shove in the back as she hissed "Be quiet will you. Why do you *always* have to show us up?"

A tall airman pushed his way through the jostling sailors then spotting the three girls he yelled. "You lot from Morecambe?"

"Yes" they all chorused.

"Then follow me" he ordered as he turned on his heel and pushed his way back to the entrance.

A large truck stood in the forecourt. The airman let

down the back flap and threw in all the kitbags ordering the girls to follow.

With hands rebelliously on her hips Edie yelled. "What... in there?"

"Of course. Unless you've ordered a staff car madam?" the airman replied sarcastically. His remarks were lost on Edie, who was already gazing around to see what else was on offer. She spotted some sailors leaning against a wall waiting to get into the one and only phone box. It was then she turned her attention back to the truck, assessing at least three to four feet between the ground and where the kitbags lay.

Basher and Phyllis were open mouthed when Edie began playing her innocent card. Turning to the airman she complained "You must be soddin' joking mate get right up there wiv this lot 'aving a butchers?"

The airman spun round on her. "Don't play the innocent with me Topsy. I can smell your sort a mile off."

"Come on Ede stop larking about. Just get on will you? We all know yer dying to show off yer legs." Basher appealed irritably. Edie clearly decided having stalled long enough to get the attention she craved the time had come to act. Lifting her skirt almost to the top of her thighs revealing long slim legs she then managed to hoist herself on to the truck. The loud wolf whistles from the sailors was music to her ears. Turning to her audience she gave a low bow whilst smiling sweetly at the now irate airman, who banged the flap back into position and slammed in the bolt. The lorry clattered along a long narrow country lane, whilst the girls clung on for dear life as the truck thrust them back and forth whilst they attempted to stand on their own two feet.

Finally it came to a shuddering halt throwing the girls into a heap.

"The bastard did that on purpose" Edie moaned as she picked herself up and straightened her skirt. Basher and Phyllis then clambered down and began to pull at their skirts and jackets in order to feel comfortable and look presentable.

Gazing around them they discovered they were at the entrance to an RAF camp, which appeared as remote as Gloucester. A tall miserable looking sergeant probably in his late thirties appeared. Edie gave him the once over before asking; "Where's this then... No-Mans-land?"

The sergeant pulled himself up to his full six foot height, put his hands behind his back clearly bristled as he replied "No... this is RAF Titchfield and your home for the next three months, whether you like it or not. However clever clogs there *is* such a place as No-Mans-land several miles from here. Now... shall we go to the guard room and get you lot registered, and then you can all piss off."

They crowded around the guard room table waiting to sign in. All in fact with the exception of Edie, who decided that the sergeant was a challenge, and she was going to make a play for him, having already worked out that he would come in very handy getting her inside the main gate if ever she was late.

Fluttering her eyelashes and wetting her sensuous lips she sidled up closely to the miserable sergeant "What's yer problem sarge, a bit short of the 'ows yer farver?" For a brief moment his expression changed whilst he mentally undressed her. Then just as quickly he glared back at her.

45

"Get that book signed lady. What's the name again... fancy pants is it?

Then tapping the side of his nose he continued "I know your sort. I've got you sussed make no mistake. And remember this... walk over that gate just one second late and I'll have you booked so fast your feet won't touch the bloody ground."

As the girls trundled toward the admin block Edie moaned "The miserable git, I was only being friendly."

It was the first time that Basher and Phyllis had experienced their mate being put down by one of her hopeful victims.

"That should teach you a lesson." Phyllis said coldly.

Edie grinned, threw back her head defiantly and remarked "He's not the only one who works in the guard room, there are others I can get to work on. It's his loss" she added cockily.

Basher sighed "You are the absolute end... you really are."

The clerks in the administrative block ticked their names from the list of prospective new comers, and then directed them to their barrack hut.

The girls had to call upon their reserves of energy to get them through the next hour. But finally with kit unpacked and beds neatly made, they sat down to view their new living quarters.

"It's a long room eh Bash? How many beds do yer reckon... about thirty?" Edie suggested.

"Easily that" Basher replied.

Phyllis wandered over to the bed in the recess at the top end of the hut, noting the extra space with some envy she queried "I wonder who sleeps here?"

"One of the cows in charge yer can bet yer boots" was Edie's polite response. Edie's eyes wandered out to the porch area. There were two separate rooms.

It was then that her curiosity got the better of her. Slowly turning the handle of the nearest door she was about to peep in... when... "Just what was it you wanted?" a voice bellowed seemingly from nowhere.

Edie almost jumped out of her skin as a sergeant pushed passed her from behind, throwing the door open wider... "Do come in! Be my guest. Take a *real* good look. But remember this lady; this is my private room, the room that is out of bounds for the likes of you. This is where I sit scheming as to how I'm going to give you and your mates a hard time. Now get out!!"

Edie crept back to her bed pulling faces to hide her embarrassment at being caught. She grabbed her cap as nonchalantly as she could, before muttering from the side of her mouth, "Come on Bash lets get the hell out of 'ere"

The vastness of the NAFFI took them by surprise. An airman was playing on a grand piano that was situated on a very large stage.

The melodies flowed one into the other... *I'LL BE SEEING YOU IN ALL THE OLD FAMILIAR PLACES... A NIGHTINGALE SANG IN BERKLEY SQUARE...*

Basher began humming to the tunes "E's a pro... Can tell 'em a mile off" Edie announced confidently.

Basher gazed enviously as couples danced sublimely around an enormous dance floor. If *only* I could dance like that she thought to herself sadly. Around the perimeter of the dance floor were comfortable armchairs. Some were relaxing seemingly content to listen to the music or perhaps waiting for a certain partner.

"Let's get a cuppa, come on Bash" Edie said as she grabbed Bashers arm pulling her toward the canteen.

A large area of tables were reserved for those who wanted a substantial meal but having got their tea and buns Basher made her way back to the armchairs with Edie following behind, precariously carrying the tray. As the two girls sipped their tea they watched the dancers gliding past them gracefully seeming to anticipate each other's movements. This was a new experience that filled Basher with renewed awe and envy. So deeply involved with her own private thoughts she became unaware that Edie had long gone and Phyllis was now tapping her on the shoulder. "Mind if I join you?" she was asking politely.

Basher shook her head slightly bringing herself back into focus. "Don't be daft of course not. I've been watching these dancers and boy would I just love to have a go." she said with passionate longing.

"You'll have plenty of opportunity to learn because we're here for at least three months." Phyllis commented.

The following morning was spent in the stores collecting battle dress tops and trousers in the formal airforce blue. Ankle boots that resembled ugly pit boots. Thick white naval sea boot stocking and polo necked seaman's jumpers. Then finally came the issue of two pairs of industrial overalls. The girls staggered back to their quarters under the weight of the newly issued clothing. Edie flung hers on to her bed and began to giggle. "Christ these are a bit butch aren't they?" she said as she held up a pair of the overalls. "We'll look a right load of dykes in these."

Not having a clue what she meant Basher retorted "Just so long as they keep us clean I really don't give a toss."

Phyllis scratched her head looking puzzled. "I'm a bit confused. Were we told we had to wear our battle dress tops and trousers for the lectures?"

"Yep... but I'm wearing me jammies under mine, cos the material is dead itchy." Edie remarked as she took off her skirt.

"Wouldn't it be less cumbersome to wear your stockings underneath instead?" Phyllis suggested.

"Good finking Phyll, see... *not* just a pretty face..." Edie replied, if not somewhat sarcastically.

After lunch they filed into the lecture room. It reminded Basher of her school days with its desks and black board and easel. So with caps upside down on the desks in front of them, they awaited the arrival of their lecturer.

As the tall blonde stunning looking young man entered the room, Basher could hear the intake of breath from Edie. Taking off his cap he lay it along side his baton on the table in front of him. His piercing blue eyes scanned around his new pupils. Then with detachment he began... "My name is sergeant White and I put up with no nonsense. We're here to work, and I would like to think that you are my best entry so far. You have chosen one of the toughest jobs known in the Royal Air Force. So I hope you are ready for this. There are eight subject for you to learn and master with exactly twelve weeks to become proficient operators."

The class pulled faces at each other. Edie nudged Basher and remarked.

"E's a bit of all right ain't 'e?"

Basher gave Edie a withering look before saying "Don't start... behave yourself for once."

The instructor was on the ball, having clearly heard the whispering he swung on Basher. "What's your name?" he snapped.

"Basher Berry sarge."

He looked first shocked then amused. "What? ...Where on earth did you get a name like that?" he asked.

Basher pointed to her mate. "She gave it to me when we first joined up. All us three joined together" Basher informed him as she pointed out her two mates.

The instructor ignored the information but remarked "I'll say this much, you're aptly named. However we'll have less of the chattering, do you understand?"

Basher's sense of injustice rose as she refused to be blamed for Edie's mistakes.

"Er... excuse me... I was simply telling *her* to shut up!" she blurted out indignantly.

"Were you now. So what exactly did she say that was so urgent it had to be answered in that moment?"

Basher blushed scarlet. "It was personnel sarge."

Sergeant White was now clearly beginning to enjoy the embarrassment of his student. He sat on the edge of his table, picked up his baton and began tapping it in his hand as he pressed the point.

"Really... well lets all hear how personnel it was... I repeat... what did she say?"

Basher felt backed into a corner so she blurted out "She said you were a bit of all right sarge."

The class erupted into uproarious laughter. Now it was the turn of the instructor to look embarrassed. As he averted his eyes to the window Basher felt it served him right for pressuring her she felt that justice had been done! His eyes then met Edie's and she smiled provocatively. He took a deep breath smacked the baton against his thigh and began pacing up and down.

"The eight subjects are as follows; Balloon technical, balloon theory. Balloon drill, wire splicing, rope splicing, winch driving, winch maintenance and balloon maintenance. You will learn how to lay out a balloon bed and rig a balloon ready for it's operation.

The little silver things that can be seen clustered over London and at various points throughout the country are not all they seem. They are monsters to deal with. Three quarters are filled with hydrogen and a quarter air. Under the belly is a large envelope pocket that allows air to flow in and out."

He picked up his baton and began tapping it on various desks before asking "Has anyone any idea what hydrogen does?"

The class stare with blank faces. "I thought not. Well let me tell you. Hydrogen is lighter than air and this is what keeps the balloon airborne. Which is fine while she is flying on a nice calm summers day, but rather a different story during high winds and gales, as you are all about to discover. Unfortunately she doesn't spend the majority of her time flying... if only she did!" There are eight rigging wires situated on both the port and starboard side of the balloon.

These are fed through a cylinder... Now this is where we come to the classified information, which at no time must you ever, discuss. Remember the slogan; *Careless talk costs lives.* I want you all to inwardly digest this slogan and have it imprinted on your minds because the following information could do just that... *cost lives...* if not adhered to.

On the inside of the cylinder is a live cartridge, which only goes off when there is enough pull on the cable. This would only happen if the cable had wrapped itself around the wing of an enemy aircraft, which would inevitably bring it hurtling to the ground. The impact of the cartridge firing, in turn, would rip the ripcord on the balloon causing it to deflate and that also would fall to the ground.

That in a nutshell is the purpose of the balloon barrage, to stop low flying bombing. However the balloons have to be maintained and that is where your hard work really begins. There is no one around to hold your hand. No blokes to lug the forty pound sand bags and ballast blocks that are there to hold the balloon in position on her bed during high winds. If any of you have been camping you will know that you have to peg down your tent and secure it with guy ropes. This works on the same principle, excepting a balloon filled with hydrogen will always be champing at the bit to get away. You have to ensure she doesn't! She will then sit like a broody old hen, her bow that is more commonly known as her nose always has to be into wind.

You will quickly learn how rapidly the wind changes direction, and every time it does - Big Bertha as she is lovingly known by her crew - has to hump her around to get her nose into wind... in the middle of the night, or whatever it is you may be doing at the time.

Her wires and strops rapidly wear out with the constant tugging. But your job is to constantly have replacements spliced in both rope and wire and our job is to teach you how.

The winch too has to have constant attention in the same way you would maintain your car. You could end up being budding car mechanics after the war.

For certain your lily white hands will be constantly covered in grease and weather beaten, and you will find muscles you never thought you had. Any questions so far?"

Basher asked "Is this the reason we've been issued with overalls and pit boots sarge?"

"It sure is. And if any of you have the notion that you'll be swanning around your operational site looking glamorous, let me disillusion you right away. You'll be lucky if you have time to wash, never mind anything else."

The instructor began pacing up and down between the rows of desks as he continued "I cannot stress too strongly how important it is to keep your balloon equipment in top order. Because your balloon will be part of a squadron.

That squadron will be strategically placed to defend places like steel works, ammunition factories, ships at sea and a whole host of important targets.

I cannot stress enough the importance of keeping everything in ship-shape order for imagine the consequence if through lack of maintenance your winch packs up, or the cable wont feed from the drum to the balloon itself, or the balloon isn't topped up with enough hydrogen, and you get a purple alert to fly her. Any ideas of what the end result might be? No? ...Well let me spell it out.

The end result could mean that bombers could get through and raise to the ground steel works, not to mention loss of life. Can you imagine how you would feel?

Quite apart from the fact that your head would roll, and at the very least a Court Martial would take place... Perhaps now you have some idea of the enormity of the task you have all let yourselves in for, and may I remind you, you have only twelve weeks to learn all of this..."

Edie gave Basher a good kick under the desk as she whispered. "It sounds 'orrible"

This time the instructor heard her. He walked over to her desk and tapped it with his baton... "You were saying?

Edie looks sheepish but is forced to repeat her remark. He walked round and round her desk whilst he explains "Oh that's the easy bit, wait till there's a gale raging, and you're tucked up in your warm bed, having just crawled in after two hours of guard duty, and are on again in another four hours...

Suddenly you're yanked out of your pit, because the balloon has to be bedded down with her nose into wind that is now changing by the moment. You then begin to drag forty pound sandbags and ballast blocks inch by painful inch! Let me further remind you, that while Big Bertha is out of wind she will bounce around from one side of the deck to the other. The sandbags and ballast blocks will be swinging like dinky toys. All this time it's pitch dark and bitterly cold.

All you have to guide you around this intricate bed of wire strops and guy ropes is a dimmed flashlight, but this is where your balloon drill is so important, you have to listen and obey every command."

He then stops momentarily before touching Edie's nose with his, whilst yelling "Because the balloon is filled with hydrogen she's like a raging dog trying to get to a bitch on heat... girlie you don't know the meaning of the word 'orrible... not yet!"

CHAPTER 6

After the first week of lectures Phyllis and Basher are sitting on their beds trying to study. Suddenly Phyllis looks up and announces "I really don't think my brain will take anymore. I can understand some of it, but by no means all. It seems to get worse as we go along." She snapped her books shut and put them away. Picking up her toilet bag she made for the ablutions.

"How much do you reckon Edie's learned then?" Basher asked with some concern. "She's never here. Seems to spend most of her time with the instructor on the dance floor"

Phyllis stopped in her tracks and in a rare moment of personal comment said. "I think it's perfectly possible he'll pass her anyway. I'm certain that's what she's hoping for."

"But that won't help her once she's on an operational site will it?"

"No I suppose not, but that's her business isn't it?" Phyllis replied as she dismissed the subject and continued walking briskly toward the toilet block.

By the time Phyllis returned from her ablutions Edie had suddenly turned up.

"Where the hell have you been? Basher asked.

"Where the bleedin' 'ell do yer fink I've bin?" Edie replied defensively.

"With lover boy no doubt!" Basher said sarcastically.

"Yer learning."

"What about your studying?" Phyllis intervened.

"What's that?" Edie asked cockily, knowing it would wind up her two mates.

Basher bristled her frustration suddenly spilled over as she yelled.

"You're a selfish cow... do you know that? You'll never get through this lot in a thousand years. Then bang goes our chances of working together!"

"Wiv my connections... wanna bet?"

"Just leave it Basher" Phyllis advised... "It's her funeral, not ours."

After lights out the nightly ritual of dirty stories being exchanged began to take place. A voice from the ablutions end of the hut was heard to say "I heard this incredible joke today, wanna hear it?"

The corporal who occupied the bed in the corner recess nearest to the three girls had constantly complained about the sordid jokes and talk that took place nightly. But it was water off a ducks back with the majority of inmates, they did it all the more and tonight was no exception. The corporal who clearly came from a privileged background and had the speech to go with it, suddenly shot up in bed and began to whine "My Daddy would have been appalled if he knew the vulgarity that I'm exposed to not to mention the dregs of humanity I'm expected to share my living accommodation with, would I fear give him heart failure."

Edie sat up at this point and hugged her knees "Well... tickle me tits... shut yer bleedin' gob will yer"

The girls all joined in shouting obscenities down the

darkened hut in response to this snobbish corporals complaints. Her life had clearly been cloistered under the wing of her Daddy who they all gathered was a high ranking Army officer having spent most of his service life in Poona. This was by no means a new scenario there had been weeks of insulting abusive exchanges when the corporal from Poona had persisted in a tirade of snobbish abuse, throwing doubt on the parenthood and environments of the majority who shared her hut.

On this occasion realising her objections fell on deaf ears she began to wail... "You *really* are the dregs of humanity."

"Ere we go, the full drama three acts and a fuckin' curtain call! Pardon me while I vomit... fink yerself lucky lady... yer actually mixing wiv the salt of the eaf' 'ere... so get off yer bleedin' perch!" Edie blurted out angrily.

When the crisis finally peaked, shadowy figures could be seen creeping out at the far end of the hut. The jokes had now ceased but the babble of intermittent conversation was rising and falling.

"What's going on?" whispered Edie to her two mates.

"Haven't a clue" Basher said as she peered over the top of her blanket into the half darkness.

Suddenly all the hut lights blazed. As the three girls shielded their eyes from the brightness they noticed the WAAF band lined up at the ablution end of the hut.

They looked hilarious with their instruments strapped over their issue pyjamas!

Then were headed by the drum major who held her mace up high as she commanded the band to strike up. Bugles blared and drums rolled as they marched bare footed looking like a teddy bears picnic until they reached the far end of the hut playing Colonial Bogey with the added chorus from the inmates of... "Bollocks and the same to you!" The corporal from Poona shot out of bed opening and shutting her mouth in one movement.

"Did you know that lot down there were bandswomen Ede?" Basher asked now in total shock at what was going on.

"Hadn't clue but I love it." Edie said giggling.

The band was now gathered around the corporals' bed and the music was brought to a halt. It was then the drum major spoke "If you would like us - the scum of the earth according to Saint corporal of Poona - to define the word rowdy or bawdy then we can provide it... we have all the necessary equipment to do so."

Suddenly the far door of the hut burst open and on the threshold stood a small but ferocious flight sergeant. Her huge bosoms heaving with rage. She bellowed as she walked slowly toward the corporal's bed. "What may I ask is the meaning of this outrage?" The corporal flung herself down on her bed sobbing. Then everyone tried to talk at once. Those in bed hugging their knees enjoyed the drama that was unfolding before them. The drum major stepped forward to face the flight sergeant.

"I take full responsibility for my band flight sergeant" she began. "But I need to point out we were severely provoked. This corporal has been abusive and insulting to the entire hut over a period of weeks and this was by way of teaching her a lesson."

"Indeed! Well now it's my turn to teach you all a lesson. From now on all of your future concerts are cancelled. You and your entire band will report to my office at nine sharp tomorrow morning, and this also applies to you Corporal Farqua-Smythe."

The drum major went scarlet before pulling herself up to her full height when she blurted out indignantly "Sorry flight sergeant but that just can't be done. We have to play at the Commanding Officers parade in the morning at eight."

The flight sergeant's bosoms began heaving once again whilst her face deepened into a dark threatening red as she swung on the drum major saying "Tough! You can explain to him personally why you cannot be present. Now get these instruments put away and I'll see you all in the morning." Then turning abruptly on her heel she marched down the hut like a guardsman on parade throwing the light switch off and banging the door as she left.

The drum major was livid and if looks could have killed the corporal from Poona would have died in her bed that night. As the band trundled back to the end of the hut, Basher heard the drum major warn her girls that there was a possibility of them all being on a charge at the very least, and a grave likelihood of them being disbanded, 'and all through that poxy cow' were the last words Basher heard as they disappeared to put their instruments away.

During the lunch break the following day the corporal was seen hurriedly packing her kit and snivelling into her handkerchief at regular intervals.

"Thank God she's going Bash perhaps we'll get some peace at last," Phyllis remarked.

One of the bandswomen entered the hut and overheard

the remark.

"We made certain of that mate. We insisted she was moved. You should have heard this bloody officer only suggested we were bordering on mutiny! They really don't live in the real world half of them." Then swiftly changing the subject she added "By the way have you heard about the dance at the end of the week." Edie's eyes lit up like a Christmas tree she turned to Basher beside herself with excitement yelling "Oh Bash we've just got to go to that"

Basher smiled at her mate's excitement and suggested "What about sussing the town out first... like tonight?"

"You're a bleedin' genius, let's strike while the irons hot" Edie said, hardly able to contain herself.

It was then Phyllis looked up from her book and asked "What iron?"

Edie stared from Phyllis to Basher her eyes flaying in her head. "Never mind dear 'eart get back ter yer book we'll tell yer when we've done all the arranging." was Edie's rather patronising response.

"OK straight after tea... Fareham 'ere we come!" Edie announced.

Having a practical mind Basher looked around the room and asked "Does anyone know how far it is?"

"About three miles I think. That is unless you are walking at night then it seems more like ten" one of the bandswomen offered. It was then that another band member entered the hut and pointed out. "By the way the dance is this Friday at a local naval base."

Edie's eyes opened and stood out like chapel hat pegs. "Did you hear that Bash?" she screamed, then with one hand on hip and giving her most provocative stance said

"He......lo... sailor... how's yer bum fer spots?"

Laughter echoed around the hut at Edie's outburst, who then turned urgently and seriously to her mate and said "This is it Bash, we definitely suss out the talent tonight in readiness for Friday. We 'ave to keep our 'and in!"

During the early evening the three girls walked out of the camp gate for the first time since their arrival. The long and winding country road seemed endless but having walked about a quarter of a mile Basher spotted a car approaching.

Edie immediately took charge, turning to her mates announced... "Leave this to me girls... watch and learn." She then proceeded to raise her skirt liberally revealing a sizable amount of thigh, with thumb poised it became evident that she was begging a lift. Phyllis blushed scarlet as she observed Edie's outrageous gesture. But to the amazement of the trio the car stopped and gave them a lift to the centre of the town. Scrambling from the car they thanked the middle-aged driver sincerely, Basher noted how he leered at Edie who promptly gave him a 'promise' the next time she saw him. "'E'll be lucky" she murmured under her breathe.

"Then why lead him on?" Phyllis almost shouted at her.

"Bleedin' 'ell... yer sanctimonious cow! Yer got yer lift didn't yer?" Then gazing around her in silent disbelief at the empty streets, she finally blurted out.

"Piss me, what kind of a one 'orse town is this then? There's nuffink 'ere"

"It's obviously a small market town, what did you

expect, neon lights and dance halls?" Basher remarked.

"There's a forces canteen over there" Phyllis suggested meekly.

"Do me a favour, 'ow many bleedin' sailors do yer reckon would be in there? Come on, lets at least take a walk down the street."

The trio scuffled discontentedly for a little way when suddenly they could hear music. Following the sound they discovered to their delight that it was coming from a quaint looking pub. Edie couldn't contain herself as she flew over the road and strained her neck to read the name of the pub.

"It's the Bugle girls" she yelled, "Tally -ho! We ought ter 'ave brought old posh drawers wiv us... but come to fink of it per'aps not. Now this is my kind of pub an old 'joanna' going. Come on... lets get in."

The low beamed ceilings were coated in brown nicotine. Sailors in navy blue suits and peaked caps propped up the bar. Whilst groups of junior ratings wearing bell bottom trousers with tightly fitted navy blue jerseys accompanied with square collars, sat around in groups puffing on their cigarettes whilst grasping their beer.

With alcohol limited they could only order half pints. The girls grasped their glasses as if they were gold dust before quickly finding seats and getting settled.

Basher sipped her beer and shuddered. "What's up don't yer like it?" Edie asked

"Not much, but no doubt I'll get used to it."

Edie began searching the room for likely candidates, but before she had the chance to flutter her eyelashes a tall good looking sailor bent over her, and asked "Mind if we join you girls?"

Before Basher or Phyllis could put forward an opinion Edie had moved over like grease lightening grinning from ear to ear said "Be our guest"

Three sailors joined the table and the good looking sailor made the introductions.

Bill was a Leading seaman and came from Waterlooville. He at a guess was around twenty, with mid-brown tousled hair and dark brown eyes that danced mischievously giving the impression of being a bit of a fly by night.

Fred the smallest of the trio only stood about five five and could only have been nineteen. His small frame showed up conspicuously in the tight fitting jersey. He had fair thin hair and grey eyes. He appeared to live in a dream world. But on the rare occasion that he spoke turned out to be the worlds worst bore. His dialect was strange and Basher certainly had never heard it before, but eventually discovered he hailed from Carlisle.

The exceptionally good looking Chief Petty Officer who Edie clearly had her eye on, was Ken. He was clever enough to dodge the issue of his background except to drift into explanations that they were all based at HMS Collingwood, which the girls learned was the host base for the forthcoming dance.

The evening turned out to be most pleasant with the Chief and Edie in competition as to who could be the most outrageous and humorous. These two seemed destined for each other. Both good looking with a similar sense of humour. And yet there was no attempt at pairing off at any time with any of the six. The old joanna struck up again and everyone joined in with the sing along despite some missing notes on the piano. All too soon the bell clanged for last orders. It was ten o clock and time to begin the long trek back to camp.

Once outside both Basher and Edie were astounded when the Chief suddenly grabbed the arm of Phyllis and walked off with her! Edie thumped Basher's arm to attract her attention before going down on one knee in the pretense of tying her shoelace.

Basher quickly caught on, and dived down to frantically tug at her own shoelaces. "What does that Chief think he'll get from Phyll? He's got to be joking!" Edie hissed in anger.

"I've not the slightest idea" whispered Bash whose experience of men was negligible.

"Per'aps 'e works on the assumption that the quietest ones are the 'ottest. But tell yer what, e's caught a cold there" Edie spat out spitefully.

"Are you two coming or what?" yelled the two matelot from way down the road who had been waiting uncertainly wondering if the two girls fancied them or not.

"Oh well... in fer a penny" shrugged Edie as she stood up. "At least we'll 'ave company to walk us back to camp it's a bloody long way Bash. Come on, but keep yer 'and on yer ha' penny."

They quickly caught up with the matelots. Bill immediately put his arm around the shoulder of Edie claiming her for his own. Which left Basher to walk with the small guy from Carlisle who proceeded to romance her with his rendering of country and western songs sung in a phoney American accent at the same time pretending to play a guitar. Basher could never remember feeling quite so bored in her entire life as this continued for the three-mile walk back to camp.

Edie and Bill had long gone and Basher was left to guess what she might be up to. But as Basher and Fred approached the edge of the camp they could hear hysterical giggling that seemed to be coming from the ditch that went around the perimeter of the camp.

Following the sounds they eventually discovered Edie lying in the ditch totally hysterical with Bill trying to haul her out.

"What's up with her?" Basher asked of her escort.

"She's pissed out of her skull" Bill laughed

"But she can't be, she's having you on. She was perfectly all right when we left the pub." Basher insisted.

"That maybe so, but she's been swigging my pussers rum and it's potent stuff. And can she put it away!" Bill giggled.

"That's real clever of you. So how the hell am I supposed to get her through the main gate in this state? It's to be hoped a certain sergeant isn't on duty because he's been waiting for this moment."

"What bloody sergeant?" Bill said getting stroppy, then pulling himself up to his full height, his body listing violently. It became obvious that he too was the worse for wear."

"Hey... don't you start Jack. Just get her out of there and leave the rest to me" Basher suggested.

Finally Edie was hauled from the ditch. She stood like a tailors dummy giggling uncontrollably as Basher attempted to straighten her uniform and brush her down. Finally she put on her cap then turned to their escorts and curtly dismissed them by saying. "Thanks boys. Perhaps see you next Friday at the dance."

Turning to her mate she said sternly. "Now listen... pull yourself together. Do you hear me, or we shall all be in dead trouble."

At this command Edie stood to attention and saluted before falling about laughing.

"Shut it!" yelled Basher now worried as to how she was going to get Edie through the main gate.

"Are you aware it's an offence to be drunk and disorderly?" Basher pleaded. But Edie was out of her skull, swaying and staggering all over the place laughing hysterically. Just then a small group approached the main gate and waited whilst the guards checked their passes. This gave Basher an idea. Pulling Edie's pass from her top pocket she grabbed her jacket from the back with her left hand, and marched her passed the guard well hidden amongst the crowd waving the passes as she went.

At last they were through! Basher gave a huge sigh of relief, until quite unexpectedly the Duty Officer appeared from the officers' mess that was situated just beyond the main gate. He halted the small crowd. "Keep your passes out!" he commanded. "Just a random check."

Basher began to sweat, clinging desperately to Edie she hissed under her breath advising her not to move an inch. Then managing to flash her own pass she prayed he wouldn't insist on seeing Edie's which she had just rammed back into her pocket.

At that point a convulsive laugh surfaced and

threatened to explode but Basher kicked Edie's shins hard to ensure it didn't happen. As they were about to be moved on Edie swayed. "Hold on... just walk straight" Basher hissed through clenched teeth. The stress of the situation now getting to her. When out of the earshot of the Duty Officer Edie asked "Hey Bash where's our mate Phyll?"

Now totally exasperated with the situation Basher gave Edie a shove before saying irritably "I haven't the foggiest idea. Just keep walking lady that's all I ask." Basher finally let go of her mate when they were well out of danger, relieved that at the last, the harassment she had been put through was at and end. Edie immediately curled up on the parade ground and went into hysterical laughter once again. This was too much for Basher. She stood over her mate and yelled "Get up and stop being so damned stupid!" At this command Edie calmly got up and found her own way back to hut twenty-five.

CHAPTER 7

Edie put her finger to her lips and said exaggeratedly. "Shhhhhh they're all ashleep." then giggling to herself she turned to Basher and began to laugh uproariously.

"Fancy ending up wiv a bloke wiv 'arf an ear, some bleedin' Van Gough he turned out to be." Basher gave Edie a shove and told her to be quiet for the hundreth time. Than as she picked her way carefully in the half light she could hear someone sobbing just as she reached her own bed.

"Ahhhhhh someone's missing Mummy" Edie giggled. But when their eyes became accustomed to the subdued lighting the laughter ceased for they could both see their mate Phyllis knelt by her bed sobbing her heart out.

"Jesus!" Edie exclaimed, "What the 'ell's up wiv 'er?"

"Shut yer rotten mouth and help me get her to the toilets." Basher ordered.

In silence both girls took an arm and directed the sobbing Phyllis to the toilets where there was full lighting. Once inside both gasped at the vision before them. Buttons were ripped from her uniform jacket, her shirt was torn and holes where buttons should be, leaving small breasts exposed. Blood trickled from a cut lip and nose, and her stockings had massive rips at the knees with great welts of exposed flesh that had dried blood mingled with fresh running down into her shoes from a wound on her shin.

Edie's hand flew to her mouth in an attempt to hide her

shock. She sobered in a flash. "Jesus... what ever's 'appened 'ere?" was all she could manage to utter.

Fresh sobs erupted from Phyllis as she wailed. "He... tried to rape me!"

"What do yer mean... tried? By the look of yer, he did!" Edie said somewhat agitated.

"No he didn't then!" Phyllis defended. "He might *think* he's God's gift, but I put up a hell of a fight. I'm a virgin and proud of it, and no poxy sailor is going to have me."

"What?" screamed Edie as the reality of the situation now infiltrated her dulled brain cells. "The dirty bastard! You of *all* people, nearly a bleedin' nun, you are."

A group of girls from the WAAF band were now standing in the doorway clearly alerted by the commotion. Some offered to help clean Phyllis, whilst the rest exchanged knowing looks then miming between themselves they returned to the hut to hold a conference. It was agreed by the majority not to report the incident to the authorities, as they preferred to deal with it themselves, and it would save Phyllis being dragged publicly through all kinds of interrogations.

Phyllis was withdrawn and very silent most of that week. Basher was aware of a great conspiracy taking place and only a few knew the plan.

The day of the naval dance arrived and Basher was approached and asked if she would agree to stay on camp with Phyllis whilst the rest of the hut attended the dance.

Basher was of course very disappointed, but aware that plans were in place although the details of which were top secret. She shrugged her shoulders and felt it was the least she could do for an old mate.

Basher and Phyllis's sleep was disturbed late that night. The hilarity of the girls all drunk with excitement of their achievement.

"Wake up Bash... Phyll... come on.... wake up!" Edie cried shaking them both. "We got the bastard and did 'im real good and proper. You'd 'ave bin proud of us."

The two girls were suddenly wide awake listening to the story of the encounter of their inmates with the Chief Petty officer.

"The dance was magic Bash, loads of lovely blokes." Edie began.

But one of the more mature members of the band quickly intervened and took up the story.

"I got Edie to point the Chief out to me. It was so easy he was putty in my hands. I played up to him something rotten, and shot him the line that my husband was away on a course and as we had married sleeping quarters I could invite him back to camp to join me for the night. It was a doddle. We all knew the plan, we were to sneak him on to our truck at the end of the dance... it went like a dream."

Phyllis began to look worried at this point. "What did you do? He's not here is he?" she asked, as she pulled the blankets under her chin for protection.

"Don't be stupid. Once the lorry got moving we all de-bagged him and beat him up. Then we threw him from the moving lorry with his trousers and cap following about half a mile later! He'll certainly think twice about attempting to rape again, we'll guarantee it" the girl from the band explained.

Edie interrupted unable to contain herself a moment

longer because this kind of drama was right up her street.

"I kicked 'is shins as 'ard as he kicked yours. I'd 'ave strung 'im up by 'is balls, but couldn't get near enough… 'cos this lot were filling their boots."

For the first time since the incident Phyllis smiled and said "That just serves him right, poetic justice, I don't know how to thank you all for your support, but thanks anyway." Then lying down for the second time that night, she slept with the peace and tranquillity of a baby.

Two months of intense theory on eight subjects of balloon operating created great uncertainty within the trio, who were now on the eve of departure to a balloon training site which to all intents and purposes was operational.

"I wonder where we're going?" Basher queried as she rammed her clothes into her kit bag.

"Aven't a clue and can't say I care very much 'eiver" Edie replied sounding down in the dumps.

Phyllis and Basher exchanged looks. "What's up Ede, going to miss lover boy?" Basher teased. "Fer Christ's sake give it a rest yer gets on me tits."

Phyllis took Bashers arm and led her to one side, whispering,

"Lay off Basher, she's bound to miss him. She's all but lived with the guy for the past two months and probably worried about who he'll take up with once she's gone."

Basher laughed. "You're joking, he'll be old news within twenty four hours, you mark my words."

The truck pulled up outside a large corner house that formed part of a square of similar types. Opposite was the balloon site situated on what clearly was once a recreational playground for children. The driver explained that this was a suburb of Southampton known as Shirley. He then handed over their kitbags and instructed them to sort out their own sleeping arrangements within the house. Unpack their kit and then report to the sergeant across the road who would no doubt be on the balloon site.

As the trio entered the house its bare floorboards creaked. They wandered from room to room. The kitchen had two beds, which Edie and Phyllis claimed at once, leaving Basher to find a spare bed in the Master bedroom upstairs.

There were certainly no home comforts here, every available inch of space had been utilised with camp beds and a locker for each girl. Basher quickly unpacked her kit and joined her two mates downstairs.

"Blimey Bash, not exactly 'ome from 'ome is it?"

Basher then noted the close proximity to the sink from Edie's bed. "Not far to throw up, when you've had a few."

"Chance'd be a fine fing, didn't cop sight of a single pub on our way 'ere" she said with some disgust.

Phyllis had been silently but meticulously unpacking her kit, putting it neatly away in her usual orderly fashion. Now she was ready so turning to her two friends suggested.

"Come on you two, it's about time we went over the road and met the rest of the crew. I can't wait to see what a balloon site *really* looks like."

The nissen hut seemed small in comparison to the barrack room back at camp. The sergeant was patiently waiting for everyone to assemble, before he began his introductory talk. A short wiry man with small features resembling either a ferret or a rat. His face was weather beaten with sharp small brown beady eyes and wispy mousy coloured hair. Basher would have guessed him at the very least in his late thirties, but clearly a local man with either a Hampshire or Dorset accent, Basher could never define the difference.

"I would like to welcome you to this training site. I'm sergeant Pringle. You will find that everything that is done here is identical to any operational balloon site anywhere in the country. We now put into practice all the theory you SHOULD have learned over the past eight weeks."

Basher and Phyllis exchanged knowing looks and smiled as they nodded toward Edie. The sergeant rubbed his chin as he glanced at each girl separately before continuing "The time has come to separate the women from the girls. You *do* know that you take your final examination here once your three week training is over?" he announced, which came across as some kind of veiled threat.

He went on to explain that two girls would be the duty cooks for the next few days, pointing out that normally this duty would last a week, but for the purposes of training a few days each was all that could be allowed in order to give everyone the opportunity of this experience.

Basher and Edie began to giggle. The thought of a crew relying on a half decent meal from either of them was outrageously funny. The sergeant swung on the both and demanded. "What's your names?"

"Edie Smiff boss" she said trying hard to keep a

straight face.

The sergeants' face went crimson. His eyes blazed as he glared at Edie, then trying to control himself from hitting her, he spat out.

"Don't take the piss with me lady. You will refer to me as sergeant at all times. Do I make myself abundantly clear?" Edie went bright pink, shuffling she looked down at her feet.

Then turning his attention to Basher asked; "Now what about you. Do you have a name?"

"Yes sergeant... Basher Berry"

The sergeant folded his arms his jaw set and his eyes narrowed. "I see... we have two bloody comediennes among us have we? Where the hell did you get a name like that?"

Nodding toward Edie, Basher explained "She gave it me when we first joined up."

The sergeant paused to consider this one. Then slowly began to walk around Basher prodding and poking her body here and there, before remarking "Yes I have to give it to her it's a well chosen name. You certainly *are* a little on the large side aren't you?" he emphasized clearly wanting to intimidate and humiliate her. Then rubbing his chin added. "Well now lets see. As you both think cooking is so hilarious you can cover the next duties as cooks, which will take us to the weekend when I do enjoy my roast beef and Yorkshire pudding. Lets see how you manage that little lot!"

Then with this instruction duly given, he abruptly dismissed the two rebels.

The twelve trainees were then taken on tour of the site

and finally instructed to change into their overalls and boots so they could begin work at once.

Back at the house Basher waited while Edie struggled into her overalls.

"A right little ray of sunshine we've got 'ere, Bash"

"What you really mean is he isn't the kind of material to have an affair with." Phyllis interjected rather cattily.

"You're joking! Wouldn't give the likes of 'im toilet room. I reckon he could be a bit of a bastard on the quiet. What do you fink Bash?"

"I certainly wouldn't recommend messing with him. A bit of a sod if pushed, I reckon." Finally all rigged out in their new gear the trio made their way back to the site to begin work.

The gigantic silver barrage balloons had been a constant presence in the skies over Britain in recent years, causing much debate among the civilian population as to their purpose. They flew majestically among high clouds hiding the reality of what monsters they were to control. After the first week of hard physical work and swotting, the new crew of students began to realise just what they had let themselves in for.

The silver beauty better known as Big Bertha had dimensions from bow to stern as wide as two houses. They could at last see for themselves everything their tutor at Titchfield had taught them. The winch was fascinating, it worked on exactly the same principle as a car, with the exception that when the clutch was let out it didn't move as a car does, but releases the huge drum of cable situated behind the drivers seat, and that in turn allows the balloon to fly.

The operations room on site was combined with the general office. Who ever was on duty was responsible taking calls from headquarters. A red alert meant getting ready to fly the balloon, but if more than a gentle breeze was forecast from the Met office the crew would be at action stations hauling Big Bertha down to interim height, which was around six feet from ground level, and there she would sit, often hitting the deck depending on the ferocity of the wind. The practical work of handling the balloon meant there was no time or inclination for a social life. Instead the crew would make their weary way back to their sleeping quarters their limbs aching from the tugging and pulling on guy lines.

After a particularly tough day Basher peeled off her working clothes and got into her pyjamas before joining her mates for a yarn in their kitchen dormitory. They chatted over the events of the course so far. Edie was as usual in front of a mirror this time pinning every strand of her hair into curlers. Basher finally yawned and stretched. "Don't know about you two but I'm turning in, I'm absolutely bushed."

A terrific thud brought Basher from her deep sleep. She lay for moments trying to puzzle what it was that had woken her, when another ear splitting bang threw her from her bed to the floor. It was then it dawned. This was an air raid.

She hurriedly pulled her slacks over her pyjama bottoms, then yanked a thick jumper over her head, before making a grab for her tin helmet. Fleeing down stairs she found Phyllis just about ready, while Edie was calmly taking her hair out of curlers.

Basher stared at her mate with incredibility before urging "Come on Ede for Christ sake. Who the hell's going to notice you in an air raid? Shove your tin hat over yer curlers, but hurry for God's sake"

"You've got to be joking Bash. There might be some fabulous air raid wardens out there."

Basher clenched her teeth in exasperation pointing out that the docks were only a few miles down the road and had been targeted before. It was clear to anyone with a smattering of intelligence that gerry had returned to finish the job. But the warnings fell on deaf ears. Edie smiled calmly at her two mates and then began to apply make up to her face. Phyllis and Basher exchanged looks of disbelief then Phyllis made one of her rare comments.

"What an enormous ego you have Edie" She then swept out of the kitchen in utter disgust. Basher realised she was wasting her time for it was clear that nothing would move or shame Edie, who now hummed to herself as she continued to apply her make up.

Basher heaved a sigh before remarking; "I don't know about you but I' off. I've no objections to getting killed for something worthwhile, but this is ridiculous."

She then made a dash for the door, but was dazzled by fires burning on the balloon site. Anti-aircraft guns were booming as low flying aircraft were circling. The throb of their engines sounded menacing. Basher got as far as the pavement outside the house when another flash, followed by a thunderous bang making her instinctively fling herself to the ground. Shrapnel fell like rain around her. In a last desperate attempt to shift Edie she cupped her hands around her mouth and yelled... "Come on Edie... you'll get killed in there. The site's on fire!" But with no response Basher began to crawl across the road on her belly. Her mouth dry with fear and her heart thundering in her head.

The large feet of the sergeant came level with her eyes.

"Get up!" he ordered. "Grab a bucket of sand and throw on any of the fire bombs still burning. Keep going till they're all out. We've to get this lot under control, for if they reach the gas cylinders the lot will go up, and us with it."

"Yes sergeant" was all that Basher could manage to say. Taking the first bucket of sand she approached the first bomb with great trepidation, threw it as she had been instructed and to her surprise it simply went out. The sergeant was beside her again. "That's it Basher you've got the idea. By the way where's your mate?"

Basher swallowed hard. This was what she had been dreading. She had no intentions of dobbing her friend in, but the glaring eyes of the sergeant told her she had better tell the truth.

"She insisted on taking her hair out of curlers and putting on her make up sarge. I did try to persuade her not to" Basher blurted out.

The sergeant couldn't help but look surprised. His eyes blazed and his face went red before he bellowed; "The stupid bitch! Who the hell does she think is going to notice her in an air raid? Get over there and drag her out... right now! I need every pair of hands to control these fires. A lot of good she'll be on an operational site should she ever get there that is!" He added threateningly.

Basher raced back to the house and spilled out the sergeants threatening message.

"He can get stuffed" was Edie's defiant reply. But Basher realised that this was one instructor her mate had seriously under estimated. It was possible he had heard gossip in the sergeants' mess at Titchfield and like the one on the main gate was not wearing it.

The all clear wailed as the last fire was being put out. The crew made their way to the kitchen for hot cocoa and a cigarette. With black hands and faces the weary crew collapsed into seats for a well earned rest. The sergeant entered and immediately addressed Edie.

"Right glamour pants where do you think you've been?"

"Getting ready sarge" Edie coolly replied.

"Getting ready for what?" he persisted.

Edie didn't reply but a hint of a smile threatened. The sergeants nostrils flared and his breathing became more rapid as he got more worked up.

"I'm not sure that you were aware of the situation" he began sarcastically, "But this *was* an emergency a serious air raid was in progress... you know... bang bang... bang! It was for real, they weren't playing silly bugger to amuse Edie Smith,"

Edie stiffened. Then pulling herself up to her full height she replied defiantly "I 'aint running the bleedin' streets in me curlers fer you or no-one."

"We'll have less of the lip for a start. You may consider this one big joke but I assure you it isn't. We all have a job to do and mine right now is to train you lot into tough balloon operators. There is no time for glamour in

82

this job so you may as well all know this from the start. You'll be lucky to get wash on an operational site never mind caking your chops with that muck" he said pointing deliberately to Edie's face.

Then slowly walking toward Edie he came nose to nose with her and continued in a menacing manner... "So the quicker you get that into your head the better. Do I make myself abundantly clear Airwoman Smith?" he shouted

"Yes" Edie answered curtly.

"Yes what?" he lashed back at her.

"Yes *SERGEANT*" she yelled with sarcastic emphasis. Then defiantly picking up her mug she took a swig of her cocoa. "He sounds like my Dad" she said addressing Basher as she lit a cigarette.

"Pity I'm not for I'd tan yer arse" the sergeant quickly retorted letting her know that he never missed a trick. Then as if to humiliate her further he yelled "Oye, fancy pants put that fag out and finish that drink. Then get a bucket and spade and shovel up every incendiary bomb on the site. Dig a deep hole and bury the lot. That should keep you going till breakfast.

The look on his face told the crew that he was now satisfied to have her under his control. Edie's mouth had dropped open and if looks could have killed he would have collapsed and died on the spot.

"You wouldn't like me to bury meself whilst I'm at it, wud yer?" Edie said making certain to have the last word, for she was certainly not used to being treated like this by her men. Tears of frustration welled in her eyes and threatened to overspill, but before she humiliated herself further she turned on her heel and stormed off crashing the hut door with a terrible bang.

A smile crept over the sergeant face. He knew he had won.

"I reckon I've cracked that ego of hers, and hurt her pride in the process. But there goes one vain but promising balloon operator." he explained to Basher.

CHAPTER 8

The large clock that hung over the centre of St Pancras station London had hands that visibly moved. This helped passengers check the accuracy of time so as not to miss their train departures. The warm June morning was a pleasant change from the more arctic conditions the girls had endured the last time they had left London earlier in the year.

Basher waited restlessly for her two friends to join her. The kitbag that was propped up in front of her was bulging with extra winter clothing that had been packed so tightly it had left no room for her overcoat that she carried over her arm. Then glancing at the clock again she realised with some anxiety that it was now turned half past eleven. Where on earth were her mates? she wondered. They had agreed to meet at a quarter past, because their train was due to leave for Sheffield at twelve five. Her eyes frantically searched all entrances. She watched as passengers merged on to the platform to await the arrival of the Sheffield train. Then just at the point of deciding to go she spotted Edie trundling through the north entrance dragging her kitbag behind her as usual.

"Where the hell have you been?" Yelled Basher before Edie could reach her.

"Got 'eld up in the tube. They found a bomb or somefink" she explained totally unperturbed. Then looking around she asked. "Where's Phyll then? Don't tell me's not arrived 'iever?"

"Nope" replied Basher as she searched again the crowded station.

"Not like 'er to be late." Then suddenly Edie's face lit up. "I know where she'll be, I'll lay bleedin' odds on it 'old on Bash, just watch me kit won't be long." she said as she chased off in the direction of the ladies waiting room.

Within minutes the two girls emerged. "I was right Bash, sat there as large as bleedin' life... *reading IF* yer don't mind."

"What the hell did you think you were doing? Didn't you know the train is due to leave?" Basher urged hysterically.

"I arrived at eleven sharp but didn't fancy hanging around the station you never know do you? It felt safer in there. I simply lost track of time." she explained meekly.

"Come on for Christ's sake the train's been in ten minutes and I don't fancy standing all the way to Sheffield."

They finally settled into a carriage with a table fixed tightly between them. Their kitbags and overcoats had been neatly stacked in the racks above their heads. They placed their caps on the table in front of them, and undid their tunic buttons finally getting comfortable for their long journey north. Edie had grabbed an aisle seat, she needed the room to cross her long legs, always with the fond hope of catching the attention of any male who happened to be nearby.

"Well then 'ow did it go?" Edie asked of her two mates.

Basher looked puzzled. "What do you mean... our

leave?"

"What else yer berk, unless yer went on a bleedin' cruise?"

"Do me a favour," Basher said shrugging her shoulders. "It's not been that exciting. My Dad was on leave for a weekend so it was good to catch up with him. He's been posted somewhere near York. He reckons it's not far from Sheffield so I'm hoping to see more of him now. He was pleased about me passing my exams. But apart from that and doing the three times a day service at the Sally Army last Sunday nothing much else happened in fact boring, would be a better word for it." she explained with a sigh.

"'Ope yer went ter confession and told the boss upstairs about yer drinking, smoking and swearing habits" Edie remarked smiling.

Basher bristled and replied defensively. "We don't have confession in our religion stupid. In any case you're enough to make the Pope swear."

Phyllis looked up from her book and remarked "I'm glad to hear that you've not ditched your religion altogether Basher. It will stand you in good stead."

Edie pulled a face before bubbling over with her own good news she blurted out "Guess what... I've met this dead gorgeous bloke at our club. It was the first night 'ome an all."

Basher smiled and said... *REALLY* you *DO* surprise me!"

But now fired with enthusiasm Edie ignored Basher's sarcasm and continued "He's a real hunk. A sexy Yank! Look... dig the *silk* stockings girls!" she announced as she moved into the aisle, then cocking her leg up to rest on the table, she pulled her skirt almost to her crotch, then looked around her and smiled.

Phyllis blushed. "Put your leg down Edie, everyone's looking."

"That's the idea mate. If yer got it flaunt it."

In a desperate attempt to ignore Edie, Phyllis turned to Basher and asked, "What did you mean when you said your Dad had been posted near York? Does he do some special war work?"

"Oh sorry, I should have explained, he's in the Air Force too."

"What?!" interjected Edie. "How old is 'e for God's sake?"

"To be honest I don't really know for sure. He was called up with the forty age group and he's been in well over a year now, so at a guess he must be around forty-one or two. I know that my Mum got herself in a right state when he left. She's one of those women who relies on her man to do everything, and to make matters worse my baby sister was only six months old when he was called up. I thought poor old Mum would have a nervous breakdown she was that upset."

"Blimey, yer old man obviously likes 'is oats." Edie remarked cheekily.

Basher blushed and bristled once again. It was her turn to change the subject for she felt this to be intrusive into the privacy or her beloved father's life.

"What about your parents Ede, were they pleased you passed your exams?" Basher enquired.

"Yep I suppose so. They aren't all that interested in

what I do. Tell you what though Bash, yer didn't fink the bastard was going ter pass me did yer?"

"No I didn't. You had me worried there for a while still we all got there in the end." Basher said.

"Yep and aren't we lucky ter get the same posting?"

"Don't count your chickens we've not been allocated sites yet" Phyllis warned.

"'Ere we go ever the bleedin' optimist."

Basher opened her bag of sandwiches. "Anyone want one? I'm starving."

The girls shared sandwiches and cakes that Basher's mother had baked. They continued chatting about the events of their leave and the anticipation of their new career.

Then glancing out of the window Basher noticed the stark change of scenery. Large factories were belching black smoke and huge wide chimney stacks were emitting white clouds of steam as the train flashed past power stations.

The steam from their train wafted passed their window every now and then blocking the view. "I reckon we're due in shortly." Edie announced as she began to button up her jacket and fasten the belt around her waist. Phyllis and Basher shuffled in their seats elbowing each other through lack of space in an attempt to prepare for arrival. Out came Edie's powder compact and the ritual of making up her face began.

As the train slowed down in preparation for entering the station they passed row upon row of terraced houses, the brickwork black and net curtains that had turned a muddy grey no doubt from black smoke that emitted from tall chimneys not to mention the coal fires that burned within the homes.

"What a bleedin' depressing place. It's worse than London, and they 'ave the cheek to call that the 'smoke'? Compared to this?" Edie complained before they had even entered the station.

The train finally pulled into platform one spilling out hundreds of passengers. The three girls heaved their kitbags on to their shoulder and made for the exit barrier. "Weren't we supposed to be met?" queried Phyllis.

"I've no idea. Just keep walking till we get off the platform" Basher shouted as she strode off in front of her two mates.

A WAAF sergeant and corporal then came into view holding up a sign, which read: *ALL BALLOON OPERATORS REPORT HERE.* The trio made their way toward the sign, and soon a small group of girls surrounded the NCO's.

"Move through the exit, turn left and wait there for us" the sergeant ordered. Finally about a hundred women stood in groups awaiting the arrival of the two NCO's.

Ten minutes later armed with clipboards they arrived. Giving instruction that as names were called they were to follow the corporal to wait for transport. Phyllis's name was on the first list. Edie and Basher held their breath, then exchanged horrified looks. "Blimey don't say that after all this time we're being split up." whispered Edie hoarsely.

"It sure looks like it" Basher said feeling sick as a wave of panic swept over her.

The next list of names included Basher and Edie, but

Edie wasn't listening Instead she watched the first group like a hawk. Then as they past the exit and stood on the pavement edge waiting for transport to arrive she picked up her kit and fled station catching up with Phyllis just as her group were climbing into one of the trucks. Leaping forward she caught the arm of the corporal and demanded

"Where's this lot going?" The corporal looked surprised. "Why?"

"Cos she's me mate, and we've been togever ever since we joined up." Edie said now close to tears as she pointed to Phyllis.

The corporal glared at Edie. "No time for sentiment in this game. But for your information they are going to Squadron Headquarters at Hillsborough. If you contact them they'll tell you what site she's on." Then dismissing Edie abruptly she banged on the side of the lorry.

Edie waved a sad and tearful farewell to Phyllis as she called "Keep yer pecker up mate. We'll be in touch, don't worry... good luck."

Phyllis looked detached and unemotional as she whispered a simple 'Goodbye' then the lorry lurched forward and moved slowly from the forecourt of the station.

When Edie turned around she discovered her group had caught up with her, and were on the pavement edge waiting for the arrival of their transport.

"Well... you take the biscuit," Basher roared, "For months she has irritated you beyond words yet here you are bawling now she's gone. We can always visit her for Christ's sake. Think yourself lucky; at least you and I are in the same squadron. It's just to be hoped we get the same site, or I'll roll up and die!" Basher remarked with some feeling.

"But I wont 'ave anyone to torment now, will I?" Edie whined.

"I'm sure you'll find someone before long" Basher commiserated.

"But it wont be the same she's me mate like you, we've been togever all this bleedin' time and now she's gone. It don't feel the same Bash."

Basher put a comforting arm around Edie just as the lorry arrived.

It rattled through the dismal city streets. The smell of hops emitted from the vast breweries in the centre of the city filling the air with a stench that made Basher want to vomit.

The sun that had shone so brilliantly in London was now obliterated by haze and heavy cloud. The inhabitants went about their daily business, pale faced and pinched with apparent anxiety. Black smoke billowed out of tall chimneys that surrounded this vast industrial area, and acres of flattened land spread out where homes and factories once stood. The bombers had visited twelve months previous, and had massacred this once booming city of steel putting the fear of God into it's people.

The wheels of the lorry skidded over tram lines, then moved over to allow the clattering trams to trundle on their way under Wicker Arches their once bright cream body work now tinged in a dirty muddy grey.

Edie and Basher silently took in their new surroundings. Then after passing a second balloon site Edie blurted out. "Bloody'ell... 'ain't it filfy Bash?"

"You can say that again Ede. I can't face coping alone on one of these mucky looking sites" Basher said near to tears, and clearly becoming engulfed swiftly into a melancholy mood.

Edie recognising the unhappy mood of her mate attempted to cheer her up with a reminder of the WAAF officer's words at Morecambe... *Be proud to know you are helping to defend this great island of ours."* she said laughing at her own ability of being able to talk posh.

Basher smiled for the first time since their arrival, whilst the girls in the truck giggled.

About six miles north of the city the truck pulled into a long drive the wheels of the lorry crackled as they drove over a driveway of stones before stopping abruptly outside a large rambling old house. Edie peered out of the back and remarked.

"What's this then, the bleedin' vicarage?"

The driver smiled as he pulled down the back flap. "This is it girls, home from home. Your squadron headquarters."

Once inside the routine of checking names began at once. A Flight Lieutenant entered the room and everyone stood rigidly to attention. He was a short stocky man in his early forties. His face rose like the rising sun under his peaked cap. But it was impossible to see the colour of his pig like eyes as he squinted around the room.

He acknowledged the newcomers with a salute and asked them to stand at ease before he began to address them in what was without doubt, a patronising manner.

"Welcome to Sheffield and in particular to this

squadron. We trust that your stay will be a happy one. You all have a hard but splendid job ahead of you. A job to be proud of, and one that in future you can tell your grandchildren how you helped to defend this glorious city of steel" he enthused with great panache and drama.

"What a pratt" mumbled Basher to Edie. "Who does he think he is... Errol Flynn?"

"Do me a favour mate, he couldn't act the goat never mind a film star. I reckon e's got shares in the steel works."

Basher smiled at Edie's humour as the officer drivelled on...

"This is your own squadron headquarters the very heart of all your future activities.

"He's so up 'imself this one." Edie whispered.

He continued in his well spoken whine. *"You'll be paid once a fortnight. The pay parade takes place right here, and I'm your officiating officer."*

"Boy can't wait! ...I'll 'come' on the spot" Edie said from the side of her mouth.

The officer paused and glanced around the room trying to detect where the chattering was coming from but was met with a wall of silence from his new intake. He shuffled irritably before continuing. *"To save time you can bring your laundry and collect any items on the day of your pay parade. Your chocolate and cigarette rations are issued on that day as it must be obvious that there are no NAFFI facilities on balloon sites."*

"You don't bleedin' say" muttered Edie irritably.

"Good luck in your new postings, I trust you will be happy working here with u" he paused and saluted before

abruptly leaving the room.

A WAAF sergeant took over and began checking her list. A murmur of babbling voices rose to a crescendo. "Be quiet!" she bawled. Then as she began to read out names, Basher and Edie exchanged furtive glances putting their hands behind their backs and crossing fingers.

"The following girls will report to the Princess Street site... Smith and Berry." The two girls let out a huge sigh of relief. When the list was completed Edie asked "Where is Princess Street sarge? It sounds posh."

The sergeant smiled "Atterclife" she replied simply.

"That could be Timbuckto, I'm none the bleedin' wiser." Edie said in muffled tones.

But the sergeant overhead the last remark and said rather knowingly as she nodded her head... "You will!"

CHAPTER 9

The driver once again helped the two girls down from the back of the transport then handing them their kit he left them on the threshold of a large nissen hut explaining that they would find a sergeant and crew inside.

During the past hour or so they had toured many balloon sites in the area dropping off the new crew from squadron headquarters. Now as it was getting dusk they stood silently viewing their first operational site. This was Princess Street Attercliffe. In the fading light they could just see the outline of a factory that dominated the corner of the street. A row of dingy looking terraced houses stood along amongst acres of flattened land that must have been the homes of many Sheffield people. The only familiar thing was the balloon and she was flying at interim height wafting gently in the summer breeze reminding them of their training site in the green and pleasant land of the south of England.

"Bleedin' 'ell this can't be real, tell me I'm fuckin' dreamin' Bash" were the first words that Edie could utter.

The coal clinker that covered the ground of the entire site crunched under Basher's feet as she stood first on one leg, then the other, trying to take in the enormity of what lay before her.

"Come on mate better see what delights are inside this 'ole," Edie suggested as she picked up her kit and opened the nissen hut door.

The entrance was dark. They passed the operations office on the left, but it was empty. Edie poked her head around the only other available door and gasped;

"Wait till yer get a butchers at this little lot!" she whispered to her mate.

They entered the room quietly and found a form just inside the door. Placing their kit in front of them they sat down and gazed around them before exchanging looks of utter incredibility. Four members of the crew sat at one of the long tables playing cards. They wore greasy dirty overalls with blue ribbed jumpers underneath. Their ugly boots looked as though they hadn't seen polish since the day they were issued. Basher observed their grimy hands and weather beaten faces that were devoid of any kind of make up. She glanced at her mate and wondered how she would survive this little lot. The training sergeant had been dead right for it was obvious that this crew hadn't seen soap or water for weeks!

The card players were so immersed in their game that they were oblivious to the newcomers. A huge belly stove roared ferociously in the corner of the room, it was stifling. Mugs of dark liquid stood on tables that were stained with cocoa rings and the remains of the previous meal.

The door suddenly burst open and on the threshold stood a gaunt girl with short cropped greasy hair that clung to her head. Her weather beaten skin highlighting her already ugly features. She eyed the new comers with great interest asking "Are you waiting for the sergeant?"

"Well, we are certainly waiting for someone." Edie replied sarcastically.

"She's just checking the balloon. She's a fussy cow. I'll go and tell her you're here," As she got to the door she yelled to the card players. "Oye corp, is there enough bread to make some toast?"

"Yep, help yourself" the corporal replied without taking her eyes off of her hand of cards.

Basher nudged Edie and whispered "My God what a way to talk to a corporal. She'd have got done for that back at camp."

"Yea but this 'aint camp mate. Watch points 'ere, this gets interesting."

The skinny girl finally returned with a huge mound of bread and a bowl of dripping. She sat in front of the stove and with a long fork commenced to toast the bread over the hot belly stove.

So fascinated were Basher and Edie watching the goings on in their new surroundings that they were unaware that the sergeant had arrived and was standing in front of them.

"You must be my two new girls." the sergeant said in her soft Scottish accent.

"Both girls immediately stood and blushed with embarrassment. The sergeant's smart appearance in contrast to her crew was so blatantly obvious. Her battle dress was pressed to perfection and she wore a crisp clean shirt along with the issued black tie. Her boots shone and her cap badge dazzled as it caught the electric light.

"So..." she began as she referred to her list. "I see your names are Berry and Smith but we don't stand on ceremony here, so what do your friends call you?"

"I'm Basher. My real name is Muriel but she re-named

me a few weeks after we joined up." Basher said shrugging her shoulders with slight embarrassment.

"Very apt don't yer fink sarge? By the way, I'm Edie."

The sergeant smiled. "I'll show you where you will be sleeping. So come on, pick up your kit, I'll then introduce you to the crew."

As the trio trudged over the clinkered site, the sergeant explained "You will find life very different on an operational site. I'm aware that my crew appear lazy and unkempt, but it's not all it seems. We work long hours and the work is tough. There is no time for formality. I pride myself on having a good team, so if you both work with us you'll soon fit in."

There was a strong smell of polish as they entered the nissen hut. It was a great improvement on the dining area. The floor shone and the table in the centre was scrubbed white. Six double bunks were arranged around the walls of the corrugated hut. Two members of the crew were sleeping whilst another was writing letters. The sergeant put her finger to her lips and whispered. "Don't make a noise these girls are tired out. Just drop your kit and follow me. You can sort yourselves out later."

As they were leaving the girl who was writing looked up nodded and smiled at the newcomers.

Once outside the sergeant continued her explanation "The girls have had a very hectic few days. We've been short on the crew compliment, but now you have arrived we can ease up a bit." she said as they re-entered the dining hut.

She approached the corporal who was still playing cards and requested that some supper be organised for the two new girls.

"Right sarge" the corporal said with little concern and still concentrating on her hand of cards.

The sergeant wasn't impressed so leaning on the table she said "OK girls give it a rest. I want to introduce you to our two new crew members. They are straight from training so I rely on you all to help them. This is Edie Smith and Muriel Berry who prefers to be called Basher."

The crew lay down their cards, exchanged looks and smiled. Then the sergeant began her introduction of the crew to both girls. "This is Jessie Obens, Carrie Spence... she's one of our favourite cooks by the way... Marion Brown and Violet Nicholson, over there making toast is Bobby Owen. Two are fast asleep as you could see, and the other two are on guard duty, the last one was writing letters in her sleeping quarters that is Millicent Martin." Then turning to Jessie the sergeant said "Run along to the store cupboard and get some sheets and pillowcases for the girls. Here's the keys" A bunch of keys landed on the table and the sergeant made for the door abruptly. She hesitated at the threshold before asking "Will someone show them where the ablutions are please. Don't forget their supper corporal". Then the door shut.

The corporal eyed the two girls for a moment before asking Basher. "Do you play cards?"

"Never played in my life wouldn't know where to start."

"You'll quickly discover there's a lot of bleedin' fings she ain't done" Edie interrupted.

Violet shot a rather menacing look at Edie before asking sarcastically. "Meaning... you have?"

"Nor 'arf" Edie replied totally oblivious to the sarcasm being dished out.

"We've 'ad some smashing times 'ain't we Bash? Never bin apart 'cept for leave of course."

Basher looked embarrassed, "Let's say there's never been a dull moment."

"And what about you Ede can you play? Or need we ask?" the corporal's tone made it obvious that they weren't that keen on this cocky newcomer.

But Edie unperturbed waded in with... "You name it I can play it. Probably show yer a few tricks fer good measure."

The crew exchanged unbelieving looks; Basher could read them like a book. But the corporal turned deliberately to her and promised; "We'll teach you Basher, but not tonight. You must be bushed after your long journey. Go and unpack your kit. I'll send Jess over with the bedding and by that time your supper will be ready."

"Thanks corporal" Basher responded as she nudged Edie to leave.

"Not such a bad bunch once your get to know them." Basher remarked as they made their way once again across the site.

"Spose not, but I reserve me judgement." Edie replied

They began to fill their lockers not daring to speak for fear of waking the sleeping crew. Jessie arrived with an armful of bedding and a bag of garments. Whispering to them both she said "Here's a few warm things like jumpers, scarves, balaclava helmets and socks all hand knitted. When you've spent a winter in this cold hole you'll realise what a boon they are."

"Thanks" both girls chorused.

"Don't be long your supper will be ready directly" Jessie told them before leaving them to it.

"Where do you reckon she's from?" Basher asked of her mate.

"She's a janner."

"A what?"

"A bleedin' janner. Sod me yer don't know nuffink. She comes from Cornwall yer berk.

The midnight guard duty had just finished. Edie and Basher dragged their weary legs to their sleeping quarters. Just kicking off their boots and taking off their jackets they lay on their beds and immediately fell into exhaustive sleep.

Suddenly the hut door crashed open and the corporal bawled "Out crew... purple alert... gerry's approaching... come on... man the balloon and that does mean NOW!"

The crew automatically jumped from their beds and like robots silently put warm clothing over their nightwear. Basher glanced at the clock over the door and then yelled irritably to her mate. "Christ... we've only been in bed an hour!"

Edie pulled her tin helmet over her curlers and retorted equally as irritated. "Tell me about it! But come on or 'aggis face'll 'ave yer guts fer garters."

They stumble into the darkness of the night and made for where they imagine the sergeant might be. Edie just avoided crashing into a hut door. "Piss me, it's like the blind leadin' the bleedin' blind!" she curses.

The red glow of the steel furnaces light up the distant

sky like a glow worm. Basher viewed this with terror. "Just look at that lot Ede, we're a sitting target if you ask me."

The sergeant was by the winch giving orders to her crew. She overheard Basher's remark and retorted "Nobody is asking your opinion Basher. Just climb into the winch and drive it... like *now!*"

Hauling herself into the drivers seat Basher is perched six feet from the ground covered in a cage of rigid steel mesh. The enormous drum of cable is sitting behind her. A gust of wind momentarily rocks the winch and Basher claws at the overhead wire mesh. She mumbles to herself "My god this is all we need, a threatened bloody gale when we have to fly the damned thing."

Having now got adjusted to the dark and as comfortable as it's possible to get, she pulled the starter motor and the engine flew into action and throbbed satisfactorily.

In the distance she can hear the sergeant giving orders over the megaphone. The curtains from nearby houses begin to move and bedroom lights can be seen peeping behind blackouts as the locals check the activity.

The factory on the corner is billowing smoke into the night sky. Basher continues to mutter to herself. "Fat chance we've got with this lot sending up smoke signals!"

The sergeant's voice rises from the darkness. "OK Basher... ease her away."

Letting out the clutch Basher feels the balloon tugging as she eases her from her bed. Then... a massive bang as she bounces from one side of the deck to the other. Big Bertha is raring to go! The sergeant yells urgently "Hold it Basher..." More drill can be heard in the distance. "Check those guy ropes, get them clear of sandbags and ballast blocks. OK we're all clear"

Then turning the megaphone toward the winch she yells "Take her away to fifteen thousand feet Basher."

As Basher let out the clutch the cable unwinds and the drum revolves violently behind her. She keeps an eye on the dimly lit meter to keep a check on the height. Suddenly there is a terrific jerk and the winch leaves the ground swinging like a pendulum! Basher's mouth is dry. Her entire body is shaking with fear. The sweat begins to trickle down her spine. Big Bertha was bouncing from the roof of the steel works! Will she free herself? Basher asks herself urgently, and if so, will she go flying off into the night sky winch and all, maybe meeting 'gerry' on the way?

As these questions flew through her mind the winch finally hits the ground and shudders violently... The sergeant is beside the winch screaming her orders to Basher who was now in danger of losing her nerve completely. "Foot off the accelerator and brake *NOW!*" she screamed.

Basher's clammy hands grip the controls but fear took over and her nerve went completely. Suddenly she turned off the engine calmly before climbing down. It was then she lost it. Totally out of control she yelled at the dumb struck sergeant "If you think you can drive it any better then bloodywell get in and drive the soddin' thing yourself, cos I've finished!"

Basher then turned and ran in the direction of the sleeping hut. Sitting on the edge of her bed she trembled with shock after such an ordeal. She lit a cigarette and drew on it nervously, mumbling to herself. "I hate this rotten job. I'm sick of this rough uncouth lot. I detest this dirty city... I'm going home. They can lock me up I don't care... I'm off... first thing tomorrow."

The crew returned interrupting her angry thoughts. The sergeant barged in pushing past anyone in her way. She stood in front of Basher clenching her fists in anger.

"Off your bed and you listen to me. When we are manning the balloon you will heed my instructions at all times without panic. We have a serious job to do here, and do it we will whatever the cost. With the application of the correct balloon drill there should be few problems."

Basher stood looking at her feet very near to tears. But felt she was being unjustly treated so barged in saying "Excuse me sarge, with respect. The drill I've done up till now did not include the balloon taking off and wrapping itself around a factory chimney, dragging the winch and me in it! ...I was dangling mid air, I've never been so scared in me life."

"Maybe not" said the sergeant, "But that's just one of he hazards of the job. You surely were warned that this was a tough and dangerous job during your training? And so it is. So let's have no more of this kind of outburst. We are here to work as a team and you are part of that team. Do I make myself clear?"

Basher muttered not too convincingly "Yes sergeant."

The sergeant turned on her heel and abruptly left the hut.

Marion does a rude version of the victory sign before turning to Basher saying;

"Don't take any notice of her Bash. We've all been scared at some time especially when we first started. You'll soon get used to it and with a bit more experience and a few more rollickings from old 'aggis face you'll be as tough as old boots in no time."

Edie intervened saying. "She's right Bash. Come on cheer up. We've bin fru a lot you and me. Yer aren't going to let a stupid fing like this get yer down are yer?"

Edie and Marion had a similar sense of humour. In a final attempt to raise Basher's spirits Marion picks up the poker from the hearth and uses it as a pretend cigar before going into a rendering of one of Churchill's famous speeches... *"Nevar... was so much owed... by so many... to so few...*

You do realise he meant us when he uttered those words Bash? Come on we're famous mate. When old 'aggis face nags remember his words and be proud to be one of the few"

Violet yells from her bunk. "Will you shut up and give it a rest, we're trying to get some sleep. And in any case you've got it all wrong as usual. *NEVER IN THE FIELD OF HUMAN CONFLICT WAS SO MUCH OWED BY SO MANY TO SO FEW."*

Marion bristled at being shown up, so she shouted, "Get'er... big 'ead."

But Violet retorted. "Shut up and bugger off! Lets get some sleep will you?"

Marion, determined to have the last word yelled "Piss off!"

CHAPTER 10

During the following weeks there was no let up with the relentless duties. Working continually amongst the hardened tough crew, made Basher feel sorry she had ever left home. For never in her life had she felt so tired and exhausted.

Depression swept over her and hung like a huge black cloud. Breaking point finally came. Making her way to the privacy of the toilets she gave way to her weariness and sobbed from her boots. Finally emerging red eyed she bumped straight into Edie.

"What's up Bash has yer muvver died or what?" Edie remarked looking amazed at the state of her mate. Basher shrugged her shoulder trying hard to control the outburst of tears that were threatening to erupt.

"I'm so bushed Ede. I never realised how hard this lot could be. Haven't slept properly for weeks. What with air raids, guard duties, then having to get out of bed in the middle of the night to pull the damned thing into wind. It's just too much. I wish I'd listened to me mother and never left home."

Edie thumped Basher's arm saying "Don't talk like a prat. Just think of what you'd 'ave missed... me fer a start. Yer sailor wiv one 'ear... Come on Bash keep yer pecker up. This 'aint like you, we'll get fru you'll see. Don't let the bastards get yer down is what I always say."

Basher smiled a weak smile and added "I could cope if

I got me quota of sleep."

Edie laughed and said. "I can fink of somefink much better than sleep ter buck yer up. Never mind yer day will come and you'll remember me words. Better than finking of England I can tell yer! It's yer afternoon off ain't it? Right... jarmas on and get some kip. That'll set yer right.

After lunch Basher dragged herself back to her hut and got undressed into her pyjamas. Laying her lower bunk bed, she placed her hands behind her head. Her eyes quickly became heavy. She was suddenly woken with a commotion and screeching of laughter in the hut. As she focused her eyes she thought she was seeing things, for opposite her leaning against the hut wall was Bobby in the nude posing for photographs. One of the crew had a Brownie box camera!

Bobby looked grotesque Basher thought. Her skinny body had no shape, no waist, no breasts. Her ribs protruded and could be clearly seen. Indeed with such unfortunate ugly features she could have been taken for any one of the male species.

As Basher was considering why on earth this girl should consider herself beautiful enough to be photographed, she discovered Bobby glaring back at her. What transpired was clearly brought about by reading the wrong signals. For suddenly Bobby lunged herself at Basher and lay on top of her pressing her lips aggressively on to Basher's attempting the thrust her tongue in her mouth!

Basher fought like a tigress! She hadn't the foggiest idea what this was about but instinctively knew it appalled her. They rolled on to the floor and kicked and punched each other like two animals. Finally Basher freed herself and screamed at Bobby "You filthy cow! You keep your hands to yourself do you hear? Or I'll report you make no mistake!"

Basher then grabbed her clothing and rushed to the toilets to get dressed. There was no way she would ever trust that Bobby again she swore to herself.

She made her way to the kitchen to get a cup of tea and found Edie playing cards. Edie took one look at Basher's face and realised something was wrong. So excusing herself from the card school she approached Basher and asked "Fought you were 'aving a sleep mate?"

Basher went into detail about what had transpired. Edie threw back her head and laughed hysterically. Basher went scarlet with temper.

"Aw come on Bash, surely you must have sussed out she was a dyke?"

Basher looked uncomfortable but decided to come clean. "I don't even know what a dyke is?"

Edie lowered her voice for once and explained in some graphic detail what it was she needed to know about life. Basher shuffled uneasily before blurting out, "Well they needn't think they can try it out on me because I'm not interested thank you!"

Around ten thirty that night Basher was checking the balloon bed with the aid of her torch. Both her and Marion were on the ten to twelve guard duty. Marion had opted to listen for the phone while making some tea and toast while Basher did the rounds on the site. Suddenly a strong torchlight beamed into her face, startling her and blinding her momentarily. "Halt! Who goes there!" she bawled.

"Gi' 'oer it's only me" the voice replied.

"Who's me?" Basher asked.

"Local bobby of course. My God you girls don't 'arf take things seriously."

It was Basher turn to shine her torch on him. He was only one of the 'specials.' They weren't the regular police force but because of the shortage of man power these guys volunteered to do police work in their spare time.

"Excuse me" retorted Basher, "But we need to take things seriously these are serious times. Anyone could have been hanging around the site, even German spies."

The policeman laughed. "You've been reading too many books lass.

Basher's blood boiled at this remark. What a berk this man was she considered.

"I wouldn't hurt you to do a bit of reading, because clearly you seem to have no idea of what is going on around you."

Suddenly the policeman grabbed Basher by the shoulders and pushed her against the wall of the nissen hut. "You're a feisty bird and no mistake... coome here." he said as he attempted to kiss her hard on the lips, pushing his body up against hers at that same time.

In one movement Basher pushed his face away from hers with one hand while lifting her knee automatically where she had been taught it would hurt. "I've just about had enough for one day, first a dyke and now you, you dirty bastard."

The policeman reeled at this attack, but backed off

pleasantly attempting to strike up a reasonable conversation. Basher suspected he was afraid she just might report him. After some moments of apologies the policeman changed the subject asking questions about her job and seemed genuinely surprised to hear about the toughness of the work.

"Eee lass I never thought it involved so much. I take me 'at off to yer."

"I suppose you'd like a cup of tea?" Basher asked, feeling certain this was his idea in the first place.

"Wouldn't say no."

Marion looked surprised but delighted as they both entered the warm kitchen.

"Brought in a waif and stray mate. He wants a cuppa and some toast."

"Not a problem" Marion said as she smiled sweetly at the new comer.

"By the way I'm Marion and she's Basher, but I expect she's already told you that."

"She hasn't as a matter of fact. Been too busy explaining what you girls have to put up with. Then turning to Basher he said "That's not a very complimentary name for such an attractive girl."

Basher blushed. "Compliments will get you nowhere. A mate of mine christened me with it days after we joined up, and it has stuck."

The policeman turned his attention to Marion as he sipped his hot tea.

"And where do you come from Marion?" he asked as his eyes twinkled with anticipation.

Marion flushed at the attention he was giving her and

said "Me? I'm a Londoner born and bred."

Basher wasn't included in the conversation from then on, so she collected the empty mugs and washed them up before clearing around the kitchen generally.

The relief arrived at midnight. Basher said her goodnights to her friend Marion who was still in deep conversation with the police officer and took off for her bed. She had just four hours sleep before she would be shaken to commence her next duty between four and six in the morning.

Marion was shaking her violently. "Come on Bash get up quick before the duty cooks arrive."

Basher stretched and glanced at the clock it was ten to six. "What's happened why didn't you call me at four?"

"You were dead to the world so I hadn't the heart to wake you." Marion explained generously. "Hurry Bash the cooks will be here any minute" she said as she fled the hut.

"Be there in a tick" Basher replied pulling her trousers over her pyjamas.

As she left the hut she noted that Marion's bed hadn't been slept in!

CHAPTER 11

The majority of the crew were in the dining area playing cards that afternoon waiting further order from headquarters. A gale warning had been received. Basher's deck of cards were gripped firmly in her hand as she concentrated on her next move. Nobody would have guessed that only a few weeks previous she would not have known an ace from a king.

"Come on Bash 'urry up" urged her mate before she broke into a fit of the giggles.

Basher looked puzzled, "What's up with you now. What's so funny?"

"You are... Christ I've never seen such a change in anyone in me entire life."

She continued to giggle more frantically as she watched Basher draw heavily on her cigarette.

Then turning to the crew Edie went on. "Do yer know, when we first joined up butter wouldn't melt in 'er bleedin' mouf. Little Miss Prim she was. She even wore a Sally Army bonnet!"

Basher went scarlet as she watched the crew exchange amused looks.

"You never!" yelled Marion clearly shocked by the revelation.

"Yes she did. Na look at 'er, fag in mouf and swears like a bleedin' trooper. It's a good job Phyll can't see yer, she'd 'ave a fit" Edie added now enjoying the obvious embarrassment her mate was showing.

"Who's Phyll?" Marion asked, as she tried to concentrate on her next card move.

"She's our 'ovver mate that we joined up wiv. Don't larf but she was worse... a rotten Sunday school teacher that one. I tell yer somefink she was yer classic narrer minded bigot. A plain Jane and no nonsense, and a bleedin' book worm to go wiv it! Imagine me between these bleedin' two! But boy I loved winding 'em up."

"So where is this Phyl now?" Marion asked.

"Over 'illsborough way somewhere." Then nudging Basher she reminded her that they really must find out where she was because they had been promising to visit her ever since they arrived.

"Tell yer what, 'ow about if we ask sarge fer a day off togever. We can go and find 'er then. Wonder what she's doing at 'er end?" Edie asked with a far away look in her eye.

"Come on concentrate its not a bloke we're talking about here. It's only another balloon operator" one of the players remarked impatiently.

Edie threw her card as she remarked. "Yes I know, but the person you've been wiv since yer joined is kind of special, and we've 'ad some ups and downs wiv 'er 'aint we Bash? Remember that time when she nearly got raped?"

The crew lay down their cards. This subject was much more interesting than a card game.

Edie realising she had the floor went into full flow giving a vivid account of the night the three of them had their first night out from RAF Titchfield.

When she came to the bit about the naval dance, and how the girls in the hut dealt with the Chief Petty Officer the drama increased to outrageous proportions.

The phone rang just as the crew went into peels of laughter at the antics of their two new mates.

"Shut up!" yelled the corporal from the office doorway, "Can't hear myself think in here."

Then after a brief conversation the corporal left the office and the crew resumed their card game. Quite suddenly a voice boomed from the doorway making them all jump. "Out crew, we have to move Big Bertha into wind."

The crew sauntered out moaning and groaning rubbing their hands down the back of their overalls to ensure they were quite dry before beginning the task of heaving and shoving the monster into wind. The corporal was in charge of this operation. She detailed the crew into their positions. One by the stern guy rope, one at the bow, while the rest hung on to a line each. Then putting the megaphone to her mouth she bawled. "Number one to five... HAUL!"

They dragged the massive creature around the bed inch by painful inch.

When she go about half way into wind she rocked and banged about shoving the crew to the ground, while sandbags and ballast blocks rose in the air and swung like dinky toys.

Finally the corporal wetted her finger and held it up in the air to test the wind direction. Big Bertha sat motionless.

"Right that'll do... thanks... now back to the hut"

"Till the bleedin' wind changes again" Edie moaned as she rubbed her sore hands.

"I'm not so bothered in the day time it's when we're dragged from our warm beds that I could commit murder." Basher remarked.

The crew seemed in a mischievous mood as they resumed their seats. Jessie put the kettle on to make some tea, whilst some fumbled with the card pack.

"Hey Bash come and read our cards." requested Marion.

Basher look horrified." I can't read bloody cards. What's up with yer?"

"You don't believe in that rubbish do you? Jessie queried as she stirred the cups of steaming tea.

"Well it's good for a laugh" Marion defended. Then turning back to Basher she pleaded. "Come on Bash give it a go."

Basher hadn't the foggiest idea where Marion had got the idea that she was some kind of Gypsy Rose Lee. But being the dare devil she was she decided to give it the full drama. Picking up the cards she professionally shuffled them before spreading them into a fan shape. The crew member who sat directly opposite Basher could have been an entire stranger for Basher had little to do with her in any way. She began giving off everything that came into her head along with dramatic eye shutting and holding her head in deep contemplation making it sound all very mysterious.

She would have won an Oscar for her acting. Until that is she happened to glance at the recipient of the so-called card reading who was now looking like a zombie with all colour drained from her.

Basher looked alarmed and asked. "What's up?"

"Well so far, most of what you've given me has already happened." she said in a frightened whisper.

Basher's heart began to thump. She threw the cards across the hut yelling, "That's it... so much for your little joke Marion. That's the last time I try anything like that again. It's scary and gives me the shits."

The day dawned when Edie and Basher were granted some time off together.

The sergeant explained that she could only spare them for half a day it was the very best she could do.

As they changed into clean shirts and well pressed uniforms Edie moaned.

"I don't why she couldn't 'ave given us the full day everyone else seems to be able to 'ave their days off wiv their mates."

"It can only be one of two things." Basher began, " Either their face fits or she considers us the creme de la creme of her crew and can't do without us. So be thankful and stop yer chuntering, thank god for small mercies as my grandmother used to say.

"Yer might 'ave somfink there. She did as least ring around and finally track Phyll down for us. Come on Bash lets get the 'ell out of 'ere."

Making their way across the busy street dodging traffic as they went they scrambled to catch the tram that had just arrived. The long seat at the drivers end was the only one vacant. The two girls watched fascinated as the driver wound round the brass handle back and forth before stepping sharply on the brakes that sent hands grabbing for the leather straps hanging over heads of those standing. When it started up again the tram lurched forward violently throwing passengers against seats. Finally it swayed jolted and shuddered violently as it went over connection lines at Wicker Arches.

"These things make me fee a bit sick." Basher commented to her mate.

"Don't bleedin' throw up 'ere."

"Got nothing to throw up! Just feel a bit queasy that's all." Edie suddenly plunged deep in thought before remarking

"I wonder why our food rations have been cut down lately?"

"Search me. All I know is that last week when I was duty cook the supplies dwindled by the day. It became a nightmare trying to share out what food there was to make a decent meal. It's a good job my Mum taught me how to make a meal out of next to nothing." Basher said proudly.

"The sarge needs to pull her bloody finger out and ring headquarters."

"You can say that again. She's not behind the soddin' door at telling us off. But something has to be done, we can't be expected to work on thin air. They're quick enough at telling us it's the toughest job in the RAF." Basher said with some feeling.

"Fitzallen Square... we don't go any further... all out" the conductor bawled.

The girls clambered down the two steep steps to the pavement. Edie turned back to the conductor, who was busy collecting his sandwich box and bits and pieces. She asked of him "Where do we get a tram for 'illsborough mate?"

The conductor stuck out his chest with an air of authority remarking "Aye oop tha's from Looondon 'ain't thee lass?"

"Brilliant! Ten out of ten for observation" Edie replied sarcastically. But not in the least worried by Edie's sarcasm, he continued with his knowledge of local dialects.

"Can tell tha knows, it's thee accent luv, a dead give away."

Edie's eyes rolled in her head with exasperation. She turned to Basher with great agitation and said, "What a bleedin' berk! Come on Bash, we'll find it ourselves."

The landscape around them was beautiful with rolling green hills and sheep grazing lazily and an occasional squirrel scampering along the thick branches of the tress. This was something they hadn't seen in a very long time, but they agreed it was well worth the hours journey from the city centre. Edie gazed around her taking in these beautiful surroundings, then commented with some concern.

"This can't be right Bash. They wouldn't 'ave a balloon site out 'ere. What the bleedin' ell would they be defending?"

Basher shielded her eyes from the early Spring sunshine. In the distance the sun caught the shining silver of a balloon swaying gently in the light breeze.

"Hey look there it is! This must be the furthest region of the squadron. I reckon this is what they call a remote site. Ah! I've got it. They place a ring of sites around the perimeter of the city then another ring closer to the city, all strategically grouped around steel works. See... that's us amongst the filth" Basher explained as she pointed toward the city they had just come from.

"Trust Phyll to get a jammy site. I'd swop wiv 'er any day." Edie moaned.

Basher grabbed Edie's arm. "I've heard the saying somewhere that Sheffield is a dirty picture in a beautiful frame... Now I understand what that means.

"Piss me... get 'er... going all poetical." Edie said as she kicked a large stone irritably. "Anyway 'ow much farver 'ave we got to bloodywell walk?"

"Stop moaning we're nearly there."

They finally came level with the site entrance. Both girls stared in disbelief. Not a clinker in sight but beautiful fresh green grass and not a single thing out of place.

A member of the crew answered the knock on the hut door.

"Is Phyllis Bourne in please?" Basher enquired.

"Yes of course, come in" invited the girl.

She knocked gently on the office door it swung open at her touch. Phyllis was pouring over some paperwork with the site sergeant.

"Excuse me sarge... visitors for Phyll." the girl explained.

Phyllis swung around and went scarlet on seeing her two old mates standing on the threshold. The sergeant greeted them cheerfully before turning to Phyll dismissing her and suggesting she show her visitors around before making them a cup of tea.

Edie immediately switched in to Phyll's embarrassment and decided to rub it in somewhat, and so in her usual forthright manner blurted out...

"Ow's it going then me old mate? ...It's only us yer needn't blush."

Phyllis looked extremely uneasy and responded in a clipped and agitated manner. "I'm fine. Come on I'll show you around."

The two girls couldn't get over Phyll's appearance. She was immaculately dressed, her uniform pressed to perfection, with boots and cap badge sparkling in the sunlight. She reminded them of their Scots sergeant. As the trio ambled around the site they also noticed that this balloon bed and it's equipment was faultless, even the wire strops attached to the ballast blocks shone with new grease!

It was clearly too much for Edie who blurted out "You really are a jammy cow! I always knew that if you fell in a bucket of shit you'd come up smelling of fuckin' roses!"

Phyll physically winced at Edie's remark, although puzzled by her attitude, "What's the problem Edie? We're all on balloon sites doing the same job. Frankly I don't understand?"

Edie was now near to tears with envy and frustration. "You would if you were on our site mate. We're amongst the filthy factories. Our balloon is plonked on a derelict bomb site where 'ouses once stood. The site is covered in black cinders from the local pits and dirt doesn't even begin to describe it. Furver more, our poxy sergeant has no sense of humour. All she ever finks about is teamwork and keeping the site spotless which for the record is bloody impossible. So pardon us if we appear ever so slightly envious of you, and your lot Phyll. Yes we're all balloon operators but there are *sites* and sites mate. If you 'ad a butchers at ours then you'd understand."

"I'm really sorry to hear this because I'm so happy here. My crew are a pleasure to work with and the sergeant is perfection. She and I are quite friendly because we share our Christian beliefs."

"Ah, well na, that explains it. It was pretty obvious when we came in yer couldn't 'ave crawled up 'er arse much furver."

Phyllis stiffened before pulling herself up to her full height. Then looking down her nose at Edie remarked, "I wasn't crawling as you so delicately put it, the sergeant was showing me some of the paperwork that's required for an NCO's job."

Edie and Basher exchanged unbelieving looks. "But you ain't an NCO" Edie insisted.

"That's where you are quite wrong. I've just got my stripes and awaiting a new posting." Phyllis announced rather smugly.

For the first time that afternoon Edie laughed uproariously. "I'll tell yer what, it would serve yer bleedin' right if yer got a site like ours, then yer'd know what *real* work was."

Being keenly aware of the icy atmosphere Phyllis attempted to turn the conversation around, as she addressed Basher. "What about you. Are you still hanging on to your religious beliefs?"

"You've got to be bleedin' joking!" Edie chipped in, dying to shock her pompous mate who appeared to be in imminent danger of turning into a first class snob.

"She smokes, she drinks and swears like the rest of us... good old Bash, always up for a lark. Even 'ad a fight wiv a dyke and 'ad to deal wiv a flasher on the site. See mate we live in the *real* world, and she's learning fast."

Phyllis glared at Edie then asked Basher "What does your mother feel about the new you Basher?"

Basher hung her head praying for the subject to be swept firmly under the carpet as she managed a rather meek, "She's not too happy."

"I don't suppose for one moment she is" replied Phyllis. Then aware of Basher's obvious embarrassment and guilt she turned her attention back to Edie and asked of her. "What about your man from America, is he still going strong or have others taken his place?"

Edie's eyes narrowed as she thought Phyll sounded just like the poxy bird from Poona at RAF Titchfield. What a short memory she's got she thought.

But answered quite firmly. "He's still going strong, in fact we're getting engaged on me next leave."

"Glad to see that at last you appear to be settling down." This last remark from Phyll was followed by a somewhat pregnant silence. Basher began racking her brains for more conversation to lighten the atmosphere but instead she blurted out. "Suppose next time we see you you'll be a Flight sergeant?"

In actual fact I've been recommended to train as an officer" Phyllis finally announced.

This announcement caused Edie and Basher's mouths to fly open with shock.

"What... an officer... am I 'earing right? ...yer joking"

Edie yelled.

"I've never been more serious." Phyllis retorted.

At this point Edie became really agitated. "Think we should be making a move Bash. It takes bleedin' hours to get back on those bloody trams."

"Don't you want a cup of tea then? "Phyllis asked politely, although it was abundantly obvious she was hoping they would refuse.

"No thanks we don't have time" Basher quickly replied, being anxious to get away before Edie could inflame the situation any further.

They both finally said their goodbyes and wished Phyllis luck, with tongues firmly placed in cheeks.

Basher was aware that Edie was about to explode so she briskly got out of earshot and only just made it, when Edie yelled... "That takes the fuckin' biscuits. Who'd ave thought a frump like 'er would end up an officer? She's betrayed us Bash... the bleedin' Judas." she rampaged as she kicked yet another stone firmly down the road.

"Hold on a minute," Basher said. "She was recommended for an officer but she didn't say she was taking it did she? If you remember she said she had been accepted as a sergeant with a new posting so get yer story right. And talking of a Judas, what about you? You cried buckets when we first got here when you realised we were being split up! So what were they, crocodile tears? Come on lets be fair. Although I don't think you need worry for I reckon that's the last we'll see of her. All the same I think it's a bloody shame."

CHAPTER 12

Marion had begun her daily collection of money for the orders from the chip shop.

"Get me sixpennyworth of chips and some pork scratchings." requested Basher.

It was Carrie's turn to be duty cook that week. She liked nothing more than to turn her hand to some delightful West Country dish. But her frustration had reached boiling point when the sergeant appeared fussing about some papers she had mislaid.

"Never mind those. Isn't it time something was done about these dwindling rations?" Carrie exploded.

The sergeant looked at her in amazement. It was so unlike Carrie to complain, she was always so reliable, keeping her head at all times and normally working wonders in the kitchen.

"What ever is the matter?" was all the sergeant could utter.

"Don't tell me you've not noticed? Carrie replied with some incredibility. The sergeant shuffled uncomfortably aware that the entire crew was now watching.

"I've noticed a few wee thing have been missing from the daily ration allowance, yes "she replied rather meekly.

Carrie erupted into anger yelling, "A few wee things! A few wee things? Get real sarge, we're down to the bones of our arse!"

The sergeant eyes opened like an owl at this outburst,

but Carrie hadn't finished...

"We're lucky if we get a loaf a day to feed this lot on and that's apart from the fact we have received no meat, eggs and a mountain of other stuff. How aware are you that your crew are resorting to buying from the local chippy for their lunch each day? They are hungry sarge, and it's not on. You should be doing something about it." she finished breathlessly.

The sergeant's eyes met every member of the crew as she blushed to the roots of her head. She didn't utter a word but walked briskly to the office and picked up the phone.

Marion arrived with the order from the chippy. She threw the parcels on to the table and the girls dived in ripping open the paper too hungry to wait for plates. They stuffed their mouths with chips and an assortment of fish, fish cakes or scratchings depending on their individual financial circumstances.

Marion had also acquired a loaf of hot new bread from one of the neighbours. She cut it into doorstep portions and shared it amongst the crew who ate it greedily.

"You want to keep well in with her" remarked Basher as she stuffed the last crumb into her mouth.

"Yep she a good sort old Ethel. Often invites me over for a plate of her home made stew and it's bloody lovely I can tell you."

Bobby was watching Basher like a hawk. She hadn't forgotten their fight of some few months previous. It was obvious to everyone that she still fancied Basher. The knowledge that her lustful thoughts not only repulsed Basher but could only ever remain a pipe dream which caused Bobby to resort to spite.

"Hasn't anyone ever told you that chips are fattening, and God knows you're fat enough as it is." she said with a smirk on her face.

Basher glared at this grotesque girl and spat back. "So... there's nothing else to eat, what do you suggest?"

"If you starved for the next six months you'd still be competing with Big Bertha" came Bobby's bitchy response.

"I'd rather look healthy than some undernourished bloody bean pole!"

"I reckon you're pregnant if the truth be known." Bobby lashed back at her.

Basher's face went crimson with temper. She knew that the assumption was that she had been having sex. She may have broken every other rule that had been taught her since childhood but sex was not one of them. It had never entered her head and so far she had no desire to test it out. She had been taught that only cheap undisciplined people did this kind of thing. She therefore considered this to be the ultimate insult. In that moment she could have killed Bobby but instead she screwed up her chip paper and threw it into Bobby's face yelling tearfully...

"Well I'm *not* then! And one thing for absolute certain you're never likely to get pregnant for nobody would have you... you ugly bitch!"

Bobby let out a loud false laugh before turning to the crew and appealing…

"Will someone please tell the ignorant cow that people like me actually don't *want or even like* little brats."

"You vile trollop." Basher seethed.

Carrie thought it time to call a halt to the tirade of abuse, so she announced "Hey listen, sarge has rung headquarters and they've promised to look into the problem of the shortage of rations. Now perhaps we might get somewhere." Then sitting down she turned to her mate Jessie and suggested "If you dig up some carrots, swedes and tatters Jess, I'll make some soup later."

Those in the crew who were keen gardeners had found a small patch in the corner of the site that clearly had been once someone's pride and joy, but that was before their homes had been bombed to the ground. The crew had dug it over and vegetables had been planted and yielded some surprisingly good crops in the past.

"There's not much left Carrie. Some girls have pulled stuff up and eaten it raw they were so hungry." Jessie declared.

Carrie looked disgusted at such a state of affairs shrugged her shoulders and said; "Well, just get what there is."

Edie had been listening intently to this conversation and thought it a good idea to lighten the situation up a bit, so turning to Basher with apparent great sincerity she said loudly; "Bash, go and give Phyll a ring, ask 'er if we can borrer 'er bloke who fed the five fousand, cos we sure could do wiv 'im 'ere."

The crew tittered amongst themselves at such an outrageous suggestion.

Later that afternoon Basher decided it was time she caught up with some writing. Her weekly letter to her mother explained the plight of the crew, explaining how hungry they all were. She added that she found the job much tougher than she could ever have imagined. Then with pen in mouth she visualised her Mum cooking her lovely warm soft buns and an apple pie that melted in the mouth. Turning back to her letter she went on to explain how some of the crew had resorted to eating in cafe's and pulled home grown vegetables from the site garden and eaten them raw. But most of the time they were all living on chips! Basher finished her letter by asking her mother to send her a food parcel.

A week past with no sign of a parcel. There was no significant increase in the daily ration allowance either, despite the sergeant's so-called complaint. The controlling of Big Bertha was now becoming a strain on them all with lack of proper nourishment.

The daily inspections were in full swing that morning, the pulleys and wire strops on the balloon bed were being greased. A heavy gas cylinder was being dragged by two of the girls in readiness to top her up with hydrogen. The lack of energy and enthusiasm was very apparent

"Good morning sergeant. I'm looking for my daughter."

The voice sounded familiar to Basher as she crawled from under the belly of the balloon. It was then she froze. It was her father talking to the sergeant! A wave of panic swept over her. What was he doing here? What would he think of her dressed like this? She felt like a beached whale. He'd have a good laugh at her expense Basher decided as embarrassment swept over her. But there was only one way to deal with this she decided. So standing up and rubbing her oily hands down the back of her overalls she stepped courageously forward. She had to admit to herself that her father did look handsome, as he stood tall in his RAF uniform. His dark hair combed back from his forehead with blue/grey eyes sparkling with apparent joy at seeing her.

Basher was learning to face up to crisis so walking directly to him and interrupting his conversation with the sergeant she greeted him rather loudly.

"Hi, what you are doing here?"

He smiled as he lifted up a huge box that was sitting at his feet yelling. "This... it's for your crew!"

Basher could hardly contain herself as she spluttered. "Is it grub?"

"It most certainly is." her father said clearly delighted that it should bring such joy and relief. Some of the crew had stopped what they were doing realising something unusual was taking place.

"Grub's up!" Basher yelled deliriously.

Never had so many, come from nowhere, so fast! Someone snatched the box and the crew charged across the site yelping with delight, their clumsy boots tearing up the cinders in their eagerness to get to the kitchen and open the box. Tears of gratitude welled in Basher's eyes as she watched the joy of her crew.

"You're a good sort dad, we're so hungry." she choked. He took her in his arms and hugged her the pride and love he felt for his eldest daughter shone from him like a beacon.

The sergeant walked slowly toward the hut with Basher and her father as they entered the hut Marion jumped on to the table waving a bottle of sauce yelling... "Three cheers for Basher's dad!"

When the excitement had calmed down the sergeant turned to the airman and asked; "How did you know we were in need of food by the way?"

His story came tumbling out to a very intentive crew. He explained that when Basher's mother received a letter explaining how hungry they all were, she was so angry that she sent the letter to me, and I was furious.

"I didn't give permission for my daughter to join the forces to be treated like this. I sent a letter of protest to Air Ministry... of course in my capacity as her father you understand."

The crew clapped their approval of his actions.

"Good old dad about time someone woke that lot up!" Marion commented.

But he hadn't finished his story. He went on to explain that the news had somehow travelled around the local Yorkshire village where he was stationed.

He was forced to gather that as far as the locals were concerned this was a national crisis and very typical of village life. Rumour had become rampant that Sheffield Balloon Operators were starving, and they certainly couldn't have that. So they set about food collecting from their already meagre rations, which included the local grocery store who added his contribution of goodies, some of which hadn't been seen for years! The local farmers too had included some fresh eggs, butter, chickens and a bit of pork, as there had just been a kill.

"So it's to be hoped some of you can cook! Well there you have it and this is the result of their collection."

Basher's Dad concluded clearly feeling proud of his achievement.

"Yes we have some very good cooks among us particularly those from the West country. But thank you so very much. Please convey our heartfelt gratitude to the village people on your return. Let's hope that your letter of complaint is more effective than my efforts. Something is very wrong, very wrong indeed, I have to admit" the sergeant said finally shaking her head in dismay.

"It most certainly sounds as if someone's on the fiddle." Basher's Dad remarked before adding "By the way may I take my daughter out for the afternoon please sergeant? We don't get a great deal of time together."

"Why of course," the sergeant said as she fawned all over the man. "Would you like a cup of tea while she gets ready?"

"That would be most welcome." he said as he settled himself down to wait.

CHAPTER 13

As Spring emerged into Summer the nightmare of the past months faded as the daily rations gradually resumed normality. Basher pulled the covers firmly around her as she snuggled down to enjoy the luxury of a lie in.

Suddenly the sergeant burst in and whipped the bedclothes to the floor yelling "Come on Basher up you get!"

Basher's eyes opened like saucers before swinging her legs automatically out of the bed. Then glaring at the sergeant she said "But sarge... it's me day off."

The sergeant made for the door agitatedly. "Check! it's *your* day with all the trimmings. We are about to receive a visit from high ranking officers from Air Ministry. I could well do without this hassle. This is what becomes of writing stupid letters home! This site is to be cleaned as it's never been cleaned before. There are fire buckets to paint every scrap of rubbish to be picked up. You can start by raking over the cinders... and I *do* mean all of them!" she exploded.

"What the *entire* site?" Basher questioned with incredibility.

"That's what I said, the *entire* site, I'll make you sorry you ever opened your big mouth, Now get a move on. We've got only until midday then you will all parade with shoes and cap badges shining and your best uniforms pressed to perfection. So move it!!" she yelled as she flung herself out of the hut banging the door loudly behind her.

Feeling sick with fear and bewilderment Basher urgently pulled on her clothing her eyes smarting with tears as she muttered, why did Edie have to choose to be on leave at this precise moment? If ever I needed her support it's right now.

Once outside she began the fiddling task of raking over the cinders. She came level with Marion who was painting the fire buckets.

"What a turn up for the book" Basher said trying to make light of the situation.

But Marion just glared at her remarking "You can say *that* again, we could have done without all this bullshit... thanks for nothing!"

Bashers mouth dropped open and the tears welled up again as she turned away in dumb disbelief.

As the morning progressed she became acutely aware that her entire crew had long forgotten the kindness of her father in bringing food when they needed it most. She also gathered that she was about as popular as a 'pork chop in a synagogue'! Her ultimate punishment was to be sent to 'Coventry' by the entire crew.

The site was spotless. The crew were now standing in two neat lines unrecognisable in their clean shirts with starched collars and neat black ties that were folded inside of their jackets. The creases in their best trousers were as sharp as a razors edge, and shoes that shone from the elbow grease afforded them that morning. The sergeant was standing some yards in front of her crew with head held high, clearly proud of her site and her neatly turned out crew who were now stood at ease.

A small group of civilians were gathered at the entrance to the site, it was obvious that something unusual was happening. They didn't have to wait long before two gleaming motorbike escorts followed by a long black limousine complete with RAF pennant flying from its bonnet appeared from under the railway arch. Then an assortment of staff cars and jeeps followed which made for an impressive motorcade. Basher's eyes were fixed on the pennant flying from the bonnet for she then knew for certain that some very high ranking officer was about to emerge. Her stomach turned over she felt sick and thought she was going to faint.

The group of officers made their way toward the sergeant. Basher then recognised their commanding officer followed by a tall distinguished man whose uniform was adorned with wide rings at the end of his sleeve and thick gold braiding around the peak of his cap. The confirmation that this was undoubtedly the Air Vice Marshall himself caused Basher's bowel and bladder to almost erupt.

The sergeant clicked her heels and stood as straight as a ram rod. He slowly approached her. She gave the perfect salute. They exchanged a few private words, which Basher assumed would be a welcome to her site, before she about turned very smartly giving full thrust to her voice she yelled her order for her crew to stand to attention.

The entourage of officers slowly walked toward the crew for inspection.

With only ten of them plus the corporal it wasn't difficult to hear what was being said.

The high ranking officer did his inspection and was

asking each girl the same question. "Are you hungry? Have you ever been hungry since you've been here?"

Basher's anger mounted as she heard the constant reply of "No sir"

The gutless spineless lot! she fumed to herself. Just wait till it's my turn, I'll show 'em.

The tall handsome and distinguished officer was now stood in front of her with apparent amused disbelief... Finally he spoke. "I don't suppose by the remotest chance your name would be Berry would it?" he said with more than a hint of sarcasm.

Basher stood tall and answered directly and defiantly. "It most certainly is sir!"

The officer then walked slowly around her with his hands clasped firmly behind his back. Basher had to admit that she hardly *looked* undernourished, much more like a heavy weight boxer. Stroking his chin in deep contemplation he finally stood in front of her. It was obvious that he was trying to understand with incredible disbelief how this enormous balloon operator had found the audacity to complain of being hungry. Basher began to feel intimidated by his silence.

"Don't tell me that you are the only one who has suffered the pangs of hunger?"

"No sir, I wasn't the only one, *we all did!*" came Basher's forthright response.

He grunted before quickly passing to the next girl.

Five gruelling days of a Court of enquiry was set up on the site, with every crew member interviewed privately and intensely. When it became Basher's turn she was appalled at their attempt to persuade and cajole, trying to put words into her mouth in an attempt to get her to sign papers that was effectively saying that her father's complaint had been somewhat exaggerated.

But Basher stood her ground, they hadn't reckoned on her strength and honesty. She explained that in her most wildest dreams she could never have envisaged that a request for a food parcel could cause so many problems. She stated categorically that she would never have made such a request for a food parcel had she not have been hungry. As were the rest of the crew.

Their final attempt to twist her words was to suggest that because she was perhaps on the big side she needed more than most to fill her up, or was it possible that her parents had misunderstood her?

The fight with words went on and on, until finally she was asked to leave the room whilst they concluded their deliberations.

After an hour of keeping her waiting she was ordered to return to the Court of enquiry. The senior officer in charge of the investigating team fiddled with some papers before he spoke. "I regret Berry that as not one member of your crew can substantiate your father's allegations this enquiry can go no further."

Basher had in the past felt intimidated by authority. But this was the last straw, she was so angry she blurted out... "This spineless gutless lot have allowed themselves to be intimidated by people like you. Shall I tell you something they were glad enough of the food parcel my father brought, and sung his praises to high heaven. You are never likely to get to the truth because they are afraid of authority. Can't you see that? ...No I don't suppose you

139

can... or won't. It clearly suits your cause!"

The officiating officer held up his hand to interrupt Basher's flow.

"Thank you airwoman Berry that will be quite enough."

Then gathering his papers he nodded to the rest who abruptly left the room and the site.

As Basher emerged from her ordeal she bumped into the sergeant.

"Satisfied now Basher?" she asked.

Basher shook physically with anger as she yelled back. "If you had all spoken the truth it would have helped."

The sergeants eyes blazed and she quickly intervened. "You need to learn that there's a time to speak and a time to be quiet.

"And this wasn't one of them! How *could* you be so hypocritical? You fawned around my father never stop thanking him. As a matter of interest I wonder what his local villagers would think of you spineless lot now?"

It was apparent that to a degree the sergeant knew Basher to be right for she had the grace to blush, but in order to cover up the multitude of sins she scored the highest marks for putting the boot right in as she explained...

"By the way your friend Edie has been posted!"

This was the final straw. Basher's eyes welled with hot tears as she appealed to the sergeant. "Where has she gone?"

"I have no idea" the sergeant lied, "Her posting came through while she was on leave and she had to report to her new site at the end of it. It could be in Timbucktoo for all I know or care for that matter."

The darkest cloud engulfed Basher. She was lost without her mate, and none of this lot would speak to her. The sobs erupted from her very soul as she fled to the corner in the toilets where her sorrow and anger overflowed.

Basher hardly slept that night but came to some definite conclusions about her future.

The following morning she made her way first thing to the office where the sergeant was filling in her log book.

"Excuse me sergeant. I would like to apply for a transfer please."

The sergeant swung on Basher and with a rather smug look replied "Don't worry Basher it's all in hand. You are to go straight to squadron headquarters and pick up a railway warrant. You are on seven days leave as from today and your will be advised of your new posting whilst on leave. So ensure you take everything from here as you wont be returning."

Basher nodded and left the office mumbling "Thank Christ for that!"

The new site looked awesome in comparison to the one Basher had left seven days ago. This was Staniforth Road in the district of Attercliffe amongst a more populated area of steel works.

The site was vast. At a guess Basher reckoned it had once been either a large housing estate or massive steels works, but whatever it was it had been bombed to the ground. The domed shaped nissen huts looked larger than those on Princess Street and there were more of them. The kitchen looked more like a double garden shed, as did the workshop. The balloon bed appeared miles away from the living quarters indeed the entire site looked a wilderness of expanse.

The rumbling of a train could be heard nearby indicating they were near to a railway line. Basher heaved her heavy kit bag on to her shoulder and trudged through the familiar clinker. Standing on the threshold of the kitchen she heard voices coming from the direction of an office. Tapping on the door she called,

"Is anyone at home?"

A pleasant fresh faced sergeant opened the door and invited Basher in. A handful of girls smiled warmly before leaving the office. Basher turned to the sergeant and asked "How did you know my name sarge?"

The sergeant looked amused. A petite woman of no more than five foot three in height, a complexion devoid of make-up but with the healthy well scrubbed look and cheeks rosier than any apple. Her thick dark eyebrows needed badly plucking, with long straight dark eyelashes that framed her deep blue eyes that shone with kindness and as she said "I do get lists of the new staff being allocated to me. More important than that, we do have a mate of yours on this site who has never stopped yaking about you."

Basher's eyes lit up for the first time in weeks. "It's not Edie is it?"

The sergeant grinned showing a set of even white teeth. "It sure is. She has gone on and on about you. Your reputation has come ahead of you."

Now hardly able to control herself Basher wanted to know where she was. The sergeant explained that she was pulling Big Bertha into wind, and furthermore had no idea of her arrival.

"See I needed to be certain it was you before anything could be said. It was obvious you were good mates and I didn't want to disappoint her"

"Oh boy, what a shock she's in for!" Basher said relieved at finding her old mate at last.

"I do believe you had a rough time on your last site?" the sergeant said clearly needing some confirmation about what she'd heard on the grapevine.

"You could say that" Basher replied as her face clouded over at the thought.

The sergeant touched Basher's arms saying;

"Another time. Lets get you settled in first we can chat later. This is a good site you'll find with a real good crew. You'll be happy here." she reassured Basher with warmth and confidence.

For the first time in ages Basher began to feel comfortable. She stood by and watched as the sergeant sorted through some papers, the turning to Basher said "Come along lets get you sorted out with a bed. You can unpack because the girls will be back from the balloon bed at anytime now, and no doubt you'll have jaw ache trying to catch up."

Basher was allocated a top bunk. As the sergeant was leaving she said "By the way my name is Mary. My preference is to be called by this name, although most of the crew call me sarge... it's up to them. But I warn you, in front of officers is must be sergeant. OK?"

"Of course" Basher said as she watched the sergeant close the door.

A Babble of voices came closer as Basher had just about finished filling her locker. A group of the crew entered stopping abruptly when they saw Basher.

"Hi" they all chorused in a friendly manner.

There was a pregnant silence for a moment before a lone girl sauntered in. She glared at Basher as if she was seeing a ghost. Then stopped dead in her tracks... finally her face lit up like a beacon as she exclaimed "Fuck me... it's Basher... good old Bash, what yer doing 'ere?"

She then lunged forward and clumsily threw her arms around the neck of her friend and hugged her. The rest of the crew recognising this to be a special reunion made for the door. As they were leaving one of them announced.

"We're going to the kitchen for tea Ede, it's nearly time so don't be long."

Once alone Edie rubbed her hands in anticipation "Right mate, come on, lets 'ere what the fuck 'appened when I was on leave. What's the bleedin' story? Tell me it 'ain't true that yer 'ad blokes from Air Ministry visit yer? We 'eard bits of gossip but thats all."

Basher took a deep breath and went through the entire saga leaving not a single item out. Finally summed it up by explaining "Ede it was bloody awful. The entire crew sent me to coventry, I've never been so unhappy in my life and old 'aggis face layed it on thick and heavy, taking great delight in telling me you had been posted. When I asked her if she knew where? She reckoned she had no idea where. The lying bitch."

Edie stood up with hands on hips yelling. "Do you

mean to tell me that the whole bleedin' lot turned Judas?"

"Yep! Every man jack of them. They were gutless and I told the bloke at the Court of Enquiry as much. I said not only were they gutless but frightened of authority, and had lied through their teeth from beginning to end. To be honest I thought he was going to have a nervous breakdown or break a bleeding blood vessel at the very least when I blew my stack and told him a few home truths."

"Good old Bash! Knew I could rely on yer. It's a bleedin' good job I wasn't there. They'd 'ad 'ave me fer insubordination or bad language at the very least. Come to fink of it BOTH" Edie said laughing her socks off.

Then not wanting to miss a single moment of this saga Edie asked "So...'ow did yer manage to get this site after all that trouble?"

"Simple... I asked for a transfer couldn't work with a crew who resented me that badly."

Edie looked puzzled and scratched her head. "I don't get this. What was it they resented for gawd's sake? Yer only asked yer old lady for a bleedin' food parcel for christ's sake!"

"To be honest I didn't even do that. I simply wrote and explained how hungry we all were and how nice it would be to taste her home made cakes and pastries. I gathered from the comments I got from the crew their resentment was the big clean up and the knobs coming from Air Ministry. They also deeply resented the Court of Enquiry probably because they knew they would be faced with awkward questions, and were so afraid of authority they found it easier to tell porkies. Believe me Ede, I really did stand alone, and when they found out I had asked for a transfer they couldn't get rid of me quick enough.

Within an hour of my request I was sent for at Headquarters and told to go on seven days leave then to report here at the of end of it."

Edie was perched on the end of her bunk listening intently to her mate's account of her most recent experiences.

"I reckon old 'aggis face' ad me moved to spite you,"

"That's for certain! By the way what did happen to you? One minute you were on leave the next gone for good, or so I was told. They even hinted you weren't in the same area anymore. I tell you mate I thought I had lost contact for good." Basher said sadly.

Edie frowned before standing up her anger clearly rising. "Do you know what. It's as obvious as the nose on me face this lot was all planned. Now I come to fink about it old 'aggis face waited till I was leaving the site before she called me back and made it appear as if it were somefink she'd forgotten. Telling me I was posted and 'ad to report 'ere at the end of me leave. She even organised the transport to take me tot he station making damned sure I had no contact wiv you. I naturally fought you would be 'ere when I got 'ere. I'll swing fer that bleedin'cow." Edie said as she shuffled her feet the deceit and intrigue suddenly hitting her. The one thing she could not abide was being taken for an idiot.

Basher was shaking her head. "Leave well alone Ede"she advised, "I'm just glad to get out of it. Never did like the site and wasn't keen on the crew either, particularly that bloody Bobby, what a revolting cow she was."

Edie's mood changed at once and her eyes began to twinkle mischievously. "At least yer learned one fing Bash."

"What's that then?"

"Yer know what a dyke is!" she exclaimed as she burst out laughing.

A crew member put her head around the door at that point and shouted "Come on you two, grubs up. It's been ready for ages."

"Coming" they both shouted in unison.

Their feet crunched over the cinders and they both walked toward the dining hut. Basher asked of her mate "So, what's it like on here?"

"Fabulous! The girls are great, and the sarge... well she's somefink else. I can work wiv 'er. She's one of us, nuffink too much trouble, nuffink she won't do. Smashing she is" Edie said with deep sincerity.

The conversation coming from the dining room was deafening. All twelve crew members were jabbering at once as they waited for their meal to be served. As they passed the girl who had called them from the hut, Edie clipped her around her head saying; "Fought yer said it was ready ages ago, liar!"

"Had to say something to ger you to move yer arse."

The sergeant arrived and clapped her hands to get some order. "All right girls shut up and listen. As many of you may have gathered this is the famous Basher. Edie's long lost mate who we've heard so much about. Basher has had a tough time on her last site so make her welcome." The sergeant then turned to Basher and promised to introduce her to everyone when they had eaten. "I'd be wasting my time otherwise because nobody would even listen before their bellies were full" she warned.

It was good to see the sergeant eating with her crew, very different to old 'aggis face' who always ate alone, giving the impression that her crew had the pox!

With the meal over and everyone relaxed Basher noted how comfortable and settle Edie seemed, talking first to one, then another. Always giving back as good as she got. She certainly was popular and never failed to amuse Basher with her quick wit and humour.

The sergeant finally approached Basher and suggested it was a good time for the introductions. The crew had lit their cigarettes and were enjoying their second cup of tea. She approached the first table "This is Sandy, Elaine and Joyce better known as Blondie. Sadie comes from your neck of the woods, and Margaret better known as Scotty for obvious reasons."

Basher's head began to reel as they approached the second table. She was dog tired having travelled from London since dawn. Names were now spinning in her head, she thanked the sergeant for her help, before turning to Edie and announced she was going to turn in because she was knackered.

Edie's eyes rolled in her head as she laughed.

"Fat lot of sleep yer'll get mate. Most of 'em are going out wiv their fellers and that means a lot of din goes on. But yer welcome ter try."

As Basher was about to clamber into her bed she noticed a shelf running around the hut situated a couple of feet above her. She noted this held gas masks and tin helmets. She had put her tin helmet and gas mask under the bunk. Scrambling down she retrieved them from under the bed, but as she clambered back the bunk swayed and rocked. Whoever slept on the bottom was in for a shaky ride she considered, particularly when she turned over in bed!

Having put the items in their correct place she slid into bed and pulled the covers up under her chin and prepared to sleep.

The hut soon became a riot of activity with girls chattering excitedly about their proposed appointments. The ironing board came out and noisy put up as someone yelled to be the next in the queue to use the iron. Shirts and collars were now being pulled from lockers whilst others rubbed away at the buttons on their best tunics. The smell of boot polish filled the air, which reminded Basher of her early days in training.

Different hairstyles were tried out and foundation powder and lipstick was being liberally applied, whilst an exchange of viewpoints as to who looked the best was taking place. Edie had been right there was little chance of sleep. Finally one by one they left. At last it was silent. Basher was about to lie down when the sergeant entered the hut.

"You all right Basher? Thought it might be a good moment for that chat" The sergeant suggested, before explaining that she wasn't suppose to let so many crew go off all at once, but we have a real good team here they really do pull their weight, so she felt confident that if an emergency arose the crew that were left would cope. That way, she explained "I'm happy, my girls are happy and there's nothing like a happy crew for success." Basher couldn't help making a bitter remark telling her sergeant that her previous Scots sergeant should have tried this method.

"Each to his own Basher, but you do get more out a crew if you work with them. At least I find it works for me. Now, what about you, I'm given to understand you had some fun and games on your last site over some food. Do you want to talk about it?" the sergeant enquired.

The intense tiredness that Basher had experienced had now left her, so she considered it best to get the explanation out of the way.

During the next hour she explained in detail her experience on the Princess Street site over the past months.

The sergeant listened intently. She needed to understand her new crew member, making her own judgements. She so wanted her to fit into the network of her already successful team. One bad apple could upset the entire team, but she concluded that all Basher needed was some Just and Fair handling along with a little understanding.

Now that the subject had been thoroughly aired the sergeant put Basher in the picture about another newcomer. This was in the form of a new Pilot officer who had just joined the squadron.

"He's a pompous old fart. Fresh from training and certainly likes to feel his feet. At the moment we are humouring him he'll quickly get the message from my crew that we no longer parade on balloon sites or turn up for work in shirts collars or ties. You know the kind of bull

that I refer to I'm sure. He'll learn and fast with my lot!"
the sergeant explained as she patted Basher's arm before
adding. "I must go have heaps to do. Get your head down
Basher and enjoy a few hours kip" she then left the hut
quietly.

CHAPTER 14

Moans groans and swearing came from under the blankets when for the second time that night the new duty officer had hauled the crew from their warm beds to turn the balloon into wind.

"The bald headed old bastard!" Basher cursed as she pulled her slacks over her pyjamas once again.

"Why 'e didn't keep us up all bleedin' night and done wive it, I'll never know, what wiv guard duty till midnight, and now this 'e might as well 'ave!"

The two mates that now shared a bunk were nearest the door and their voices could be heard a mile away.

The sergeant stood inside the porch entrance. She danced up and down as she attempted to mime to the girls that the officer was outside the door, and could hear every word. But nothing would shut them up.

"If truf be known 'e doesn't know the first 'fuckin' fing about balloons or wind direction" Edie continued as she grabbed her woollen balaclava helmet and yanked it over her head. The duty officer could be now heard stomping impatiently back and forth crunching the cinders as he went.

The sergeant's eyes now riveted to the ceiling as she prayed for a cessation of her crew's anger. Then fearful as to what else the officer might hear, she called "Come on girls... hurry up, the sooner it's done the quicker you can return to your beds."

As Basher emerged the sergeant plunged the megaphone into her hand.

"You can give the drill Bash you've the loudest voice on the site and apart from anything else it'll keep you out of trouble. That mouth of yours will get us all hung!"

It was obvious that this was said for the benefit of the seething duty officer, for the sergeant seemed quietly amused by the entire scenario.

For the next hour the crew pulled and shoved Big Bertha around the bed inch by painful inch. Then finally the officer held his finger in the air to test wind direction. Then finally gave the order to stop the drill as the balloon according to him, was now well and truly into wind.

The crew stood with hands on hips complaining that he didn't know his arse from his elbow.

"Just leave it. Let him find out the hard way." the sergeant whispered.

Basher sidled up to Edie and exclaimed "He's a first class prat!"

Edie rubbed her sore hands down the back of her trousers. "I'd like to string 'im up by 'is balls! We've tugged and pulled the pissin' fing but it's obvious to any idiot that the way Big Berva rocks and pulls like a dog on 'eat that she's no more into wind now than when we started. 'E's a bleedin big 'ead!"

The two girls watched speechless as the officer strode around the balloon bed touching guy lines here and there, before finally rubbing his hands together with complete satisfaction.

"That's it sergeant, that's how it should be done. I have to say that your crew are the most undisciplined lot I've every come across. I therefore want them on parade tomorrow morning at nine sharp." Having made his point he saluted and left the site abruptly.

The sergeant shouted as loudly as she dare for her crew to stay put. The moment his jeep disappeared into the darkness she yelled down the megaphone.

"Now lets get the bloody thing into wind properly. Sorry girls, start heaving again, the quicker we get her into wind the quieter she will be."

A very disgruntled and tired crew appeared for breakfast some few hours later.

"How much longer 'ave we to put up wiv that stupid old fart? 'E keeps us up 'arf the bloody night pulling our guts out fer what? It wouldn't be so bad if the stupid pillock knew what 'e was doing, but 'e 'asn't got a clue!" Edie announced speaking directly to the sergeant.

"Can't we report him sarge?" Sadie asked.

The sergeant looked troubled. She hated the effect this new officer was having on her crew. They were justified in their criticism. It was then she remembered the memo she had received during the last few days.

"Leave it with me girls. There's a new Squadron Leader arriving and he certainly does know what he's talking about. I happen to know on very good authority that he's come through the ranks, so he's had plenty of experience at balloon operating. Once he's settled I'll have words with him."

Then glancing at her log book she continued; "Oh yes before I forget, we have to parade at nine sharp this morning on his Lordship's orders."

Cries of "You've got to be joking?" but the sergeant

continued, "I wish I were. He thinks you are an unruly lot, and he intends putting it right, or so he informed me."

"He needs a good 'butchers' at the Princess Street crew, that'd teach him!" Basher said with some feeling.

The sergeant clapped her hands. "Right girls off you go and smarten yourselves up for this bloody parade. Shirts collars and ties please, and don't forget the elbow grease on your boots. Lets humour the silly sod. And by the way I almost forgot Edie, Basher, Sandy and Sadie you all have a dentist appointment tomorrow." She left the room and disappeared into her office.

At nine sharp the crew lined up into two neat rows. Edie and Basher being the tallest were as usual at the back. The jeep arrived and the new Pilot Officer approached the parade with the aplomb of an Air Vice Marshall.

"Who the bleedin' 'ell does 'e fink 'e is?" Edie said out of the side of her mouth.

"Dunno, but he winds me up something rotten. I'd like to put a squid up his arse." Basher retorted with some venom. The officer carried out a full inspection before deliberately standing in front of both Edie and Basher. He glared at first one then the other, clearly wishing he could belt them both. But instead he walked to the front in silence. Both girls giggled.

Then throwing his shoulders back he stood erect before beginning his lecture "It would appear that you have all lost sight of the reasons you are here. An important job has to be carried out. At all costs we have to preserve our balloon so she will be ready to defend this great city of steel." he began.

"Three acts and a curtain call" muttered Edie.

He glared in silence at both girls. It was clear he had heard the comment for his full rounded face went purple with temper before he spat out... "My job could be made easier if I were not constantly having to suffer the indignity of abusive language. When I order a job to be done, it will be carried out. Is that clear Berry and Smith?"

Neither girl moved a muscle, instead they stood as straight as ram rods looking directly ahead of them in silent insubordination. His eyes narrowed as he viewed them with controlled frustration. It was abundantly clear that if he could have charged them he would have, but he knew he couldn't win. Instead he gave his salute to the sergeant, turned on his heel and walked briskly to his jeep.

Once inside he banged the door and revved his engine as if he was entering a race at Brands Hatch. The moment he was out of sight the crew threw their caps in the air and cheered.

"Fancy going for a drink tonight then Bash?" Edie asked

"Can't I'm on guard duty till eight and then again at midnight." Basher explained.

"We can still go after eight. What about you Sadie, fancy it?" Edie asked of the other cockney.

"Why not, I fink I've got half a crown left... last of the big spenders, lets live dangerously... Yep count me in mate."

"We're not tarting up are we?!" Basher enquired.

"Do me a favour, battle dress'll do but no bleedin' boots. Never know who we might meet" Edie said her eyes dancing with anticipation.

Basher and Sadie exchanged looks. "Oye we're only

going for a quiet drink we aren't on the 'knock off'" Sadie pointed out.

It was a short distance to the local pub in a heavily populated working class district. The cobbled streets had row upon row of dirty sooty brickwork buildings surrounded by towering factory chimneys that emitted black smoke. The streets of terraced grimy houses converged on to the main shopping area. It made for a depressing picture.

The trio reached the pub it was the nearest to the balloon site and right at the beginning of the shopping centre. A pawn shop and small tobacconist were squeezed either side of the pub with their gas lamps burning behind dark shutters. All still open in anticipation of the arrival of steel workers as they came off of the next shift.

A familiar blue police box stood along side the red public phone booths outside the pub.

Having ordered three halves of beer and finding suitable seats the girls lit up their cigarettes and began to relax, It was good to be away from the demands of Big Bertha Basher considered, as they all sat in silence enjoying their smoke.

Three soldiers sat at the next table, all huddled together as if in a private conference. Basher became increasingly interested in their behaviour. What a good job that Edie had her back to them for they wouldn't remain in conference long if it were left to her, Basher considered.

It was then that one of them caught Basher staring at them. She quickly averted her gaze but it was too late, he took it as a signal of some interest and before she had time to blink the three soldiers approached the girls offering to buy them a drink. Edie of course moved over quicker than grease lightening, and soon they were all chatting. All that is, with the exception of Basher whose unease increased as she noted the lack of identification flashes on their uniforms. She became even more alarmed when one of them asked if they worked on the balloon site around the corner.

"Sure do" Edie blurted out, clearly unaware that they might be fishing for information.

"That must be hard work" one of them remarked sympathetically before adding, "What holds the damned thing up?"

At this point Basher felt compelled to kick Sadie sharply on the shin, hoping she would get the message as she announced "Will you excuse me guys I need to spend a penny."

"Sure!" they all chorused not taking their eyes off of Edie who was lost in adoration as usual and clearly oblivious to what might be going on under her nose.

Sadie had got the message and excused herself at the same time. Once in the toilet Basher quickly explained what she had observed.

"But what can we do?" Sadie queried.

"You go back and keep them talking. I'll nip outside and ring Squadron Headquarters and ask their advice.

As Sadie reached the door Basher called urgently. "For Christ's sake be careful, no top secret leaks and try to keep Edie from opening her great 'gate' She can be so stupid that one, especially if men are involved."

Having made her urgent call Basher was advised to return to the group and keep them talking. They had just re-filled their glasses when Basher put in an appearance. "Where have you been? Got the runs or what?" one of them asked rather cheekily.

Basher had to think quickly. "Felt a bit faint so went outside for some fresh air, but I'm all right now Edie gave Basher a concerned look and was about to comment, when one of the guys asked Basher a direct question.

"You know that cylinder thing that's attached to the cable of the balloon what part does that play during and air raid?"

Basher couldn't believe her ears for there was nothing subtle about this question and the soldier was watching her response with menacing interest.

"You seem remarkably well informed, when so far you've only shown a passing interest in our work." Basher said, stalling for time.

He laughed a false laugh before remarking. "In view of the fact that we were at the manufacturing end of things I was merely testing." he said smartly.

Basher's response was quick off the mark. "If you were involved in the manufacture as you claim then you should be able to tell me the hydrogen capacity and amount of cable per drum." she added cockily.

He blushed to the roots of his head, and Edie clearly thought that Basher was trying to be clever.

"Come on, how the bleedin' 'ell did we manage to get on to the subject of work? We came 'ere to forget it." she added naively.

It was then that the pub doors suddenly flung open and three military policemen walked in grabbed a soldier each and marched them unceremoniously out of the pub.

Edie's mouth flew open and her eyes shot out like chapel hat pegs.

"What the pissin' 'ell's going off 'ere?" she yelled.

Basher swung on her mate and raising her voice said "All you have eyes for is what they have in their trousers. I on the other hand had noted the lack of identification flashes on their uniforms. Then all those questions they were asking. God love me, a kid of three could have sussed them out" Basher concluded in exasperation.

Then catching site of the pub clock she added, "Christ lets go, I'm on duty in half an hour!"

The sergeant was talking to the new Squadron Leader as the three girls entered the office to sign in.

"Would one of you be Basher?" the officer asked smiling.

"Yes sir, I am." Basher responded.

"So it was you lot who apprehended the so called soldiers?"

"Yes sir" they all chorused. Basher thumped Edie on the back to remind her she could not take any credit for this. But the officer addressed all three by saying;

"This is what I like to hear, girls who are observant. Your suspicions were well founded, they are all suspect spies! The enemy must be getting desperate for these three weren't exactly clever were they? Never mind, well done!"

As he rose to leave the girls stood to attention having clicked their heels smartly.

When he reached the threshold he turned back and remarked.

"Cut the bull! We're here to do a job you're not still in

training."

Edie's face broke into smiles as she said to the sergeant. "My kind of bloke that. No bull shit. Just gets down to the nitty gritty."

"Did you mention fart face?" Sadie asked.

The sergeant smiled. "He won't be bothering us again, he's been given Princes Street site as a special consignment. Are you quite sure you're not psychic Bash?" she asked.

"That's what I call poetic justice. It couldn't happen to a more deserving bloke" Basher said as she threw her cap in the air.

CHAPTER 15

A huge wave of nausea engulfed Basher caused by the aroma of lunch cooking, as she made her way to the office. The sergeant looked up from her paperwork as Basher slumped into the nearest chair and began spitting yet more blood into an already saturated rag.

"We're all back sarge" Basher finally managed to say.

"So I see. What did they do take all your teeth out?" she queried.

"No sarge, just two big ones at the back, and a filling on a double tooth at the bottom. It took an hour and frankly hardly worth saving, for the filling seemed to outweigh the tooth that was left!"

"Where are the rest, are they as bad as you appear to be?"

"Sadie had two out but Edie only had fillings the jammy sod. They are in the dining room waiting for lunch."

"Would you and Sadie like some soup?" the sergeant asked with concern.

"I can't speak for Sadie, but I don't want anything thanks sarge. What with the cocaine and the tram ride I feel quite sick, but would appreciate a lie down."

"Off you go then. I'll check the others" the sergeant said as she rose from her seat.

After a few hours sleep both Basher and Sadie felt better, although Basher's sickness had given way to some throbbing pain.

Edie came bouncing in full of excitement. "Hey... just 'eard, there's a dance tonight at Cutlers 'all. Anyone game?" she then stopped in her tracks and looked pained as she noticed her mate's swollen cheek. Basher managed with difficulty to explain "I don't somehow think it would be wise not tonight, but ask Sandy I bet she'll go."

The sergeant entered the hut and broke up the conversation regarding the dance. She took a quick look around the room before asking; "Is every here?"

Basher looked around and said, "Hold on, where's Blondie?"

"Gone to the loo." Edie replied

The crew looked puzzled. They knew by her tone that something serious was about to break. "There isn't too much time so you can explain to Blondie when she returns. You all need to be in the dining room in about ten minutes. The C.O. is coming to talk to you all. Also I've had to re-organise the roster I'm sorry to say, that means that Basher and Sadie are on guard duty this evening."

Basher and Sadie exchanged horrified looks. "Come off it sarge, we're the only two who've had teeth out today." Sadie remarked.

"Sorry it can't be helped." the sergeant said before abruptly leaving.

The volume of chattering reached an enormous crescendo as the crew queried between themselves the slightly threatening message the sergeant had just delivered.

"Wonder what the C.O. wants?" queried Edie

"We've probably been posted overseas" Basher

suggested.

"Or sent back to Morecambe even" Edie teased.

"Anything but that!" retorted Basher.

The crew duly assembled in the dining hut and as the Commanding officer entered the sergeant ordered "Crew... atten...tion!"

The crew stood erect. "Be seated," he ordered seeming rather irritated. Then taking of his cap he perched on the edge of one of the tables.

"I'm the bearer of some interesting news, but whether you consider it good or bad is I suppose, up to each individual, so much depends on how happy you are as balloon operators."

Edie nudged Basher as the C.O. continued his explanation.

"If you've been following the events of this dreadful war you will have realised that it has now swung from the defensive to the offensive. I'm certain that the 'powers that be' have many a plan up their sleeve. But what the hell has all this to do with us? You may well ask."

"It means that we have now played our role in the defensive program and are about to become redundant."

A murmur of disapproval and gasps of surprise came from the crew. But he hadn't finished... "Clearly a huge network of defence such as ours cannot be dismantled in five minutes. It will take time and planning. In the meantime I want to thank you for the magnificent part you have played. You will have by now discovered that the job has not been an easy one, but I trust if nothing else, it has helped to build stronger characters as a result. Your patience and tolerance has been tried to the limit. Your physical strength has been tested to an enormous degree. I personally have been proud to have been in charge of women like you, and want to be the first to thank you. You have given your all to this country but the time has come to consider a new trade. Give it careful thought for if you are half as successful in your future work as you have been as balloon operators you will have done well. Now, are there any questions?"

"How soon will this happen sir?" Sadie asked.

"As far as I know this site will be one of the last to go, so we are talking in terms of perhaps six months. I cannot be more specific."

"What trades will be open to us?" asked Sandy.

"Most of them. You'll be receiving more information about this and will have ample time to study your options." he explained.

The questions and answers went back and forth for over an hour. The C.O. thanked them for their time and moved into the office to have a private word with the sergeant.

During the evening meal the only topic of conversation was the closing down of the sites.

It had come as a bomb shell to the crew, who had never considered the possibility of closure. A feeling of extreme sadness engulfed them as they considered their options.

Edie glanced at the kitchen clock and announced their was still time to get to the dance if they got a move on. This was her way of pushing the unpleasant future prospects under the carpet, and it worked as their was a sudden dash to the sleeping quarters to get ready.

"What time are yer on guard duty then Bash? " Edie

asked as she polished her buttons.

"Eight till ten" replied Basher as she held her face for every now and then the pain seared through her gums.

"I reckon sarge ought to 'ave found someone else tonight, it's not fair putting you two on. Yer the only bleedin' two whose'ad teef out! Not like 'er to be so thoughtless" Edie moaned as she put even more elbow grease into polishing her shoes.

Sadie passed a couple of asprins to Basher and told her to get them down her before they went on duty, she felt they might help.

Sadie watched flabbergasted as Edie pulled on a fine pair of grey silk stockings

"Where the bleedin' 'ell did yer get those from... hlackmarket?"

"Cheeky sod! Get yerself a bleedin' Yank and bobs yer flippin uncle."

Where the 'ell did yer go to meet a Yank?" Sadie enquired.

"It's a long story. We're getting engaged on me next leave" Edie explained as she checked her make - up in her small mirror.

"Then what the 'ell are yer doing going out dancing?"

"Get real. Keeping me 'and in, can't get out of practice now can I?"

"You're a saucy cow and no mistake." Sadie remarked.

Basher had begun to search her locker for her balaclava helmet and scarves.

"What are doing?" Sadie asked.

"Getting ready for guard duty. We must keep our mouths covered Sade. If we get cold in this lot we'll know all about it" she said with some urgency.

"You sound just like my mum. A proper old woman you are!" Sadie replied.

The girls who were going dancing were about to leave the hut. Basher called out to them. "Have a good time, don't forget if you can't be good be careful!"

While Sadie added; "And keep yer 'and on yer 'a ha'penny!"

Basher wandered around the perimeter of the site, checking here and there and flashing her torch to make certain nobody was lurking around the balloon bed. Truncheons hung from the belt of their slacks making a huge bulge in the side of their overcoats.

Sadie a well built lass but with no excess flesh, which compared to Basher gave the appearance of being reasonably slim.

She was attractive with large brown eyes that beamed from a full rounded face and a sensuous mouth with a row of even white teeth that had a slight gap in the front. But tonight the only part of her face that could be seen was her eyes. A scarf had been wrapped tightly around the mouths of both girls and the balaclava helmets pulled over the top. With layers of warm clothing underneath, a huge top coat made them look like wrestlers waiting to go into the ring.

Two men had been hanging around the gate for some time and the guards had been observing. Now they felt it time to investigate.

"Do you wish to see someone or are you waiting for one of the girls?" Basher asked.

The two blokes looked surprised at being questioned, and even more astounded at the apparitions that stood before them.

"We aren't waiting for anyone. We simply stopped for a chat and were discussing the merits of your balloon. But tell me for I'm intrigued, why are you both so well covered around the face? If you don't mind me saying so you look more like bandits." one of them said without a hint of an accent indeed sounding rather posh Basher thought.

Basher explained about their visit to the dentist, and an interesting conversation developed between them. They were to discover that one was called Simon and the other Paul. They were to learn that Simon was a trainee accountant and Paul was hoping to become a solicitor. Both lived locally.

During this very interesting conversation Sadie kicked Basher's shins several times, which Basher took to mean that she didn't fancy either of them and wanted to be off but Basher found their refined manners refreshing.

The church clock came to Sadie's rescue. As it struck ten she shot off like grease lightening. "We are now off duty and have to report." Basher explained.

"Shall we see you tomorrow?" Simon enquired.

Basher flushed under the layers of clothing. It has been a long time since anyone had shown any interest in her, so she quickly agreed to see him again.

Sadie was making two mugs of cocoa as Basher entered the kitchen.

"You're not serious about those two plonkers are yer?" Sade said as she laughed her high pitched laugh.

"I thought they were rather nice." Basher replied defensively.

"Ugh! Not my type, two little squirts if yer ask me."

"Haven't you heard that good things come in small parcels? You don't know class when you see it that's your trouble."

"Give me a six foot cockney any day. But hey I know somebody who would just love that Paul bloke."

"Whose that then?" Basher asked.

"The snob of the site, our friend Sandy. He'd be right up her street she's a toffee nosed cow at the best of times. " Sadie suggested.

"I'll have to see if I can do a bit of match-making then" Basher suggested as she went dreamily to bed.

"Pass the cornflakes Ede." Basher requested.

"How many for toast?" asked one of the duty cooks.

The entire crew put up their hand. They were so intent in shoveling cereal into their mouths they had no time for words. The cook looked alarmed and called to her mate. "Christ year's better stoke up the fire! Twelve slices needed for starters."

"What's the new bloke like then Sandy?" one of the crew asked

Quietly stirring her tea she shrugged her shoulders. "Not bad, very polite and well bred."

Sadie intervened. "He wasn't my type at all. But 'e 'ad a good set of come ter bed eyes, I have ter say."

"Cods eyes, more like" Basher said chipping in.

Edie gave Basher a rather interesting look before asking; "Hey Bash, what about your one... come on... spill the beans!"

"Good looking and a budding accountant with a Bond Street flair would just about sum him up." Basher said laughing.

"Get 'er... more like the Duke of Darnall."

The sergeant listened to the banter of her crew as she ate her own breakfast. She smiled at times at the exchanges of wit and humour. The phone rang. She left the table and entered the office. On her return she proceeded to finish her meal. Some of the crew got up to leave. The sergeant put down her knife and raised her voice so as to be heard above the hub-bub of conversation. "Hang on a minute girls I've something to announce."

A mutter went around as girls returned to their seats and sat down heavily wondering what was to come next.

"Now what?" Blondie asked as she threw her leg over the form to sit next to her friend Elaine.

"I've just got some news. Three of you are to be transferred to Worthing Road site. They need help as they are closing down. It's only temporary, so Basher you Edie and Sandy are to go."

The three girls exchanged glances and moaned between themselves. The rest offered condolences before asking permission to leave the hut.

They had all become accustomed to sudden changes in their working lives but hated to be uprooted from the security of their own site.

"How long is this for then, sarge? Basher asked.

"About two week from what I can gather" the sergeant replied.

Sandy nudged Basher. "What about the boys? They are suppose to be meeting us here tonight" she whispered.

Edie overheard the comment and asked of the sergeant.

"When do we' ave to go?"

"Right now, so chop chop, get your kit packed and get

going" the sergeant urged.

Basher and Sandy exchanged looks of horror.

"What are we to do about the blokes? Sandy asked.

"Search me, haven't a clue" Basher replied despondently

Sandy suddenly turned to Sadie having thought of a really good idea.

"You're on guard duty early this evening aren't you Sade? Would you mind telling them for us? They know the district and will be able to find us... please!" she pleaded. Sadie smiled, "Anything fer a quite life. Leave it wiv me." she promised.

CHAPTER 16

Worthing road site was much the same as their own, not as vast but had been cleared of bomb damage where houses once stood, leaving rows of back yards that the bombers had missed.

As the trio entered the site they were met by a small framed girl with a neat and orderly appearance. Her confident manner indicated that she was perhaps in charge. Her frail looks subsequently proved to be deceiving.

"Thanks for helping us out girls" she began warmly as she herded them through the entrance to the office. "I'm really short of crew and there is so much to do. By the way how experienced are you at cooking?" she asked as she glanced at them individually.

"Don't look at me I'm 'opless, but these two are fabulous cooks." Edie announced.

"I wouldn't go that far, but we'll certainly have a go, won't we Sand?" Basher said looking at her colleague for confirmation. Sandy nodded her agreement.

Basher and Sandy lay on their bunks listening to the howling wind as the eight o clock pips shrieked from the radio that evening.

"They're not coming. I wonder if bloody Sadie gave them the message, she doesn't like them you know, so I wouldn't put it past her." Basher announced despondently.

"I'll tell you what, if she hasn't then we have definitely had it" Sandy said sounding disappointed.

The door suddenly burst open and a crew member put her head around the door and asked; "Are you two from Staniforth Road site?"

"Yes... why?" Basher said jumping from her bunk.

"Cos there's two blokes out there who want to see you."

Basher panicked. "I've got to make my face up yet." she said grabbing her toilet bag.

"Don't worry, I'll ask them to wait, they won't mind" Sandy said calmly as she brushed her slacks and pulled at the crease to make it stand out. There was nothing slovenly about his girl. Her shirts and collars were always clean and well starched. Her uniforms were pressed to perfection be it her best suit or her battle dress outfit. She reached for her cap and made a quick exit.

Shaking with excitement Basher hurriedly applied her make up, then rubbed her shoes with the elbow of her jacket before putting them on. As she was about to leave Sandy returned explaining that the boys wanted to take them for a drink. "Can you find sarge and get permission to leave the site?" Sandy pleaded.

The small room in the local pub had a coal fire, which added to their comfort. Basher drank cider. She had discovered it was far more palatable than beer.

Sandy on the other hand sipped tomato juice from a long stemmed glass with an air of sophistication.

The two young men seemed more than content with their half pints of beer, and their arms around the shoulders of the two girls. They lowered their voices so that the conversation became a little more intimate. Simon enquired as to whether Basher would be free the following

Sunday, he wanted to have her visit his home for tea, but seeing the look of surprise on her face he quickly explained. "I simply thought such a gesture might ease the pain of missing your own home."

Basher blushed with embarrassment hoping she hadn't given a false impression she hurriedly said. "How kind and thoughtful, I would love to, thank you."

The time sped by and once outside the pub they broke off in two's. Paul and Basher chatted about the family she had left behind in the South of England. At last they past the last alleyway before the site. Simon guided Basher just inside the narrow entrance away from prying eyes of the public. His hand reached out and tenderly touched her face before pulling her closely to him kissing her gently.

The clock struck four the following Sunday afternoon as Basher made her way across the site. Simon had given her instructions on how to reach his home. She made her way down the cobbled street with it's terraced houses, and realised it was only just a few streets from her Staniforth Road site. Number fifty-two had a side alley, rather like the one that Simon had taken his first kiss a few days previously

She smiled as the thought of those moments warmed her. Then making her way up the darkened alley she was then confronted by a high locked gate. She poked her head over and discovered a small latch.

But before entering she had a good look around. She noted the long zinc bath hanging on the outside wall. This was familiar from her own childhood days. But the large zinc tub with the wooden dolly peg that stood inside of it was something new to her although obvious that it had something to do with washing clothing.

She had already observed that the people from the north appeared poorer and a little behind the times in comparison to her own experience in the South. Perhaps through lack of funds or opportunities she concluded.

A small petite lady came to the doorway her pasty face seemed filled with pain that had etched deep lines into her cheeks. Her jet black hair was brushed neatly to one side and held in place with a hair grip. Basher noted her hands were red with chilblains. She had to look up to meet Basher's gaze. She glared through dark piercing eyes taking in every contour of Basher's body. There was a vague resemblance to her son Simon until she spoke, and there the resemblance ended.

"You must be Simons' young woman. Cum in luv" she said in her broad Sheffield accent.

Although this was a hot summers day an enormous fire roared up the chimney of the black Yorkshire range that shone brilliantly from an obvious daily black leading.

The brass knobs of the fender mirrored the flames of the fire and shone bright from the sheer hard work of keeping them sparkling clean, A large black kettle sat on a shelf that was attached to the fire grate and appeared to be constantly boiling.

"I'll mash tea. Simon will be down in a minute. My son is very fussy about his appearance" Then with a disapproving look she blurted out, "Although goodness knows what for, in this instance?"

Basher cringed and felt vulnerable in the presence of this woman who took control the entire time it took for Simon to appear. She was to quickly learn that Simon was the eldest of three boys, and he was clearly her special son. He had been born under special circumstances to her and left handicapped when polio struck following an attack of childhood measles. It also became apparent that this mother protected her son and was totally dependent on him. The man he knew as father had died when he was only eleven, and he had to be responsible for conducting all of his mother's affairs. His mother went to pieces, but his academic abilities got him through. All of this information was made available to Basher whilst they waited for the arrival of Simon. Basher quickly concluded that who ever took this man on would always have his mother to contend with.

A challenge that Basher would rather not contemplate as she had already been stung under the scrutiny of this lady in a very short space of time.

During tea Paul's mother continued to stake her claim in no uncertain terms, leaving them both feeling uncomfortable.

Simon finally suggested they retire to the front parlor where they perhaps could be left in peace. When alone he made it clear to Basher that he was glad to get away from his over protective and possessive mother.

"Don't take too much notice of her, She thinks she owns me" he explained.

It did occur to Basher that perhaps if he explained to her how he felt, she might just back off. Her thoughts were interrupted by the haunting melody of Beethoven's Moonlight Sonata that Simon was playing on his piano. Suddenly his face etched with a sadness that seemed deeply hidden inside of him.

The kitchen was a buzz of activity the following morning as the guards changed over duties, and cooks turned up for the beginning of their day.

"There's some fresh tea in the pot." one of the guards advised.

"Thanks" Basher said as she poked the fire furiously before puling out the ash pan and taking it outside to empty it.

"Bring the coal hood in, we may as well make the fire up before we start the breakfast." Sandy suggested.

The tea was poured. Basher wiped her hands on a cloth before grabbing her mug and swallowing it down in one go.

"Blimey you got an asbestos throat?" Sandy enquired.

Basher laughed, "Nothing like the first cup, that was good. Now... what's the order of the day?"

"Well we've got some steak and kidney should we make a pie for dinner for a change?"

"Yep good idea. I'll prepare the meat and get it in the oven while you sort out the breakfasts. Have we any onions by the way?"

"I think I saw some in the pantry the other day." Sandy replied as she got the bread ready for toasting.

"Tell you what. When I've put this meat in, I'll take over the breakfast preparation and you make the pastry. It will then be a joint effort eh?"

"Fine by me" Sandy said as she poured the cornflakes into twelve dishes.

As the crew hungrily tucked into their breakfast one of the crew enquired;

"What's for dinner today Bash?"

"Steak and kidney pie like yer mother used to make" Basher promised as she rubbed her hands in anticipation.

A huge gust of wind blew around the hut rattling all the windows. A couple of the girls jumped up and peered outside.

"My God! Listen to that lot. Don't tell me we're in for yet another gale."

"How the hell are we expected to deflate Big Bertha in this high wind?" someone asked.

The shrill of the phone coming from the office sent the sergeant dashing to answer it. Within seconds she screamed. "Out crew, we have to fly her!"

"I thought we had to deflate her? "one of the crew yelled.

"Seemingly not. It's a red alert." the sergeant yelled as she dashed outside.

Basher was pleased to be duty cook. All other duties were excluded. Except in circumstances of emergency.

The aroma from the cooking meat smelled delicious and the pastry was now rolled out ready to make the pie. The wind howled around the kitchen rattling doors and window shutters. The shouting of orders and the cursing from the crew could be heard as they battled to unleash Big Bertha.

"They sound as if they're having fun" Sandy commented."

Basher looked deep in thought before commenting "This is one of those days when I'm glad to be duty cook. Although I've got one of my 'feelings' about this lot."

"You and your 'feelings'" Sandy remarked as she smiled to herself.

"You can scoff my friend but my 'feelings' have never let me down so far."

With an egg cup placed in the centre of the dish to keep the pastry away from the bubbling meat Sandy carefully placed the completed pie into the oven, whilst Basher prepared the morning cocoa for the crew.

"That looks good enough to eat" Basher remarked as she made for the door to inform the crew that their drinks were now ready.

But the moment she appeared a harassed sergeant yelled... "Drop everything and give us a hand, we've nearly lost the bloody thing twice. What soddin' idiot suggested flying her in this gale must be off their head!"

"It won't be the Squadron Leader because he knows better." Basher yelled back as she dashed into the kitchen to fetch Sandy. As both girls rushed toward the balloon bed they could see Big Bertha bouncing from port to starboard and then nose diving on to her bow. The corporal hung on to the tail guy rope at the stern in an attempt to control her, but a strong gust of wind caught the balloon on her undercarriage making her dive forward. She tipped right on to the tip of her nose flinging her tail in the air carrying the corporal with her!!!

The crew stood open mouthed watching in horror, as the corporal was hurtled over the kitchen hut and falling with a sickening thud. At the same time the guy ropes and wire strops made an ear splitting crack as the balloon was wrenched from her moorings flying into the street and finally wrapping herself around a lamp post. The mini whirlwind had also stripped the roof from the kitchen hut and had blown it into the road.

The world appeared to stand still as everything seemed to happen in slow motion. It was then that the sergeant took control; "Will someone go to the corporal please while I phone for an ambulance and inform headquarters that we've lost our balloon."

As she made for the hut she yelled... "Someone certainly needs reminding that they don't know their arse from their elbow when it comes to balloon operating."

The corporal lay motionless. Her face grey and her lips tinged blue. Two members of the crew had covered her in blankets as the bells of the ambulance rang.

Some of the crew attempted to unwrap the balloon from the lamp post. By the time a duty officer arrived with two strong airmen Big Bertha had been released.

"At least it saves you deflating her" the duty officer offered.

"There are easier ways sir!" Basher remarked.

The wind died down as quickly as it had arrived, and was now replaced by a deluge of rain. Basher and Sandy viewed the mess in the kitchen.

The hissing of the rain water as it splashed on to the red hot stove, accompanied by a strong smell of burning that came in the direction of the oven suddenly reminded them both of the masterpiece they had left to cook before going to the aid of the crew.

"My God the pie!" Basher exclaimed.

"Never mind the pie how about keeping dry for a start." Sandy said as she made a dive for the office to find the only available umbrella.

Basher opened the oven door cautiously. She blinked in horror for the pie was no more. Instead a mass of bubbling meat with not a sign of any pastry!

Sandy bounced back into the kitchen covering herself with the large umbrella, she sniffed and asked "Well... how is it then?"

Basher burst out laughing. "Can we all share the joke?" Sandy asked icily.

"Take a look for yourself." Basher suggested now convulsed into fits of laughter.

Sandy opened the oven door and then let out a shriek "Bash what are we going to do?   It's ruined... the girls will kill us!"

"We can't afford to let them see this lot so why don't we put up the blackout boards." Basher suggested as a few ideas were beginning to come to her.

Sandy looked puzzled, but driven by desperation went along with the idea.

They began the task of fitting the blackout boards to each of the outside windows. As they turned the last peg to secure the final board Edie shouted.

"Whatcha doing. What's going on?"

"Having a bloody orgy what do yer think we're doing? Keep yer nose out" Basher yelled as she tapped the side of her nose.

"We're drawing attention to the fact that we have a problem. I don't think this such a good idea." Sandy said in her panicky high pitched voice.

Basher swung on her and yelled "Trust me! There's no bloody time for inquests, just do it!"

As the two girls returned to the kitchen Sandy was really rattled and demanded of Basher "That's just my point, do what exactly? The meal is ruined and we have exactly half an hour before the rotten crew pile in here expecting a lunch of steak and kidney pie!"

Basher suddenly catapulted into action. She removed the pie from the oven. It looked revolting as bits of pastry swam around like dead fish. The egg cup stood proudly in the centre with a smattering of pastry clinging desperately to it. Basher could no longer hold back an eruption of violent giggling, while Sandy glared at the dish and appealed. "I repeat... what are we going to do?"

"Get some flour from the pantry and some fat. This is going to be the best stew they've ever tasted" Basher announced now peaking with creativity.

"Fine, but how do we explain away the change of menu? And how do we deal with the bits of pastry floating in the gravy?"

"They'll blend in with the dumplings. The change of menu is due to unexpected gales. Just tell them we didn't have time to make the pie... simple."

It was then that Edie appeared from nowhere having obviously overhead the conversation.

"You silver tongued bastard" she accused as she grinned at Basher.

"Had a good tutor mate!" came Basher's swift response.

The duty officer entered the kitchen and began to sniff rather violently.

"What ever it is you are cooking smells absolutely splendid," he said rather condescendingly. Basher and Sandy exchanged amused glances but before they had the chance to explain he asked "Are you three from Staniforth Road site?"

"Yes sir" they all chorused.

"You can return tomorrow. No point staying on here. The crew can cope now they've no balloon to deflate. But thanks for your help anyway."

"Thank you sir" Basher offered on behalf of her colleagues.

Then looking at the roof he announced; "I'll get someone down as quickly as I can to fix the roof" then picking up his cap he abruptly left.

"As if we care about the bleedin' roof. Come on girls lets get packed." Edie yelled.

"Er... excuse me... but we have dinner to serve first." Basher reminded her mate.

CHAPTER 17

The following afternoon the three girls were relieved to find that they had missed the hard slog of balloon duties as they sat comfortably in the kitchen of their home site. The news of the accident on Worthing Road had gone around the sites like wildfire.

"Boy did that corporal go down with a thud, enough to break her back. Any update on that corporal, sarge? Basher asked after the crew had been debating the ins and outs of the accident.

"That's precisely what she has done, broken her back. Of course that will have ended her career pretty abruptly, and no doubt she will be relegated to a wheelchair for life."

Sandy look horrified "It doesn't bear thinking about. We go out there and hang on to those guy lines for grim death... it's dangerous and frightening." she declared with some passion.

The sergeant looked pensive before stating. "To be honest the corporal should never have hung on to that guy line in that gale, but I suppose it's easy to say after the event, but I trust it's been a severe lesson to all of you?"

Basher sat upright in her chair and joined in the debate. "I can cope during the daylight hours it's the night time that bothers me. You can never tell in the pitch dark where the cable is. I've got a thing about the cable winding itself around my neck. I have nightmares about it."

Edie burst out laughing. "It'd take more than the bleedin' cable ter strangle you, more like going round the world twice with the thickness of that neck. Do me a favour, that cable's got no bleedin' chance." she said still laughing at the prospect.

Basher looked pained and hurt by her mate's remarks because her fear was very real to her.

The dreams of the crew were disturbed the following morning when the sergeant bellowed from the doorway; "Come on crew rise and shine, the wind's getting up and we all know that what that means!"

"Give us a break sarge we're knackered after our stint on Worthing Road" Sandy remarked.

Moans groans and swearing came from under the blankets. Basher crawled out feeling tired and bad tempered. She banged on the side of the bunk to shake Edie.

"Come on mate up yer get, can't leave it all to sarge."

"Get er... little miss fuckin' goody two shoes." Edie spat out irritably.

But once outside they took great gulps of air to help revive them, then hurried to the kitchen to grab their first cup of tea, listening half heartedly to the general instructions of duty being given by the sergeant.

The arrival of the postman during breakfast caused momentary excitement, but soon ended when Blondie's mate Elaine fled the hut in floods of tears.

Then when the news of the presumed death of her fiancee who she was to have married in a few weeks broke, a mutter of abuse came from the crew blaming the war and Hitler for such tragedy, and depression settled over them like a big black cloud.

The sergeant quickly got the message. She closed her log book with a bang and stood up announcing "Right girls let's get to work... like now!"

As Basher entered the workshop her thoughts were raging. What the hell was the sergeant thinking of, where had her sympathetic nature gone? It was so unlike her. Poor Elaine had lost her bloke almost on the eve of her wedding!

Basher became so wound up she began acting out the drama in her head as if it were a play. Her eyes travelled around the workshop with its bench, vice, rigging ropes and tools that were needed for repair work. She clamped a wire strop into the vice and began splicing. It took a lot of strength so she was able to air all of her pent up feelings. The door suddenly burst open and Scotty stood on the threshold. "Can I no come in?" she asked in her soft Scottish voice.

"Of course with pleasure" Basher reassured her, and relieved to have some company. The opportunity of getting to know this gentle Scott was something she had wanted to do for some time, but the chance had always eluded her.

Scotty took a seat picked up some rope and began splicing. The two girls chatted amicably about their families and backgrounds.

"Where exactly do you come from Basher?" the Scot asked.

"I was born in Wimbledon but my parents now live in West London. You're from Scotland aren't you?" Basher asked, stating the obvious.

"Scotland's a big place. I come from Edinburgh." Scotty told her friend.

"I've never been to Scotland. Come to think of it, I've not been to many places but I'll make up for it after the war." Basher said with some sincerity. She then took a photograph from her top pocket and passed it to her colleague. "That's my baby sister."

As Scotty reached to take the photograph Basher noticed a dark red scar that went from one side of her neck to the other. There was a pregnant silence until Scotty finally asked "Is it ma neck that intrigues ye?"

"Well... yes... what on earth has happened to you?"

Scotty shrugged her shoulders and said nonchalantly "Och, I had a wee ride on a balloon with the cable round ma throat... almost took me to heaven!"

Basher's stomach turned over and her hands felt clammy. She had witnessed accidents in the past, girls flung and badly cut, bones broken, but this was horrible and her worst nightmare. This gruesome discovery was interrupted with Edie bursting in; "Bash I've got news." Her tone indicated that the war had come to a sudden end. She stood on the threshold of the workshop with one hand on the door ready to bolt. "We've got to bed the balloon down, a gale warning 'as just come in. Come on 'urry up sarge is waiting ter 'ave our guts fer garters." she urged. Basher put down her work and followed the other two declaring. "What's new? The sarge has been in a bad mood for days."

The crew's routine jobs came to a stand still. All orderlies and cooks had been rounded up. Nothing mattered except to get Big Bertha bedded down.

The sergeant approached Basher suggesting. "You've the loudest voice on he site, give the crew their orders, even in this gale they'll hear you at squadron headquarters."

"Who the hell has rattled your cage?" Basher muttered as she took the megaphone, but the sergeant ignored the remark and joined the rest of the crew on the balloon bed.

"All right winch... roll her in." Basher bawled.

She felt a bit self conscious as the spectators gathered and all eyes seemed to be on her. Her size had not diminished but as promised when she joined up she was even bigger!

An hour passed as Basher shouted the prescribed drill. She then overheard one of the men in he crowd remark "Christ... she's a voice tha knows that would freeten the daylights out of 'itler!"

Basher pretended not to hear the uncomplimentary remark instead she kept her eye on the crew. A perfect team working as one, dealing with masses of intricate guy ropes and rigging, pulling dragging and tugging. Finally Big Bertha gave up the fight and lay quietly as a sleeping babe.

The spectators continued to chatter amongst themselves. One was heard to say "Jesus... those lasses 'ave some tugging ter do lad, should make childbirth by comparison a piece of cake!"

After tea Basher and Edie sat huddled around the belly stove. The howl of the wind didn't help to ease their troubled thoughts.

"Stone the flippin' crows sounds like trouble blowing

up Bash. Must know we're on duty. Still the balloon's bedded down for the night, unless of course gerry decides to pay us a visit."

Basher snapped "Shut up will you! Why are you always so bloody pessimistic? We've not had an air raid since we've been here, so why now eh?"

The thought of having to fly the balloon in this gale filled Basher with terror, for that cable loomed before her like a re-occurring bad dream. Her thoughts flew to the accidents she had experienced of late, then there was Scotty's hideous scar... her thoughts rampaged on... the very cable that could cut into the wing of an aircraft and bring it hurtling to the ground could easily strangle her too!

The crash of her steel helmet on to the floor wasn't exactly a tranquilliser to her already troubled thoughts. Then amid the apologies from a clumsy member of the crew the sergeant bellowed from the doorway...

"Action stations... we have to fly her... enemy aircraft approaching... come on jump to it!"

Having yanked on jackets the crew rushed outside. "Who's driving the winch sarge?" Basher enquired.

"You can drive Bash because Blondie went on leave this afternoon."

As she sat huddled in the winch she murmured a silent prayer of thanks for Blondie's absence. She never could work out why Blondie always had the job as winch driver, because apart from her obsession and fear of the cable she really did enjoy winch driving. Then revving the engine to a roar she could vaguely hear the sergeant shouting her orders. Her command bellowed down the megaphone and rang through he air like a whip. "Ease her away Bash... be careful now, she's reeling."

As Basher let out the clutch the balloon pitched and tossed like a ship in an angry sea. Then when she reached twenty feet from the ground she bounced back on the deck... a scream of... 'Duck!' came from the direction of the balloon bed. Basher imagined that someone had experienced a nasty moment. But minutes later Big Bertha was flying at one thousand five hundred feet, and there she was to stay until further notice.

A sigh of relief was breathed as the crew made a mad dash for the hut. Some cursed the wretched alert as they rushed around madly having now been made late for their 'dates'. Those left on duty kept their ears open for the sound of the siren heralding the arrival of the enemy... but all was still.

"What no date Bash?" one of he crew asked.

"No, he's studying tonight, and in any case I'm duty crew."

Midnight struck as Basher's guard duty came to an end. She poured the tea for the next shift then said her goodnights.

As she was about to crawl under the blankets she was surprised to see Sadie enter the hut looking very solemn. She took up her position in front of Basher's bunk and dramatically bowed before announcing "The Duke has arrived madam and wishes the pleasure of your company."

Basher shot out of bed. "Tell him I won't be long" she called, as Sadie disappeared into the darkness.

The mouth of Scotty dropped open. "It's all right you'll get used to this" Basher explained, as she pulled her slacks over her pyjamas.

"BBBut who on earth is the Duke?" Scotty stammered.

"My boyfriend. He's a posh budding accountant hence the cracks... must go can't keep him waiting." Basher said as she fled the hut.

The nightmare of the past hours left Basher as she was locked in the arms of her Duke. Their future together was the security she yearned for, someone to love her in spite of her puppy fat. They were young and optimistic and although the world around them was being smashed to the ground, nothing could break their confidence.

The clock tolled its half hour and reminded Basher of the three and half hours sleep that was left before her next guard duty. She clung desperately to her Duke. "See you tomorrow darling." he whispered before disappearing into the darkness.

The urgent voice of he sergeant penetrated Basher's beautiful dreams and bedclothes were suddenly yanked off.

"Come on girls, jump to it, we're losing the balloon, so move!"

As Basher drifted out of her deep sleep she was aware of the buzz of excitement going on around her intermingled with swearing and moaning. The hut was a beehive of activity. Sea boot stockings were being pulled on, jumpers, slacks and battle dress tops. Finally Basher jumped out of her bunk, grabbed her slacks and steel helmet and emerged into the blackness of the night.

The crew stood rooted to the spot... they were too late... their beloved Big Bertha had gone! The sergeant came rushing toward them "It's on the railway line girls, hurry please or there'll be a terrible accident." she yelled urgently before disappearing into the darkness.

Edie suddenly appeared and stood beside Basher "What a turn up for the book" she said overcoming crisis as usual in her typical cockney style. "This is it Bash... fame at last... come on run for it."

They ran in the direction of the railway line. Basher suddenly heard a loud whistling sound like a bomb before it hits the ground. It couldn't be she argued with herself, there isn't a raid on.

It was then that fear gripped her and her heart pounded as she came to a dead halt. "What's up Bash?" Edie shouted as she realised some yards ahead that her mate was not with her. A petrified Basher was just about able to utter "WWWait a minute Edie, don't go another step, that damned cable's around here somewhere, I can hear the wind whistling down it."

Edie stood deadly still... "I can't 'ear anyfing" she yelled after a few moments.

"Neither can I now" Basher said feeling annoyed at having made a fool of herself.

"But please, let's make certain" she begged.

The pair walked around like sleep walkers, hands outstretched feeling for he cable. Then down on their hands and knees grovelling like a pair of hunted animals in a frantic search for the death trap they imagined waited for them.

"Come on" said Edie, "You're bleedin' imagining fings, there's no fuckin' cable round 'ere."

"No I'm not! I swear I heard it!" came the now frustrated Basher. So once again they started to run to join their crew. As they gathered speed, to Basher's horror she heard it again, but this time so loudly that she didn't bother informing her mate, instead she turned on her heel and ran hell for leather in the direction of the nissen huts. Swaying on the threshold of the office in a state of collapse she found herself looking into the forbidding eyes of the Squadron Leader. "What do you think you're doing here?" he asked.

"Well sir..." Basher stammered "it's the cable... her whole story tumbled out.

The duty officer began to laugh hysterically. "Basher!" he commanded, "Take off your tin helmet." As she did the middle dropped out and rolled across the floor.

"What happened to that?" he asked.

"It was then that Basher remembered the helmet being dropped earlier that evening. "Er... it had a bit of a bump sir."

"It did," the officer said stifling another threatening eruption of laughter, "And the screw that bolts the two parts together came loose. So when you ran the wind whistled through the two divided parts, the faster you ran, the louder the whistle became. What you *thought* was the cable was no more than the wind!"

The officer took out his handkerchief and wiped his eyes as he convulsed into more peels of laughter.

Basher stood silent for she could never remember feeling quite so stupid in her entire life. Then seeing the distraught look on her face the officer added "Never mind Basher, you stay here and look after the phones, it's just as important as deflating the old balloon."

Then picking up his cap he made for the door. On the

threshold he hesitated before saying "Basher when you choose your new trade, make certain there are no cables to strangle you, but... keep it under that tin hat!"

CHAPTER 18

The crew ambled back one by one. Some poured tea from the pot that Basher had just made, whilst others made their weary way back to their beds. Edie and sarge were the last to arrive.

"What happened then sarge, did you manage to get it off the railway line?" Basher asked as soon as they had a mug of tea in their hands.

The sergeant's eyes flew into her head with exasperation. "We eventually dragged it to the embankment and out of danger of the trains. But we weren't allowed to deflate her." Edie was hanging on to the sergeants every word and finally not being able to contain herself a moment longer she butted in...

"And guess what Bash? We 'ad to wait a full 'our because some poxy officer wanted to deflate her very first balloon wiv a knife! She 'ad come wivout it and had to drive back to headquarters to borrow one from 'er mate. When she arrived back you 'ad fought she was launching a bleedin' ship I fought I was 'earing fings when she pulls out this bleedin' knife and announces; "I've waited my entire career for this moment..." yer know Bash all fuckin' posh like... the stupid cow."

Basher glared from Edie to the sergeant in total disbelief at what she had just heard, then finding her tongue asked "What was wrong with the correct procedure of pulling the bloody rip cord?"

Edie threw her arms in the air, "Oh no... that's too bleedin' easy. Lady bloody muck just *had* to use a knife. No doubt she finks she'll be awarded the Victoria Cross for bravery. I was 'oping the wind would sneak into Big Bertha's belly and inflate 'er fer a moment. I'd have loved to 'ave seen 'er ladyship 'anging on the end of the tail guy!"

Basher smiled at Edie's poetic description of the scene she had just witnessed. Then Edie suddenly swung on Basher and asked the dreaded question "What 'appened to you? I turned around and yer'd gone."

Basher blushed, but not wanting to explain her stupid mistake for she knew she would never hear the end of it, she changed the subject rapidly by suggesting it was time to go back to bed.

An air of speculation was present the following morning during breakfast. Finally Edie confronted the sergeant and asked "Does this mean we'll be closing down now sarge?"

"What makes you think that?" the sergeant replied as if playing her cards close to her chest.

"Well Worthing Road site did the moment the balloon went. That was it, closed within hours." Edie stated with a confident air.

"We're due for closing anyway aren't we sarge?" pressed Basher.

The sergeant looked agitated with the barrage of questions and irritably replied "We are the last to go in the squadron. Carrisbrooke are deflating today so no doubt their balloon will come to us."

"Oh my God!" moaned Blondie. "That means another

full inflation process.

The sergeant shrugged her shoulders and said "Yep that's about the size of it."

The ringing of the phone interrupted the barrage of questions and the uneasy atmosphere all the changes had caused. The sergeant seemed relieved for the break as she rushed off to the office, but returned quickly and announced "Basher it's for you."

"For me? Nobody rings me on site." Basher remarked as she fled to answer the call. Basher emerged after a few moments searching for Edie who was eventually found sitting on the step of the hut having a fag.

"Hey guess who that was on the phone?"

"'Aven't a clue, 'itler at a guess." Edie replied smiling

"Silly bugger. It was Phyll. She wants us to meet her in the city tomorrow evening for a meal. She's been posted already, so wants this final meal" Basher explained.

"What after the forty days and forty nights of silence? Is this 'er idea of the Last Supper?"

Basher smiled to herself before entering the office. The sergeant was sitting at her desk pondering over some papers.

"Sarge... can me and Edie have the evening off tomorrow only one of our mates we joined up wiv wants to have an evening meal with us before she's posted.

"I don't see why not" then tapping a pile of leaflets on the table she handed them to Edie who had been hovering in the doorway. "Hand these out please, the girls need to be deciding what their next trade is to be."

"Fitzallen Square... terminus" he conductor yelled as passengers got ready to leave the tram. As they queued to leave Edie was bobbing up and down trying to catch a glimpse of Phyll through the window. "There she is Bash" Blimey she's only a bleedin Flight Sergeant.... look at 'er."

Despite her superiority in rank the two girls greeted her in their warm manner, but Phyll stiffened slightly attempting to keep her distance both emotionally and physically. This rankled Edie who could never keep her mouth shut when it came to Phyllis, it was a truly love hate relationship.

"Ere we bleedin' go" she muttered clearly feeling snubbed, but Phyllis appeared unaware of Edie's agitation as she announced "There's a nice little restaurant over there."

Edie's eyes followed Phyll's then she blurted out. "'Old on 'ere, we aren't all on Flight Sergeants wages yer know. The nearest pub'll do me."

Phyllis jerked her head back in shock. "Oh no not a pub! I'd rather pay for the meals myself if you are that short. You can always pay me back later. I'll leave my forwarding address."

Edie's mouth opened and shut in one swift movement. Basher waited with baited breathe for her to hit the roof, but to her total surprise Edie simply burst out laughing. "Do yer know I rumbled yer the first day we met in London. I could 'ave prophesied 'ow yer'd turn out and I'm not bloddywell wrong 'eiver. Tighter than a ducks arse with the piggin cheek of old nick" But Edie hadn't finished she turned to Basher "I told yer, the quiet one's always 'ave somefink up their sleeve."

Phyllis never could keep up with Edie, whether she was slagging someone else off, or having a go at her. It was as if her brain couldn't keep pace and more often than not she lost the plot. This was one such time she could not comprehend the judgment that had just been dished out to her. Edie knew this, so took advantage by grabbing Phyllis's arm and pulling her across the busy road said;

"Come on then Flight lets get some grub down us, seeing as yer paying."

An hour passed as they went hungrily through a three course meal. Exchanging experiences of the most recent months. Edie was on top form dramatising all the events finishing with three acts a curtain call and a grand finale!

When Phyllis finally got a word in she asked Edie. "Is your American man still on the scene then?"

Edie thrust her left hand across the table almost knocking Phyll's nose from her face and flashed a rather large sparkling ring announcing; "Yep well and truly! What about 'er then? Got 'erself a bleedin' accountant fer a feller."

Phyllis smiled warmly at Basher and said sincerely, "Well done Basher."

"I can't flash a ring yet cos my feller has to meet my parents at the end of next week when we go on leave, and he's a bit old fashioned, he wants to ask my Dad first."

Edie butted in and asked Phyllis. "What trade are yer changing to then? No don't tell me, yer going ter be a bloody officer." she said sarcastically.

Phyllis kept her cool and in her unperturbed manner replied.

"I did consider that option actually. But after careful consideration turned it down. I've been posted to Cranwell in Lincolnshire. I'm going to train as Teleprinter Operator and hope to work within Bomber Command."

Basher and Edie exchanged unbelieving glances before shrieking; "So are we!"

"Well sod me, we'll be togever once again, can't get rid of yer that easy eh?" Edie managed to say when the excitement subsided. Then after a momentary pause added. "We'll be the same rank again, cos you'll lose those bleedin' stripes mate."

Phyllis smiled and far from taking offence she said simply. "We can begin again at least for a short period because there is no guarantee we'll all get the same squadron once our training is over. So lets make the most of the time in Cranwell. I've missed you two in a funny sort of way."

The clock in the Square tolled its half hour. "We'd better be going Bash" Edie suggested. Then with a promise to keep in touch this time, the girls made their separate ways back to their sites.

The following morning the sergeant waited until her crew were settled with their second cup of tea after breakfast before calling order.

"I'm afraid I've some sad news for you all. We officially close this Friday. Some of you have future postings and leave organized, but the rest will have to establish theirs immediately. You will be advised of your new posting before you go on leave. Now it's all hands on deck. A lot has to be done to wind down the old site. Thank you for your help and team spirit, it's been a pleasure working with you all. Sorry I've been a bit moody lately but I knew this was coming and I personally dreaded it. It is very un-professional I know, but I cared about my work and my crew. You've been a smashing bunch..." she choked on her threatened tears and fled the room.

Basher's parents greeted Simon warmly. Her mother fussed over him as if he were royalty, whilst her father's smug grin told Basher that he approved of her choice of young man.

Simon had made his way to the bathroom for a wash after his long journey south.

"Nice bloke you got there" her father said when they were alone. "A nice mannered young man and got a good head on him too. Well done girl"

Simon entered the room and brought with him a strong aroma of aftershave. As he came close he grasped Basher's hand and squeezed it tightly before taking a seat near her father. Both men quickly got involved in deep conversation. Basher made her way to the kitchen to see if her mother needed any help in the preparation of the supper. But everything was well organized as usual in the cooking department. "You can lay the table if you like" Her mother said. "I've put a clean tablecloth on!"

Basher collected the cutlery from the drawer and began laying the table.

Her mother poked her head around the breakfast room door and remarked "He's a bit small for you isn't he? You look more like mother and son." she added giggling to herself.

Basher thought to herself 'here we go' she always has to criticise and judge. But yelled back in her defence "At least he's good looking and got brains."

"All right keep your hair on," her mother snapped as she carved large slices from the joint of beef that was now cold. She lay out portions carefully on each plate before turning to her daughter and ordered "Get out the pickle and pickled onions. Your know your father won't consider it supper without them."

Basher busied herself smoothing out the tablecloth and checking the cutlery was correctly in place. The pickles and freshly cut bread lay in the centre. The bubble and squeak smelled delicious as it simmered on the stove.

This was the best part of the day for Basher. It had been so for as long as she could remember. It was a time she had missed the most since leaving home. Supper time was when the entire family gathered and her father would amuse them with his funny - if not blue – jokes. Tonight was a special feast, extra food had been put on in honour of the new guest. Mother had done them proud, despite the rationing of food.

"I didn't realise you were home for good Dad" Basher remarked as they were now enjoying the feast before them.

Her father smiled; "Never heard of flat feet getting you out of the forces? - purely on medical grounds you understand?"

Basher knew her father of old, and gathered from his smug if not somewhat sarcastic attitude that he'd been up to his old tricks, having pulled a 'fast one' For she could swear he'd had flat feet all of his life!" Simon and Basher exchanged loving glances across the table. Now and then he found her leg with his foot and stroked it gently, sending shivers down her spine.

This was a new emotion she had never experienced

before, but she was to quickly feel uneasy as her father took the floor. The thought of him embarking on a series of dirty jokes would be totally un-acceptable and embarrass her beyond words. She coloured slightly until she realised her fears were unfounded as her father was now addressing her seriously.

"Did I ever tell you girl, what I discovered about your food shortages in Sheffield?"

Basher groaned; "Oh don't remind me Dad, you'll put me off me supper."

"No... listen... you'll like this one... Some weeks ago I was coming home on a weekend leave. I'd just left the camp on a very quiet country road in Wiltshire. Had no money so had to thumb a lift. It was then I spotted a car coming in the distance so taking up my position at the edge of the gutter I put my thumb out. Then to my horror a long black staff car pulled up complete with a pennant flying from her bonnet. And for the sake of our guest here, who has never been in the armed forces, a pennant flying from the bonnet means there is a very high ranking officer inside.

I nearly died, talk about the chits! Anyway I stood smartly to attention and gave one of my best salutes and managed to send me cap flying into the gutter! In my fluster I bent down to pick it up when I hear this dead posh voice say "Give him a lift driver."

I moved swiftly beside the driver not daring to look behind. Well I mean... it could have been Winston himself for all I knew. Suddenly the posh voice asks.

"What's your name airman?"

"Berry sir, I says."

"That name rings a bell," he says. Then after a short pause he suddenly bursts out with... "Ah yes... I remember now. There was an airwoman by that name stationed in Sheffield on a balloon site. Kicked up a holy stink at Air Ministry, something to do with not having enough to eat." he said thoughtfully.

"Not being able to contain myself a moment longer I blurted out. Yes sir that was my daughter."

Basher's hand flew to her mouth and her eyes opened wide as her father continued his interesting story about this liaison with some strange high ranking officer.

"Really Berry," the officer continued. "You should be proud of her. She stood her ground and no mistake. Splendid and most commendable, not afraid of authority that one, should go far... indeed she should!" the officer enthused.

Basher's cheeks erupted into deep blotches of red, whilst her eyes continued to open and shut like a barn owl as the story was unfolding.

Her father continued by explaining that the officer then tapped him on the shoulder and asked "Any idea of the outcome of that enquiry Berry?"

"No sir. No idea at all sir."

"A nice little black market racket was going on there. A few officers and several NCO's were dismissed the service as a result. You should be jolly proud of that daughter of yours Berry."

"I am sir. I did think at the time that maybe there was a bit of a fiddle going on sir, if you'll pardon the expression.

"Indeed there was... by the way, any idea who I am Berry?" he asked.

Basher's father put down his knife and fork at this point relishing the drama that was unfolding.

"I turned around to face him finally. His face was vaguely familiar but I just couldn't put a name to it. I was so embarrassed I could have died on the spot. But had to be truthful so I said simply... "Sorry sir, I know you well, but the name eludes me."

The officer smiled before saying... "I'm commonly known as Bomber Harris... but Air Vice Marshall Harris to you!"

THE

BREIGHTON

TWINS

CHAPTER 1

A biting wind took Bashers breath as she alighted from the train at York railway station. It was an overcast day in October of 1944.

Throwing her kit bag over her shoulder she made her way over the bridge to the exit. In the courtyard were some Air Force trucks waiting. Their drivers leaning against the door drawing heavily on their cigarettes. Basher was in no mood to hang around her journey had been long and tiresome.

She approached one of the group asking if they were going to Heslington Hall.

The drivers 'ummed' and 'aahed' teasing her making out they had never heard of the place. She momentarily mentally panicked she was certain that is was Bomber Command four group that she had been told to report before she was given a week's leave from her Teleprinting course at Cranwell. It had to be she told herself her railway warrant was for York. But now her patience was wearing thin so made it clear that if someone didn't make up their minds she would ring group Headquarters herself and ask for some transport. The sergeant among them realised she meant it and suggested she throw her kit in the back of the truck and then go and sit in the drivers cabin, He went on to explain they were waiting for some aircrew who were due on the next train from Scotland, and were all going to Heslington Hall.

Having got comfortable in the truck Basher rubbed her hands together vigorously to get some feeling back into them. Her feet were gradually beginning to thaw. It certainly was some degrees colder here than in the south of England.

Suddenly a lot of yahooing could be heard within the confines of the station. It was then that about twenty aircrew burst into the courtyard and cheered as the sergeant directed them to the rear of the truck. Throughout the entire journey, that took around twenty minutes, the revellers in the back were singing popular songs to their own dirty lyrics. Crumbs, Basher thought, are these the kind of characters I'll be working with? For she knew an operational squadron meant action of the most serious kind. She guessed their task was to fly on nightly bombing raids, so perhaps their rowdiness could be excused.

Suddenly the brakes of the truck squealed to a halt. They had pulled into the small courtyard of an old rambling house.

"Out you get my lovely," the driver said to Basher, before banging on the tarpaulin behind him yelling... "Everyone out!"

A warrant officer sat at a desk with pen at the ready. He smiled before asking "Name please?"

Basher reeled off her full title. The Warrant Officer smiled, advising her not to get too comfortable as transport was ready to take her to 78 Squadron Breighton. It might just as well have been tinbucktoo, because it meant nothing to her.

The same sergeant that had brought her from the station was at the doorway suggesting she got back on board because once the aircrew had reported they would be off again.

The bleak exposed Yorkshire countryside was depressing. They had driven for miles in narrow country lanes with a mist hanging low over the fields and the bare black trees looking stark against the cold grey sky. Elvington, Holme-on-Spalding-Moor, Melbourne, Pocklington. Basher smiled as she now recalled all of these names. They were on the blackboard of her training school. It was part of the general network of the intricate teleprinting system.

Small groups of aircrew had been dropped off at these vital squadrons.

At last Basher was alone with the sergeant wondering if her squadron was perhaps nearer to the moon!

"Right... now my lovely let's get you to Breighton."

"Not before time" Basher said disgruntled, as she was tired and tetchy after such a long day.

The truck rumbled in the half darkness. At the end of a long stretch of road Basher could see the gates of RAF Breighton.

The driver dropped her off at the guard room and waited until she signed in before taking her to the administrative block. This is where she was allocated her barrack room. Having taken her details the corporal disappeared from behind the counter then with arms bulging with sheets, pillowcases and clean blankets she told Basher to follow her.

On the way to her new barrack room the corporal explained that they had withdrawn the bedding from stores because they guessed she would arrive after closing time.

Then went on to explain that in the morning she had to collect a bicycle from the stores. This was an imperative piece of equipment as everything was so widely spaced. If in the event of not being able to ride a bicycle, now was her chance to learn... or walk!

Having arrived at the hut the corporal dumped the bedding on the first available empty bed, before asking Basher to step outside. Then signalling in the direction of the cookhouse, she advised her to go immediately to get a meal, or it would be too late.

As the clock struck nine in the signals section the following morning, Basher reported for duty. The corporal in charge of the teleprinting room greeted her warmly and invited her to sit at the desk next to her, so that she could explain her duties.

The room was no more than approximately twelve feet by twelve. Basher noted a small hatch just above the desk at which she was working. The door of the hatch had an inside lock on which was hung a notice in huge red letters; NO ADMITTANCE PLEASE KNOCK.

In the corner of this small room stood a pot-belly stove roaring away throwing out heat at an alarming rate. The corporal began explaining that the three teleprinter machines that were situated directly behind them had their own individual uses.

The one on the extreme left was a vital classified machine, which received the document Form B. This document contained all details of a forthcoming raid including the size of the bomb load. The rendezvous point with other aircraft, the weather conditions and the route and targets.

Basher confirmed that she did understand the seriousness of this document, as it had been a source of emphasis on her most recent training course.

The machine that was set aside for the use for these documents would alert the operator with an incessant message... FORM B FORM B FORM B...

The frequency of this signal made an unmistakable sound, so that even if the operator were out of the room she would be alerted by the SOUND of the signal and would enable her to lock the entrances to the room placing NO ADMITTANCE placards on all entrances. The handling of this document was so classified that not even the Duty Officer was allowed into the room at this time.

The corporal went on to explain that the middle machine mainly brought in incoming messages and the end right hand machine was for outgoing messages.

The corporal had introduced herself as Margery, although she made it clear that the Warrant Officer in charge of the signals department was very strict about anything that smelt of familiarity, so it would be best in his hearing to refer to her as corporal.

The next hour was spent learning how to fill in the log book, as every incoming message had to be logged, and placed in the OUT tray, and the copies of outgoing messages also had to be logged and filed.

The vital information about the receiving and sending of telegrams was explained in some detail and Corporal Margery warned Basher not to get too emotionally involved, because she would have the task of sending out bad news from time to time. Basher swallowed hard at this news because it had never occurred to her that this is what her job would involve, but she decided that she would cross that bridge when she came to it.

Just as she was getting the gist of the job, having sent out a few messages and received some, she entered everything correctly into the log book when the door suddenly burst open and a tall insipid looking Warrant Officer walked in.

He was over six feet in height and of slim build. His hair was blonde, and his complexion pasty. The blonde eyebrows were so thin it almost seemed as if there were none, and then the tiny light blue eyes that penetrated wherever he was looking, were rimmed with pink. He had nothing going for him in the looks department but clearly wore his uniform with pride. Basher thought he looked to be in his late twenties. She on the other hand would have made two of him. She stood at least at five feet ten and that was in her stocking feet! Her frame was large and she had at times been described as well built, but mostly refereed to as fat. She had a deeply rich voice that could sound like a fog horn when she wanted it to. Her personality was as strong as her build, hence she had acquired the nick- name Basher whilst serving in Balloon Command.

She was Christened Muriel, but Basher had stuck during her service career. The Warrant Officer began tapping his foot as he waited for Basher to stand, but instead she sat swinging her legs. This wasn't deliberate insubordination it was because discipline had been so lenient during her time in Balloon Command that she just couldn't get out of the habit of treating None Commissioned Officers as equals. To say this got her off on the wrong footing eventually became painfully obvious. Pulling himself up to his full height he finally asked rather sarcastically.

"May I ask where you were stationed and what was your previous job before remustering to signals?"

Having never come across a Warrant Officer before Basher was at a loss to know how to address him. To be on the safe side she decided to do neither, but went on to simply explain that she had been a Balloon Operator. The Warrant Officer nodded his head rather slowly as he spat out.

"That just about says it all. A more undisciplined lazy lot I've never come across. Well lady I'm Warrant Officer Pratt and will be refereed to as 'Sir' in future. I will not tolerate your undisciplined ways here in my section. You will report for work on time and when I enter the room you will stand to attention. You will do as you are told at all times. The moment you step out of line I'll have you on a charge so fast your feet won't touch the ground." With that he nodded to the corporal, and she followed him out.

Tears welled in Basher's eyes in sheer anger. How dare he judge the job that Balloon Operators had done. I'd like to see him cope with a barrage balloon in a gale, she furiously thought to herself. But that job was more important than stupid rules and regulations.

Our kind of discipline was to ourselves and our team, not to people who were so far up themselves simply because they had rank she thought indignantly.

The corporal returned and could see by Bashers face that Warrant Officer Pratt had upset her. She brushed her hand across Basher's back as she passed her to take up her seat.

"Listen Bash, don't listen to him. He loves to pull rank. You see in Civvy Street he was a simple Market Gardener. So to reach the dizzy heights of Warrant Officer has gone to his head. He has ideas of grandeur and thinks he is someone important. He abuses the power his rank gives him... Take my advice. Keep your head down. Do your job efficiently and answer him just a simple yes or no, then he can't get at you."

Basher nodded her agreement as she got up and tore off a whole length of messages that had just arrived on the incoming machine. As she entered each one in her log book she could smell a distinct aroma of coffee.

"Boy that smells good" Basher remarked to the corporal who was now filling the belly pot stove with some fuel.

"It's your break time Bash, off you go into the next room. The girls will give you some coffee and biscuits."

Mugs of steaming hot coffee were on the bench of a room adjoining the kitchen. Someone in the kitchen passed through a tin of biscuits and called for everyone to help themselves. There were no seats so clearly everyone was expected to stand for their break. Basher felt shy and self conscious as she stood amongst these strangers. A sergeant approached her asking her name and in which department she worked before introducing her to all those who were assembled.

They each smiled and nodded their acknowledgment before turning to their particular friend to continue their conversation.

Basher could hear what she thought was her own local

dialect, following the voice she found herself at the entrance to a door of a telephone exchange. Two operators sat on the PBX switchboard with their backs to her. It was the girl on the right who sounded like a Londoner as she answered each call. Basher was so thrilled to hear a familiar accent because not only was she in north Yorkshire she was in a hut full of Geordies mostly from the Newcastle area, and this was the first familiar accent she had heard since she arrived.

"Hi" she said meekly. "I guess you might be a Londoner?" she began.

The girl on the right turned around. "Well... West London to be honest. Where're you from then?"

"Not far from you actually, a little place called Feltham."

"Well sod me, small world." she replied as she turned around to answer another barrage of small lights that had now lit up the switchboard.

"I can see you're busy" Basher said as she glanced at the clock in the room, I'll have to get going anyway, my break is over. Can I meet up with you after work?"

"Not really" her colleague replied, "You see I'm confined to camp for fourteen days, but I get a break around seven. If you come to the NAFFI we can have a cup of coffee and a chat then."

"Fine, see you then." Basher replied as she hurried back to her own section.

At seven sharp Basher entered the NAFFI. This was one of the largest she had ever seen. It was divided into two parts. One area was a restaurant and shop while the other a massive lounge complete with a stage and grand piano sitting grandly in one corner and a large dance floor spreading out in front of it. Basher felt a flutter of excitement, I bet they have some corker OF dances in here she thought to herself. Arm chairs were placed around the edge of the dance floor with more scattered around behind, with tables and chairs for those who wished to drink. A Flight sergeant navigator appeared and sat at the piano playing all the well known songs of the day. Basher felt sure he was a professional for a played beautifully. Having stood for a few moments taking in the atmosphere and trying to get her bearings, she then heard her fellow telephonist call out. "Oye.... I'm over 'ere." Basher was to learn in a very short space of time that her colleagues name was June. She came from Ealing in West London, she was twenty four years old, single and a boozer. The reason she was on 'jankers' was because she had been found in York drunk and disorderly.

Basher took a sharp intake of breath when she heard about this. Because during her entire service career she had never been on a charge. The thought of being hauled in front of officers and given punishment petrified her. But this girl couldn't have cared less. She was about the same height as Basher, around five ten. Her build was on the big side but she couldn't be described as fat. Her round face had very high cheekbones and a natural high colouring, which may have been due to her drinking habit. She reminded Basher of a cherub!

Being a bit older than Basher she had more experience of life making it clear that nobody got the better of her. She certainly came over as a bit of a tough nut.

During Bashers Balloon operating days she had also toughened up, but hers was more of a physical toughness, she still maintained her deep sensitivity. But despite their differences in character and temperament they hit it off as if they had known each other all of their lives.

As June drained her coffee cup she blurted out, "Come across old Pratt face yet?" Basher looked momentarily puzzled, until she realised that June was referring to the Warrant Officer.

"Oh yes he's already rattled my cage."

"He's a bloody jumped up nothing, so take no notice mate." then glancing at the NAFFI clock June looked a bit alarmed. "Christ I've gone over me time they'll kill me in that cookhouse. Listen... what hut yer in?"

"Dunno the details just that it's full of Geordie cooks and waitresses, who work in the aircrew officers and sergeants mess."

"That's next door to me. See you at nine when I've finished. I'll come to the hut OK?" And with that she was gone.

CHAPTER 2

A group of airman were already at the main gate stamping their feet and throwing their arms across their chests in order to keep warm, as the two girls approached.

"What time is this bus due?" Basher asked of her mate.

"About quarter past, but it's nearly always late."

This was the first time Basher had been outside the main gate of the camp since she arrived more than two weeks ago. June had now completed her 'jankers' and was allowed off the station. They decided to celebrate Junes' freedom by going to the cinema in Selby. The two chatted while they waited for the arrival of the one and only bus of the evening. It finally arrived twenty minutes late.

June had began questioning as to whether they would actually be too late to get into the cinema. Basher was already suspicious that perhaps June was hankering after going for a drink. The two airmen who sat behind them on the bus clearly fancied their chances. But the two girls were ten jumps ahead of them and knew they were only after a quick snog in the darkened cinema, so their advances were met with an icy cold stare. As the bus pulled up opposite the cinema Basher was grateful to notice there was still a queue and with only one program nightly she felt they had an excellent chance of getting in. The strains of 'Why Are We Waiting' came from the back, and the two guys who had been on the bus were still persisting with their chat up lines.

"Hey... you two! Cockney twins!" they called as one whistled through his fingers. "Can we join you?"

"No you bloodywell can't. So sod off!" June retorted.

Basher gave her mate a side-long glance thinking, do I really look like her? But concluded it was probably because they wore the same blue uniform and were similar in build, plus they both had a London accent. Just as she comforted herself with that thought, June asked if she was ever stationed in Blackpool? Basher explained that she was for a short period. She had wanted to originally be a wireless operator but found the course too demanding and had to pack it in. June looked thoughtful before asking if she had ever been friendly with a French Naval Officer? Basher's mouth dropped open, and there was a pregnant pause before she replied. "Yes his name was John Paul Mussel. He was a lovely guy and although I was engaged at the time, this was a truly platonic friendship."

June interrupted. "It might well have been platonic as far as you were concerned, but he carried a bloody great torch for you... I met up with him in the Toc H canteen. It must have been just after you had left because he kept telling me 'You are so much like my girl friend'. To be honest he got on my nerves he wouldn't let it drop. The only reason I'm reminded of it is because those guys back there think we are twins. This French bloke kept on and on about you. He showed me your photograph. I now realise that when we first met I felt I knew you. It was that bloody photograph!"

"What a small world eh? Me and him had a ball. I remember going one afternoon to the Tower ballroom to listen to Reginald Dixon on the organ. John had been machine gunned on board ship, and was bandaged from his shoulder down to his finger tips on his left arm. He only tried filling his lighter with petrol during the performance in the pitch dark I may add and of course spilled it all over his bandages! When he lit his fag his entire bandages caught fire! There I was banging his arm trying to put it out and all he could do was laugh hysterically."

Basher was aware during her explanation that June was getting agitated and looking around frantically.

"I'm not standing here much longer. There's a pub over there that looks inviting. Shall we go Bash, and give the pictures a miss?"

At that point much to Bashers delight the queue moved along a few paces so she took the opportunity to continue the subject about the French Naval Officer.

"Did he ever tell you about his family?" Basher asked of her mate as she desperately tried to divert her attention away from the pub.

"No..." June replied, now sounding interested. Basher went on to explain that early one Sunday evening she wandered into the Toch H canteen and found John sitting on his own crying. When she enquired as what was the matter, he explained that he had just received a telegram from the Red Cross to explain that his entire family had been taken into his village square and shot. This was a reprisal for finding members of the French Resistance hiding British airmen in the village.

Junes mouth fell open. "The bastards! He never ever told me about this. In fact I really fancied this guy and could have killed you for having such an effect upon him.

I can still hear him now in his broad French accent; I miss 'er so much. She was so beautiful. You remind me so much of 'er but you are not 'er"

Basher shook her head, "I truly don't understand, because the last thing he said to me was 'When you are married you must come to Normandy with all your liddle kids'. He seemed to totally accept the fact that I was engaged."

The queue was now moving at a fast pace which disrupted the girls line of thought. As they entered the foyer June noticed it was an Alice Faye movie and she told Basher this was one of her favourite actresses. That first night clinched their friendship, and from then on they were inseparable much to the exasperation of the Warrant Officer who now made it clear he disliked them both with a passion. On the other side of the coin the attitude of both girls left no doubts that they considered him an idiot of the first order. Neither had any illusion about him, they knew he was gunning for them and would have no hesitation at putting them on a charge if he thought he could get away with it.

What didn't help their case was within the first week of Junes freedom she took off again for York without telling Basher, got drunk and found herself on a more serious charge. The Commanding Officer this time was exceedingly angry and warned her that if she was brought before him again he would have no hesitation recommending that she be dismissed the service. Basher tried reasoning with her mate during the next fourteen days whilst she continue to keep her company during her evening breaks from her punishment duties.

The Warrant Officer never allowed June to live it down. Behind her back he constantly reminded Basher that people like June would be a bad influence and rightly or wrongly she would have the same tag to her name. Realising this was ineffective he sneered that at least it would put paid to their social life for the time being. That was until one night he walked into the NAFFI and saw Basher and June together laughing their heads off. The next day Basher found her shift had changed to evenings!

The girls were to quickly learn that this man could be vindictive and spiteful. But they didn't bargain for his deceit. It was during an evening duty that Basher had made some tea. June was the only telephonist on duty. Before joining her for the tea break she made certain that the door to her section was left open so that if a Form B were to come in she would hear it. Basher's ears were now well and truly accustomed to the sound of the call sign.

The switchboard wasn't very busy. Both girls gossiped as they sipped their tea.

Suddenly Warrant Officer Pratt stood in the doorway and to their surprise began a perfectly civilized conversation. It was so out of character that it should have warned both girls. June taking full advantage of the situation began telling dirty jokes. But clearly this man was accustomed to a very cloistered lifestyle, for he hesitated at most of the punch lines before laughing uproariously, leaving both girls pretty certain that he didn't really understand them at all. But had to laugh so as not to seem foolish. It was then he made a rather unseemly remark to June, who spun around to face him and pointing her finger humorously said "I'll have your guts for garters!"

Warrant Officer Pratt laughed hysterically, then wiping the tears from his eyes said to June in his broad Devonshire accent, "Wherever did you get a saying like that?"

June glanced at Basher her eyes flaying in her head, before turning back to her senior officer and telling him he hadn't lived. Telling him that it was one of the oldest lines in the English language. The Warrant Officer left the section still wiping his eyes. June called out after him, "You'd better go before you wet yourself!" But he didn't hear it which was just as well.

The following morning Basher took June her morning coffee, only to be told that she was on yet another charge for insubordination to a senior officer! When June returned she went straight to Bashers section. She was livid as she explained that Sir had gone straight to the admin office that night and charged her... despite his hysterics at her jokes. But when charged June told the whole story and said she had a witness. The charge was dismissed much to Junes relief. During the afternoon break someone had brought in a home made fruit cake. Warrant Officer Pratt always made for his section at break times. He didn't miss a trick always taking more than his fair share of what was on offer. That afternoon he had his back to the door and was deep in conversation with the sergeant. June walked in and waited until he had taken a huge bite of his cake before lifting her index finger she poked him in the back telling him precisely with every stab just what she thought of him, not really caring if he charged her again.

He choked on his cake to such an extent he couldn't

answer her before she flounced back to her section. The girl's noted that he steered clear of them for quite some time after that little incident.

The signals section was situated next door to Flying Control and both were adjacent to the runway. During early morning duties the planes would rumble back from their night raids. Quite a contrast from the evening previous when they thundered down the runway taking off. It was during a morning duty that Basher was handed a fistful of telegrams that had to be sent out over the telephone. Without checking them she picked up the phone and asked the operator to put her through to telegrams. The telegram operator answered and asked her for the message. Basher began reading first the address and then the text ...*We regret to inform you that your husband Squadron Leader Smith has been killed in action...* her eyes filled with tears as she continued to read out at least twenty telegrams all informing mothers and wives that their sons and husbands had either been killed or were missing. Just as Basher had stamped them to indicate they had been sent, the Warrant Officer walked in, picked up the pile and checked them. Basher held her breathe for she felt certain he was going to find something wrong, but instead he simply shrugged his shoulders and said "That'll teach them, think they're the bees knees just because they fly."

Basher couldn't trust herself to comment. She was livid. What kind of mentality could entertain such thoughts? she queried.

The Form B signal interrupted her angry thoughts. She automatically asked the Warrant Officer to leave. His face went a deeper shade of purple. He clearly wanted to refuse but realised that Basher was doing her duty correctly.

He did however hang around until the absolute last minute, obviously furious that this should happen at all in her presence as he thought it undermined his authority. Yet he could not get his head around the fact that he could do bugger all about it as Basher was carrying out the correct procedure. She had opened the hatch doorway, hung the NO ADMITTANCE notices on both doors, before finally standing rather smugly with her hand on the handle waiting for his lordship to leave. As he passed through the door Basher let out a rather sarcastic "Thank you" He then sped rapidly out of the section.

Basher hung over the incoming highly confidential information that was being received at a massive speed. My god! she thought, not another raid tonight the poor sods have barely had time to get over this one and by the look of it, a massive one. It was around eleven that morning that the Form B was completed. Basher typed out her acceptance with her initials, tore it off then folded it and placed it in an envelope that she sealed and was marked TOP SECRET. There was no one around so she knew she would have to go to Flying Control herself to find the Duty Officer for this is where he mainly hung out. Having dispensed with the important document she returned to find her middle machine typing sixty to the dozen, and when she popped her head over the back of the machine she found sheets of it lying on the floor.

At an appropriate moment she tore it off, and then settle down to entering every one of them into the log book and placing them in the appropriate trays, before ringing for someone to come and collect them.

Her day had been a particularly busy one. Then just as she was preparing to hand over the phone rang. It was 'Sir' who advised Basher there was no relief as the operator had gone sick. She would have to work through until nine that evening when the night shift would take over. When Basher enquired as to how she was to get her evening meal, he said he would have it sent over from the cookhouse. There was very little for her to do during the early evening. It was now early Spring and there was still a chill in the air, so she stoked up the pot belly stove. There had been a lot of activity going on around her outside. Small jeeps could be seen rushing from place to place. The ground engineers had been working on the planes most of the day. The trailers of bombs could be seen making for the aircraft and loading up in readiness for the night raid. A tannoy call was heard requesting all aircrew to report to the Briefing room. They must be almost ready for the off Basher thought as she tidied around her office. Then glancing at the clock on the wall she realised it was only an hour to her relief.

The office door suddenly burst open and a tall young good looking aircrew officer rushed in. He had a head of bright red hair and a pink complexion to go with it. His panic was obvious, he was taking a calculating risk as he had no right to be anywhere near her department. But placing a piece of paper before Basher he said in a broad Northern Irish accent.

"Do us favour me darling. This telegram is to be sent the moment you see my aircraft's wheels touch the tarmac when we return in the morning. I'm in 'C' for Charlie'

Darling this is most important. It's my last op of my second tour, and at last I'm due three weeks leave and I'm taking my wife on our honeymoon! This telegram gives details of my arrival in London. You are on duty aren't you?" Basher nodded her head. "Will you do this for me?" Basher agreed instantly. With that he kissed her on the cheek and said. "You're an angel."

Basher coloured up and smiled. "Leave it with me I'll make certain this telegram goes... promise."

The Flt Lieutenant flew through the door as if he was on fire for he knew he was out of bounds. Aircrew were forbidden to speak with anyone other than their crews after they had been briefed. Basher placed the precious piece of paper in the top pocket of her uniform and buttoned it up. As she cycled back to her barrack room she couldn't get the young officer out of her mind. It would be sods law for anything to go wrong now after a second tour. Which means he has been on sixty fully operational raids. Christ I hope he makes it. He deserves a break poor sod. Basher thought.

A bright and sunny day welcomed Basher as she rode to work across the wide open spaces of the airfield. She could hear the drone of the aircraft as they circled ready to land after their nightly raid over Germany. She almost threw her bike against the wall because she wanted to be at the window of her section while she waited the arrival of 'C' for Charlie.

The night duty operator was already watching as the planes touch down. She advised Basher that all was well before she left to go back to her hut to bed.

Basher took up her position at the window and prayed

that Pratt face wouldn't appear before she had done what she had promised the handsome officer she would do for him. The aircraft were landing in their droves. A 'Able' B 'Bertie' come on... Basher said out loud as she scanned the skies for more. At last here it was... C for 'Charlies' wheels touched the tarmac, but wait a minute... he was going too fast to land... up he went again... he had over-shot the runway. Back he went to do yet another circuit. Just as quickly he was out of sight... then an explosion could be heard that shook the building. My god what was that? She took out the crumpled telegram from her pocket and placed it on her desk. She heard the clanging of the bells of ambulances and fire engines in the distance. But C for 'Charlie' was not returning what on earth could have happened? Bashers heart felt like lead. Surely nothing could have happened to C for 'Charlie' their wheels actually touched the tarmac they were home and dry. She looked once again at the telegram. The officer was telling his wife to meet him at three o'clock at Kings Cross station. If she didn't send the cable soon his wife would never make it for she lived in the Home Counties.

At around midday some telegrams were brought in. Basher thumbed through them. There it was Flt Lt Flannery had been killed. There was no hint that he had actually been so near to arriving safely.

Basher sent out her cables but the one that caused the heaviest heart that day, was the one to his wife telling her the bad news. Basher envisaged her opening the telegram with delight eager to know what time to meet him... but that one was still in Bashers pocket.

CHAPTER 3

The snow lay thick on the airfield at RAF Breighton on that cold crisp January day in 1945. The snow ploughs were out clearing the runway making certain that weather conditions didn't interfere with the nightly bombing raids over Germany. Because Basher and June worked in the signals section they had an idea that things were hotting up in the now defensive war. Pressure was being brought to bear on Mr Hitler. His cities were being crucified on a nightly basis by our bombers, and the Americans and Russians were closing in on the ground.

But this was Basher and June's day off. They decided it would be wiser to stay on camp, as the bus service would no doubt be cancelled owing to the bad weather conditions. Having had lunch they made for the warmth of the NAFFI.

As they sipped their coffee Bashers eyes travelled to an item on the Notice Board. "Hey what's this?" she announced as she left her seat to get a closer look.

'Anyone interested in a Camp concert? Can you sing, dance, tell jokes or act?

If so, come along to the audition next week Tuesday evening at 7.pm sharp.

"What the hell is it?" called June.

Basher returned to her seat deep in thought. "There's to be a camp concert, they're asking for volunteers" Basher announced.

"Count me out. All I can do is play the fool." June replied flatly, making it clear she was uninterested in the scheme.

"But if I wrote a script would you at least consider it?" Basher asked tentatively.

"Might do. What have you got in mind?"

"Dunno. Perhaps something like an 'Over the garden wall' gossip between two middle aged women. What do you reckon?"

June suddenly warmed to the idea, and suggested they returned to their quarters so that Basher could get to work on the script straight away.

Before leaving the NAFFI Basher purchased a thick exercise book, then grabbing their cycles they had to push hard against the biting wind to reach the warmth of their hut enthused with their new ideas.

Propping their bikes against the nissen hut, June made a bee line for her own accommodation announcing; "I'll leave you to the creative writing mate, I'm turning in for the afternoon. Give us a shout when you've done it."

"Charming!" was all Basher could say, but was quite happy to be left alone to concentrate on the script. Pages and pages were scattered over Bashers bottom bunk. She glanced at the clock, it was gone five! She put her script in order and made for Junes hut.

She was still asleep. "Hey come on lazy bones, it's nearly time for tea."

June stretched and sat up on one arm. Basher read through the script and June began to laugh.

"Christ a budding Shakespeare and no mistake. That's bloody good mate. I defiantly want a part in that"

Over the evening meal the girls debated their strategy for approaching 'Sir Pratt' about time off. Basher suggested that perhaps to request an hour for the audition first, might be the best plan because there was no certainty that they would be accepted.

The following morning the moment the Warrant Officer's voice could be heard, Basher was off her seat and confronting him. She explained the situation pointing out they were both on shift the night of the auditions, so would it be possible for them to attend?

Warrant Officer Pratts face went purple. "Out of the question!" he dismissed.

Basher pulled herself up to her full height. "In that case I intend seeing the producer of the show about this. He *is* an officer by the way." she added threateningly. Sir began tapping his fingers on the bench. He was livid, for he knew the officer would override him. What was worse, and really bugged him, was these two had got one over him.

It was written all over his face. Finally realising he had no choice, he snapped "I can't imagine why you both want to indulge in such a petty childish thing. Neither of you have any talent, so God knows what you propose doing. You can go to the audition for an hour, but you return back here by eight sharp, and not a second later. I shall personally be here to see that you do, or you will both be in deep trouble."

It occurred to Basher that they may not even be through by eight, but she wasn't about to argue the point. She had got permission and she didn't care about anything else.

She would cross any further bridges as she came to them. She simply thanked him politely before going back to her section.

The camp theatre was a buzz of excitement as both girls tentatively entered. The first four rows of seats were taken up with various bodies. A Squadron Leader pilot came to the microphone and introduced himself, explaining that he was a producer in civvy street. He spoke of his pleasure at seeing so many who were prepared to audition for his show, which he was calling *"BIRDS OF A FEATHER."*

The auditions got under way. About half way through, an airman who the girls had recognised from the Stores, was up on stage singing *"We'll run them in, we'll run them in..."* June poked Basher in the ribs and whispered, "Who is he looking at, me or you?" and with that she began to giggle.

The airman in question was certainly behind the door when good looks were dished out. He had an unfortunate bad squint, so that both eyes looked in different directions. Having said that, he had a very powerful voice. Junes remark set off a hysterical session between the two girls, possibly due to nervous tension, as unfortunately they were both on next.

They climbed the steps on to the stage managed to get one line out before bursting out laughing which quickly developed into hysterics. The producer was not amused and suggested they both leave the stage until they could control themselves.

It was five minutes past eight when they realised they should have been back in their section. This thought sobered them up instantly. They were on next. They brought the house down and were accepted immediately for the concert. As they hurriedly made their way to the exit the producer yelled asking "Where do you think you're going?"

Both girls tried talking at once explaining that their Warrant Officer had threatened them if they were a minute after eight. The officers eyes rolled in his head with exasperation. He told them to stay because he hadn't finished with them. There was an opening dance routine that had to be gone through, but reassured them he would deal with their Signals Officer!

June and Basher exchanged looks, shrugged their shoulders and sat down.

When the last person had auditioned he read out the list of names of those who had been successful. Asking them to come on stage and line up in one straight line. He had a good look along the line before moving people about. When everything was to his satisfaction, he instructed them to put their arms around the person next to them. Then to take two steps forward, a high kick with the right leg, two steps back and a high kick with the left leg. After they had practice these steps a few times he added some music and began to teach them the words. *'We are birds of a feather... 78 is our name.'*

The entrance door suddenly flung open and on the threshold stood Warrant Officer Pratt heaving so badly he couldn't speak.

The Squadron Leader Producer spun around and asked "Yes... can I help you Warrant Officer?"

Sir seemed to lose control. With a very red face he

yelled "Yes you can. I specifically told those two they were to be back in their section by eight o'clock.."

The Squadron Leader held up his hand, before explaining it was not their fault. In any event they had passed the audition and would be coming to rehearsals weekly for the next few months, so he had better make alternative arrangements to cover their duties. Sir was almost spitting blood. He then threw a wicked look toward the producer turned on his heel and marched out, banging the door loudly behind him.

The two girls stood open mouthed. The producer turned to them asking "Is he your boss?" They both nodded. "Poor sods" he muttered.

The weekly rehearsals almost caused Warrant Officer Pratt to break a blood vessel. Without fail there would be sarcastic remarks every time they attended a rehearsal. He also made sure to give them all the extra difficult duties he could conjure up. All they could do was to keep their heads down, do as they were told because they knew they could do sod all about it.

The camp concert was coming together nicely. Basher and June looked forward to the weekly meeting with the rest of the cast. They found that their high kicks got higher and less painful as time went on.

"Just think Bash, you and me could end up on the stage for good when this lot is over."

Basher laughed, "A new line in chorus girls, Tessie O'Sheas heavyweights... But be warned, things are hotting up with these raids. I can read between the lines with the information I pick up."

"What a bloody Jobs comforter you turned out to be.

There's me being all positive and you go and spoil it... you miserable cow."

"I'm only being honest" Basher remarked sadly.

When they arrived at the NAFFI after their evening's rehearsal they ordered their usual night cap. A pianist was at the piano playing *'The White Cliffs Of Dover'* and a few couples were dancing. Basher looked on enviously as the dancers gazed into each others eyes and locked in each others arms momentarily oblivious to the war raging around them.

When Basher arrived at her signals section the following morning there seemed to be an unusual amount of activity. On enquiring what the panic was about, the duty operator told Basher that she had delivered one Form B and another was due through anytime, and they had been warned it was an important one.

The middle teleprinter had signals overflowing on to the floor. The operator apologised for this explaining that she had been on the go most of the night and had never been able to catch up.

Basher looked around her before suggesting "Look leave this to me. You get off to your bed you look shattered. I'll cope with this lot."

Then mentally making a plan in her head she began by tearing off the reams of paper and sorted them out into individual signals. There were phone calls to be made, signals to log in, and in the middle of all of this the Form B arrived. Basher checked the machine to ensure there were no problems and carried out the security checks then when everything appeared to be in order she went back to logging in her signals and filling a now overflowing 'out' tray.

She rang for a clerk to pick up the signals as some appeared rather urgent. By the time the coffee break arrived Basher felt exhausted. Then just as she was picking up June's coffee she heard the tanoy blaring out. It was urgently calling all aircrew to the briefing room.

"There's something big going down" Basher said in hushed tones to June as she passed her the mug of coffee.

"I gathered as much, this board has been like Blackpool illuminations pre-war."

Basher was most surprised to find that the aircraft didn't take off until nearer to seven that evening. Finally discovering that this was due to a change in the weather pattern. The crews had been advised to sleep, and assured there would be a wake up call. Seemingly the raid was to be so big, that to be successful the weather was to play a large part.

At seven the following morning Basher awoke to the drone of aircraft. She flew out of bed for she had overslept, and only if she rushed could she possibly fit in her breakfast. Dead on the dot of eight she entered her section. Warrant Officer Pratt was stood at the window counting the aircraft as they came in.

"Yippee" he yelled, "So far five have failed to return, that's less mouths to feed and less bullshit we have to put up with from the cocky sods."

Basher ignored his disgusting remarks but tentatively asked if A 'Able' or B 'Bertie' had returned?

He turned on Basher and with a smirk asked "Do I take the reason for this urgent enquiry is because the idiots who have organised or are in this stupid concert might be among those crews?"

Basher nodded her head to confirm that this was so. He smiled triumphantly and said he hoped they never returned and that would be the end the farce of a concert party.

Bashers blood boiled at the cruel remarks of this man. But she was optimistic and knew they were still coming in every few minutes. So she pinned herself to the window staying until the squadron returned. But A 'Able' and B 'Bertie' were not among them. Her heart sank; there was no doubt now that there couldn't be a concert because not only the crews, but the producer was one of the pilots. Her boss had left some time ago so Basher rushed into the switchboard room to inform June of the dreadful news.

"Christ... Pratt face'll have a field day when he finds out. We'll never hear the last of it. He'll gloat forever."

Basher replied as she left the room "He's all ready started."

It was nearing the end of her shift when Warrant Officer Pratt strode into the teleprinter room. He lifted signals that were still on the machine and read them through. Then he checked the 'Out' tray. Basher knew he was looking for trouble.

When he couldn't find anything, he stood with his back to the window, his legs astride and hands on hips.

"Well..." he began "That's the end of your little fiasco on a Tuesday night. I've checked it out. Every single aircrew person in that show has gone... never to return!" Then clapping his hands together as if dismissing something unsavoury he added "Thank Christ for that! Now we'll have no more nonsense and you and your mate can start pulling your weight."

Basher glared at this monster and could no longer hold her tongue. "You don't possess a soul. Are you quite certain you're on the right side? Why not let our boys drop you over Germany, Hitler could do with the likes of you right now."

"Watch your tongue lady!" he fumed, then knowing he couldn't charge her he strode off and banged the door.

Basher wanted to burst into tears. Her heart ached for the boys who had gone. For their families who would have just heard the bad news. The concert rehearsals had been so enjoyable and a good laugh at times. Furthermore she had a feeling for writing scripts, and felt that contacts were important, and to have had this experience with a civvy street producer she had hoped he might help her when the war was over. Now that opportunity was lost.

CHAPTER 4

The weeks that followed seemed barren and empty with nothing to look forward to. Then as Spring gave way to early summer, Basher arrived at her section feeling more uplifted than usual, she had no idea why, she just did. It was during the latter part of the morning that Warrant Officer Pratt announced that she was to report to the admin office. Wondering what on earth she had done this time, she made her way and cautiously stood before the WAAF officer.

It was then she was told that she had to pack her kit, as she had been transferred to Headquarters 4 Group. They were desperately short of operators and Basher was considered a reasonably good operator. But was reassured it was only a temporary posting. Her heart thumped in her chest, she felt uneasy, for she hated change.

As she packed her kit she realised there was little point in giving in to her feelings. It was an order and had to be obeyed whether she liked it or not.

With kit at the ready she then knocked on June's hut door. June was having a wash and brush up before going to work. She was now on afternoons.

"What's up?" she asked. "You look as though you've lost a bob and found 'apenny."

Basher explained that transport would be at the guard room in ten minutes as she had been temporarily posted. June was outraged and blamed Sir Pratt she was certain he had suggested this to split them up. It was something that Basher hadn't considered.

"Well even if it's true, there's nothing I can do about it, at least it's not permanent."

"I wouldn't bank on that either. I wouldn't trust that bastard any further than I could see him."

Bashers chin hit the floor as a great wave of suspicion swept over her. She said her goodbyes to her best friend, and left the hut with eyes brimming with tears.

The sergeant in charge of the WAAF guard room at Group Headquarters looked as though she might have been a prison warder in civvy street. Short cropped greasy dark hair, beady dark eyes, well built without being fat. Her uniform was immaculate and her buttons shone. There was no mistaking the attitude of 'You don't mess with me'. Basher swallowed hard before giving her details. She had no desire to cross this one. Her heart was in her boots. She had a pre-conceived idea that she didn't like this place, and that was before she met the inmates or the signals section. What delights would she find there? she thought to herself.

The sergeant plonked some sheets and bedding on the table and then delegated her corporal to show Basher her sleeping quarters, and give general directions about the place.

As they entered a much larger nissen hut than the one she had been accustomed to at Breighton, the corporal warned her to be quiet as most of the inmates would be in bed as they had been on a night shift.

She urged Basher to drop her kit by an empty bunk, and then follow her so that she could show her the cookhouse, and direct her to the signals section.

The camp itself was quite small. It housed only six large nissen huts, a much smaller cookhouse in comparison to Breighton, plus the guard room. That was it, she was told.

As the two women reached the main gate, the corporal pointed to the right of them. All Basher could see were thick woods. The corporal explained that somewhere in there was the signals section. When Basher enquired about a NAFFI and entertainment, she was told there was a small shop in Heslington Hall where cigarettes and the chocolate ration could be purchased once a week. Once a month there was a dance in Heslington Hall and they brought crews in from various stations around the area. The rest of the time was work, work and more work, no time for recreation.

The corporal suggested that Basher make her way to the signals section to find out what duty she would be on. Basher thanked the corporal and began to make her way down the long and winding country road. As she reached the edge of the woods she noticed to her left a large building, there was nothing else around other than trees, so she assumed this to be the famous Bomber Command 4 Group Headquarters, signal section.

Walking into the porch she was faced with two swing doors, the clatter of machines was deafening from there, so when she pulled open the door she couldn't believe either her ears or her eyes. In front of her were several long tressle tables at which a sergeant and corporal sat checking signals.

Either side of them and across the width of the room were machines. On the wall to the left, was a massive blackboard with a diagram of all the stations in Four Group and their names.

There must have been at least twenty operators already busy at their machines, but many were empty, clearly in need of operators.

Basher moved around to face the sergeant, explaining who she was, and enquiring as to when her duty began.

The sergeant looked relieved, before pulling out a rota, and began to search. With her finger carefully going down the page she finally advised Basher that she was on night duty for a few days, and suggested she ought to get some sleep because the night shift began at nine that very night!

At five minutes to nine Basher entered her new workplace. She had slept from boredom, and eventually was awoken with the activity in the hut. She was introduced to her hut mates, who she discovered were her work mates too. They were all on the same shift. The sergeant allocated Basher her machine and was told that was the one she was to stick to. It became apparent that the corporal's job was to ensure that everyone was given enough work to keep them going. As soon as one batch of signals was completed, another pile was waiting. This became the pattern every night. From the moment you sat down at nine in the evening, you were kept going until eleven, when coffee was made and the staff got a ten-minute break, in turns. At one in the morning half of the shift would traipse along the pitch dark country road to the cookhouse for a meal. This was their hour dinner break.

Basher was to discover that the worst time during a night shift was from three until six in the morning. It took all of her will power to keep her eyes focused and open.

But by six o clock she would become wide awake, and her energy levels would heighten as she looked forward to being relieved during the next hour and enjoying her breakfast.

Sleep she discovered was difficult to come, and it would probably be around midday before she would go off into deep slumber, consequently not wakening until between six and seven in the early evening. It was always a scramble to get to the cookhouse before it shut. The food would be what was left over from a meal that had began around five, and therefore not very appetising.

After three days of nights the girls were suddenly switched to the day shift.

The sergeant and corporal on this shift were excessively strict, and had a reputation for being a pair of sods. They wouldn't allow one single error. Time and again work would be returned, and the operators were told to re-send it.

The atmosphere was tense and unhappy. Basher preferred these hours but didn't like the bosses at any price.

During the lunch break the operators from her shift sat together moaning like hell about the sergeant. Then one of the girls told them to cheer up reminding them there was to be a dance on Saturday night and the French aircrews from Elvington were to be the guests.

"You'll come with us won't you Basher?" her next door neighbour enquired.

Although Basher loved dancing she felt a bit out of her depth. They were friendly but seemed to lack sincerity making her feel like the new girl at school. But so as not to 'rock the boat' she promised she would go.

The following Saturday evening the hut was a beehive of activity. Ironing boards were out, and shirts, collars and uniforms were being pressed to perfection.

A great deal of effort was being put into the polishing of buttons and shoes. Curling tongs were being heated on top of the belly stove that was roaring away in the centre of the hut, and the ex-hairdresser amongst the girls was busy doing everyone's hair.

Basher was aware of how attractive these room mates were, with lovely slim figures. All it did for her was to make her even more self conscious of her own large frame. She felt fat and frumpy by comparison as she watched enviously at the girl in the opposite bunk who was now pulling on some light grey silk stockings. The girl must have noticed Bashers face, for she suddenly threw a pair at her suggesting she try them on for size, explaining her boyfriend was an American and she had dozens of pairs. Basher went scarlet with embarrassment, but thanked the girl for being so kind. As she admired her own legs in these wonderful silk stockings, she was reminded that this was the first time she had ever owned a pair, and she couldn't get over the difference they made to the contour of her legs.

Her legs were her only good asset, long and in good shape, even though she considered the rest of her body was pretty horrible. A wave of doubt swept over her. She suddenly didn't know why she had agreed to go to the damned dance in the first place because nobody would dance with her she told herself. She began to apply some make-up half heartedly, she never used much anyway.

The hairdresser noticed how unhappy she looked, and

offered to put a bit of curl into her hair. Off she went finally with the group from her hut, feeling the odd one out amongst such glamorous girls.

As they entered the front door of Heslington Hall the sound of the big band could be heard. Basher loved this music. Her feet felt itchy at the very sound of it.

The group climbed the stairs and entered a huge hall. The stage was filled with the Squadronairs looking smart in their uniforms. The bar was situated to one side, and an assortment of French and Commonwealth aircrew were stood several deep waiting patiently to be served.

Just as one of Bashers crowd reached the front, she turned around and asked Basher if she wanted a drink... a stranger answered for her "Not for the moment" he said, as he took her hand and led her to the dance floor.

Basher looked thunderstruck and couldn't understand why he had chosen her out of all the beauties she had envied before they arrived. Her confidence soared with every step. He was an excellent dancer.

As they glided around the floor, her partner seemed bemused, but his eyes never left her face. Then with a wicked twinkle in his eye he asked "Do you come here often?"

Basher threw back her head and laughed. "Can't you think of anything more original?" she asked.

"O.K. how about... what's your name?"

"Basher" she said with a dead pan face.

He stopped abruptly in the middle of the dance floor... "What?! ...you're kidding!"

"No I'm not. It's my nick-name. My real name is Muriel"

"Ah... now that's much nicer... but I'm going to call you Blossom.

Feeling rather embarrassed but flattered, she asked "Are you stationed around here?"

"No I'm on loan. Have been repairing the damaged aircraft" he explained.

"Hey! I'm on loan too, as a teleprinter operator."

"Not just a pretty face then, brainy too?"

At that point the dance finished and the couples began leaving the floor.

As Basher made her way to re-join her colleagues he said "Don't you want a drink then?"

"Well yes please" Basher watched him as he made his way to the bar. He was over six feet in height and of medium build, with fair hair and stunningly blue eyes. He was a handsome hunk and no mistake.

Two seats had become vacant so Basher grabbed them and waited for his return.

Then handing her one of the glasses of beer he said "Cheers, here's mud in yer eye."

"Do I detect a London accent?" Basher enquired.

"North London. Wembly to be exact" he explained as he took his seat.

"I'm from South West London. By the way do you have a name?" she asked.

"Oh sorry Blossom.... yes I'm Ron and stationed near Birmingham" he explained.

It was then the light caught the diamond that was shining from Basher's left hand. Ron picked up her hand and slowly examined the ring.

"Oh" he said with disappointment in his voice,

"Engaged I see. Who's the lucky bloke then?"

"A feller I met when I was stationed with Balloon Command in Yorkshire."

A quick step struck up at that moment, Ron grabbed Basher's hand and swept her around the floor. He seemed deep in thought as he weaved in and out of couples who were enjoying the tempo of the dance. The band then changed melodies *'What'll I do, when you are far away and I am blue, what'll I do?'*

Ron tightened his grip around Basher's waist and pulled her closer to him. Then with his head next to hers he whispered... "The next time you see your bloke, tell him he's got competition."

Bashers heart missed a beat, this had never happened to her before in her life. Ron was certainly some catch, tall, handsome and very humorous, in fact the exact opposite to the man she was engaged to.

His charm gave a boost to her ego that made her confidence rise to magical proportions. It was evident that the chemistry between them was very strong, so much so, that Basher daren't respond to his suggestion, but instead tried to desperately change the subject.

"When do you return to your base?" she asked him.

"Sadly tomorrow Blossom. You will you write to me, won't you?" he pleaded.

The dance ended and they returned to their seats. Ron took a piece of paper from his tunic pocket and said "Come on... full name and address please!"

Basher could see he was deadly serious. She gave details of her temporary address and that of Breighton her home base. As she did so a wave of guilt swept over her, as she knew that Simon depended emotionally so much upon her.

Then placing the precious piece of paper back into his pocket he took her hand once again and suggested, "Shall we go outside for a breathe of fresh air?"

Warning bells began clanging in Basher's ears. Here we go, she thought. A quick fumble is all he wants. But despite her feelings she found herself rising and being led. It was as if she suddenly lost control of her own actions.

They sauntered down the country lane until they came to the edge of the woods. Feeling somewhat uneasy, Basher began talking rapidly and pointing out the signals room where she worked. But Ron wasn't listening, instead he leaned against a tree and pulled Basher very gently into his arms.

Then running his fingertips over the contours of her face he gently brushed his lips lightly across hers. Basher trembled violently. This was a first and no mistake, she had never been treated with such tenderness. Then cupping her face gently in his hands he kissed her fully on the mouth. It was one of the most wonderful kisses she had ever experienced. Then lifting his lips gently from hers he whispered "Is there any contest with the man you're supposed to be marrying?"

With her heart pounding she wanted to cry tears of total frustration. Her reasoning was telling her she was mad. She had only just met the guy and yet the undoubted charisma between them was electrifying. Because she couldn't cope with the situation she suddenly pulled away and announced that she wished to return to the dance.

"Not a problem Blossom" he said as he put his arm

around her shoulder, and guided her back in the direction of Heslington Hall.

CHAPTER 5

Some few days after the dance Basher found herself on yet another night duty, but at least the sergeant appeared more considerate that her day time counterpart. She allowed two girls at a time to have a two hour break. They lay out on tables that were situated at the far end of the room. That end of the room was in relative darkness, and apart from the noise of the machines, they managed to fitfully sleep, and although Basher welcomed the break she woke with a blinding headache. Her bones ached and she felt nauseous. It took at least an hour to get back into the swing of things.

They came off shift at seven on that Sunday morning and wearily made their way to the cookhouse for breakfast.

The entire shift sat together. They were the only ones in the cookhouse, which was just as well because as they began to eat a hearty breakfast of sauté kidneys and fried potatoes, one girl spat out her food yelling "These kidneys are bad!"

The rest began to smell at their plates. "Too right they are" announced the corporal. "Hold it everyone, while I complain."

The cooks argued and frankly didn't want to know. It was too early for a duty officer to be on call. The girls drank their tea and threw their kidneys in the bin before walking out.

Back in the hut the inmates began moaning about their

spoilt breakfasts complaining how hungry they all were. The feet of a chair was suddenly scraped across the linoleum floor. One of the girls stood up and addressed her inmates.

"What do you intend doing about it then? Leave it, and let them get away with it?"

"No!" they all chorused.

"OK put yer money where yer mouth is. Who's willing to come with me to complain to the Duty Officer at nine o'clock?"

There was a pregnant silence for a few moments, before Basher's deep sense of justice got the better of her. "I'll come with you" she offered.

The corporal butted in. "I have to come with you as your NCO... I have no choice, thems the rules."

"Not a problem" the girl on the chair said.

The corporal turned to both girls and advised that they make a start on cleaning buttons and shoes. Then have a wash, change into clean shirts and collars. You don't give the Duty Officer the slightest reason to avoid the issue.

Basher began to regret opening her mouth as she watched the rest of the shift climb into bed. She was tired too, and could have so easily have joined them.

But instead, true to her word, she got out the metal polish and began putting some 'elbow grease' into polishing her buttons.

The girls were now fast asleep. The corporal whispered "Are you ready Bash?"

"Yep, ready, willing and able" she replied.

As they walked toward the guard room the corporal suggested that it would be best if they allowed her to do the talking. She went on to explain that the rules were, that only an NCO could put the case, the rest were witnesses. Basher had a bit of a job getting her head around that one, because that's not how it was, however 'mine is not to reason why' she told herself.

The three women marched smartly into the guard room and the corporal asked the sergeant if they could see the Duty Officer. The sergeant slowly searched the faces of the three women suspiciously before picking up her cap and fixed it firmly on her head before ordering. "Follow me."

They arrived at an office that backed on to the guard room. The sergeant knocked and entered alone leaving the door open.

The corporal appeared to know the procedure. She held her finger to her mouth indicating that everyone should be quiet. She began to fiddle with her tie and cap, making certain she looked presentable. The trio could hear the sergeant explaining that the corporal apparently had a complaint to make.

All at once the sergeants voice bellowed as if she were on a parade ground of hundreds... "Squad... atten....tion..... quick march.... one two one two... halt!"

Basher and her colleague stood either side of the corporal, who was now in full flow about the kidneys being bad at breakfast, and the girls needing something substantial after a full night shift.

Half way through the explanation the officer stopped her, and in a voice bordering hysterics shrieked "Corporal what are these two airwomen doing here?"

The corporal looked non-plussed but explained. "They are my witnesses. They've come to complain Ma'am."

"Get them out! Don't you know that more than one person complaining is mutiny?!"

Basher had a job to control her laughter. She had never heard of anything quite so farcical. But the sergeant was quick on the mark.

"Corporal... stay where you are. The rest... about turn... march out in single file... left right, left right... halt! Dismiss!"

When the two women reached the other side of the door, the sergeant shut it with a huge bang. Leaving Basher and her mate sat on the step.

Basher could no longer hold back her hysterical laughter. It took some minutes to calm down, then she asked "Does she live in he dark ages or what?"

"They make me bloody sick" her mate remarked angrily. "It's like a bleedin' comic opera. We could have been in bed asleep, instead of cleaning buttons and tarting ourselves up, and for what? That stupid old cow talks out of her arse."

The corporal appeared and said "Come on girls, let's get the hell out of here."

"Is she going to do anything about it?" Basher asked.

"She wasn't that keen, but promised to look into it. She spent most of her time bullshitting me for allowing you two to come with me."

Basher began to giggle again. "Stupid bitch! I've heard everything now... *Three girls cause mutiny at 4 Group Headquarters Bomber Command'* It would make a good film." Basher said wiping her eyes at the absurdity of the situation.

"No it wouldn't... cos no bastard would believe it. It's

too ludicrous for words!" her colleague remarked with disgust.

On the Wednesday morning of her third week Basher was woken by the noise in the hut. Her first reaction was to jump out of bed, but as her thoughts became more coherent, she realised with some comfort that she could turn over and have another sleep, as she wasn't due on duty until two that afternoon.

A great feeling of goodwill swept over her as she snuggled down. She had the distinct impression that something special was about to happen, but not being able to find a reason for this euphoria she fell asleep in a happy state of mind.

It was shouting outside of the hut this time that quickly brought her from deep sleep.

She checked her bedside clock. It was midday and time she was making a move. She decided to have a bath, she felt a bit clammy after such a deep sleep. All the bathrooms would be free at this time of day she reminded herself. So pulling clean underwear and a shirt from her locker, she picked up her toilet bag and towel and made for the ablutions.

Just as she was immersed in the warm water, a voice from outside the door called.

"You in there Bash?"

"Yes... but only just. Why what's the problem?"

"No problem just some mail for you. I'll poke it under the door OK?"

"Yep, that's fine" Basher said, as a gush of excitement welled within her.

Then reaching out she picked up the three letters from the floor. Her hands were wet so she grabbed her towel and wiped them dry, before sliding down the bath and soaking once again, whilst she read her mail.

On examining her letters she recognised her mothers handwriting. One from Simon, her fiancee and one... a mystery. She tore open her mothers letter first. She wasn't a great letter writer but kept in constant touch, relating all the family news. Simons letter reiterated how he missed her and looked forward to her next leave. He told her he was about to spend yet another weekend with Vernon his gentleman friend, who for reasons best known to himself he had never introduced to Basher. This friendship in the past, had concerned her. The air of mystery that surrounded it had made her feel uncomfortable, insecure and resentful. But suddenly it wasn't important anymore.

As she gazed at her last letter, she guessed it might be from Ron, her new friend she met at the last dance.

'Hi Blossom' it began. 'I arrived back at base but found life too dreary for words. My being is filled with sadness because I miss you so very much. I'm further troubled because I really don't like the idea of pinching someone else's girl. But you are so special to me Blossom. I know we haven't known each other long yet I feel I've known you forever. I'm kept fairly busy on camp because I don't know if I told you, but I play in the camp dance band. I'm a saxophonist. One day I want to join one of the big dance bands. I love music Blossom, and would really like to go professional. Thought I'd warn you about this, so that you know what you would be letting yourself in for should you, please god, change your mind about your present engagement. I would give the world right now, just to touch your face, to caress your lips, to hold you in my arms. There are many things I'd love to do to you, but you know I wouldn't harm a hair of your head, or ask you to do anything unless you really wanted to. Blossom please promise to come and see me on your next leave. If it's only for a weekend. There are some marvellous dance halls in Birmingham, and I'm not station too far away. I could book you into the YMCA. Please please say you'll come. I _must_ see you again.'

Basher read the letter again and again. It gave her a wonderful feeling of excitement and anticipation. He was a perfect gentleman, no funny business, no pressure, just seemed genuinely attracted to her in a most sincere way.

Finally she put her mail to one side. She'd better get a move on, she thought or she would miss lunch.

As she entered her section that afternoon the sergeant called her over. "You can return to Breighton on Friday Berry. We have now got the staff we need. They will be arriving the same day that you leave. I shall be swopping you over to the morning shift on that day. So arrange at the guard room for transport to pick you up after lunch, is that clear?"

"Yes sergeant, thank you" Basher replied feeling elated at her news.

She sat down at her teleprinter and smiled to herself.

"What's up? You look like the cat that licked the cream." her neighbour commented.

"Not exactly. But the funny thing is, I woke this morning with a strong feeling of well being. You know, as if something special was going to happen."

"And it has?" asked the girl.

"It certainly has. I've received some nice mail, and I've just been told I'm returning to my base on Friday... can't wait." Basher said enthusiastically.

"Charming! Doesn't say much for us then, does it?"

Basher blushed. "I didn't mean it like that. Don't get me wrong. I've had a ball here. I didn't think I'd like it at first, but once I got used to it, I was fine.

Basher had been keeping her eye on a signal that was coming in on her printer, when the same initials came up at the end of the transmission Basher managed to tap on the space bar to attract the attention of the operator at the other end. These initials had been bugging her since the day she had arrived.

It was a long shot, but she felt certain this was an old mate from her days in Balloon Command. They had been on the same site, were best buddies, but had lost contact. She continued to tap furiously on the space bar. She knew it was forbidden, so had to be quick. Suddenly the operator at the other end typed out... "Well... what do you want?"

"You wouldn't be Sandy by any chance?"

The reply swiftly came, and Basher could feel the excitement through the keyboard.

"That's not Basher is it?"

"It sure is mate. Hi! Where the hell are you?"

The two old friends typed out their addresses, so that mail could be sent between them. The sergeant was watching every move of her operators, but Basher took a chance and managed to quickly explain that she was on loan, and would be returning to her base on Friday. Sandy it seemed, was down South in some remote spot doing

classified work. This certainly was the icing on the cake...
What a day this had been!

CHAPTER 6

Basher reported to the guard room at RAF Breighton the following Friday afternoon and to her delight was allocated the same living quarters. She dumped her kit on her bed and made for June's hut. Poking her head around the door she found no sign of her.

"Any idea where I might find June?" Basher enquired.

One of Junes room mates looked up from her writing and said "Yes hinney, she's just back from her leave, and had a canny time by all accounts. She's down at the stores collecting her bike."

"Thanks, that's where I'm heading I'll catch up with her there, no doubt. But thanks anyway."

Basher walked into the stores just as June was wheeling her bike out.

"Hello me old mate, how's yer bum fer spots?"

"Such a dignified welcome… but great... and you... good leave?"

"Wonderful... bliss... met a dishy bloke, the man of my dreams…"

"You're joking! I got you down as a promising dyke. Who is he anyway?" Basher enquired.

"His name is Ted, he's in the regular army and stationed at Catterick, where I've spent most of my leave" June explained, grinning from ear to ear.

"I always suspected you to be a bloody dark horse. How the hell did you swing staying on the camp?" Basher asked wide eyed.

"Influence and rotten cheek mainly. What about you, how was Four Group?"

"It was bleedin' hard work. I hated it at first. The day shift sergeant was almost as bad as Pratt face. It was much stricter than working here let me tell you. But... I've got myself a *real* problem."

June caught her breathe. Then with great drama asked "You're not pregnant are you?"

"Don't be a pillock, of course not! I went to a dance at Heslington Hall and met this hunk of a bloke. He's a Londoner stationed somewhere near Birmingham. He wants me to spend a weekend in Birmingham, on my next leave." Basher said rather furtively.

"You two timing hussy" June said laughing, "But you *are* going aren't you?"

"I don't know yet. But I'll tell you this much, if I do, it's the end of my engagement."

"Why? Don't be a pratt, play the bleedin' field mate. Go on, fill yer boots, have a ball, you're only young once."

"Oh no!" Basher said in horror. "That's not my style. The fact that I would even consider going, would be enough. I'm strictly a one man woman.

"Oh boy, this does sound serious" June observed.

"I'm telling you mate, this guy has got the lot. Good looks, a sense of humour, gentle and kind, not in the least pushy. I've never been treated like this in my life" Basher explained.

The storeman brought Bashers bike through at that moment, and both girls rode off side by side, deep in contemplative thought.

"When are you next on duty?" Basher of her mate.

"Dunno and don't care either. Not looking forward to working with old Pratt face again, in any event." she stressed miserably.

"Should we call in at the guard room and give the section a ring? May as well know where we stand, then at least we can plan the next few hours."

Basher raged as they both left the guard room and made for the NAFFI. She explained to her mate that she had only just come off of nights, and he had put her on them again.

"At least you've got twenty four hours before they start." June said trying to cheer up her mate.

"Doing what?" Basher asked.

"Try writing to the gorgeous hunk for a start!"

"I think I'll come to the section with you tomorrow. I've got seven days leave to come, so I'm putting in for it." Basher stated.

There was a distinct nip in the air that evening as Basher rode toward her signal section to begin her night duty. But nothing could dampen the euphoria that she felt as she entered her office, for in little over a week she was to begin her leave. She had posted a letter to Ron telling him she was coming to Birmingham the following Friday, and was staying until Sunday afternoon. She asked him to book her in at the YMCA. With a feeling of deep satisfaction and anticipation she got down to sending the signals that were now waiting in her basket.

June popped in just before she went off duty. Basher finished off the signal she was sending, and then closed down the transmission.

"Did you manage to organise your leave after all?" June enquired.

"Yes, but as per usual, he moaned all over me about being short staffed. And hey guess what? He had a right go at me about the mess in the kitchen... as if it was all my fault. I've not been here, but that appears to have escaped his notice." Basher said sarcastically.

June seethed with anger before she burst out "He will always have a go at us, you should know that by now mate. It never entered his tiny skull that neither of us have been in the fucking section for two weeks."

"I couldn't agree with you more. But let's forget him, he's not worth the breathe being wasted on him. I'm off next Friday and I can't bloody wait."

"Have you sorted out what to do about the two men in your life?" June asked.

"Nope... I'm playing it by ear to be honest. There's something telling me to hold fire."

"Very wise. Well I'm off, my bed calls me." June said grinning.

"You're bloody evil, just look at this little lot, and that rotten incoming machine hasn't stopped rattling since I've been here. It's still not as bad as Heslington though, you've never in your life have seen so many signals. It's a wonder me fingers didn't seize up!"

June made for the door, put on her cap, then yelled "cherrio" and was gone.

For the next two hours Basher worked ceaselessly. The section was quite eerie at night. No sign of aircraft revving up, and by the look of the log book no Form B's had been received for a couple of days. At one in the morning Basher left the section and made for the kitchen. The Warrant Officer was right about one thing; the kitchen was in a rotten state. Not a clean mug available, so Basher had to wash one up before she could make herself a cup of coffee. She settled herself in the armchair by the belly stove and sipped her hot coffee whilst reading the paper. The machines had suddenly gone quiet, and possibly the combination of the silence and the warmth from the fire made her eyelids heavy, until finally she was forced to give in to the tiredness that was engulfing her like a thick blanket.

She had a vivid dream. She was back at Heslington sitting at her old machine. The deafening rattle of all the machines meant she had to raise her voice to her neighbour. "We haven't seen any Form B's for the past two days, does this mean the war is over?"

Basher suddenly woke yelling the word 'Over' and realised it was in fact her own machines that were rattling away.

She blinked at the glare of the light before looking at the office clock... it was five in the morning! Shaking her head violently and rubbing her eyes she jumped out of her chair to check the incoming signals. There must have been at least twenty of them, over flowing on to the floor.

Then with heart thumping and nausea gripping at her stomach she realised that the classified machine also had reams of paper that had over flowed and was creeping toward her under the chair!

"My god!" she said out loud, what if a Form B has come through... What if aircraft should at this moment be taking off?!

Ripping off the paper in a frenzy from the classified machine, the horror climaxed as she noticed that not one signal was eligible... the machine had broken down and instead of signals there were tiny overprinted boxes, that looked more like a pianola music script. Basher grabbed the phone and frantically dialled out for the group headquarters

"This is Breighton" she heard herself saying, sounding as if her voice didn't belong to her. "My machine has broken down. Has their been any Form B's sent since 0.100 hours this morning?"

"Just a moment" the sergeant said on the other end of the line. Bashers mind raced ahead. What excuse could she give for not noticing the fault before this? She began to perspire as she waited for the sergeants response.

"Hallo... the voice called... No there hasn't been any Form B's at all"

Basher sighed a huge sigh of relief, but the sergeant continued... "Will you give me the details of the last signal, because you do realise we now have to re-send everything that has been transmitted during the night. And as a matter of interest, why has it taken you this long to detect the fault?" she asked.

Basher took a deep breathe before explaining.

"I'd finished all transmissions and logging by between one and half past this morning. Our Warrant Officer had given me a hard time complaining about the state of our kitchens, when I came on duty last night. The fact that I had been working over there with you people for the past two weeks didn't appear to register. However as I had nothing left to do I decided to clean up the kitchen. He was right, it was disgusting, and it has taken me all this time to sort it out."

"Your job is Teleprinting not a domestic." came the curt reply.

"With respect, I hope you tell my Warrant Officer that, should he contact you about this. Basher said hopefully.

She now had exactly three hours to put her plan into action. Leaving the office door wide open so that she could hear the incoming machines running, she made a dash for the kitchen. She cleaned it as it had never before been cleaned, and ended up with scrubbing the floor. Then another dash back to the office to check all the incoming signals, ensuring they were printing on the one and only good machine. She shut down the unclassified machine and put a notice on it *U/S - REPORTED*.

The twenty signals that had just been received had now to be logged. This presented a further problem, because the time of sending had to be typed against the initials of the sender. A time consuming forgery had to take place, in order to log the signals in such an order that they tallied with the time they *SHOULD* have originally been entered in the first place. Basher was desperately working against time.

When she glanced at the office clock she found it was already seven twenty, her relief would arrive in forty minutes, and there were repeat transmissions still coming in. At a quarter to eight she began to pray, as she watched the machine still rattling signals through. Finally the machine went silent.

She handed over to the day staff confidently, as if

nothing untoward had taken place.

"By the way tell Warrant Officer Pratt that his precious kitchen has now been cleaned." Basher said as she fled the office.

Her sleep was disturbed later that day when June burst into the hut.

"Don't you start afternoons today? she enquired.

"What... eh?" Basher said as she came out of deep sleep.

"It's nearly one, you'd better get a move on, come on jump to it, let's grab some lunch. I'm on at two as well." June urged.

"Fancy making us work days, after a night shift, it shouldn't be allowed" Basher said, as she heaved herself out of bed.

The two girls chatted whilst Basher got ready. June explained that she too would be on leave the same time as her mate because Ted, the new boyfriend, had rung the night before explaining he had a 48 hour leave pass. Basher began to feel a renewed energy surging through her as they both debated their various expectations of their forthcoming leave. She was ready in record time. They grabbed their bikes and made for the cookhouse. The aroma of steak and kidney pie met them as they entered the busy cookhouse.

"Boy! I didn't realise how hungry I was" Basher remarked as they reached the serving hatch.

Then having settled down to enjoy their lunch, Basher looked furtively around making certain no one from the signals section was within earshot.

When she was happy that the coast was clear, she explained to her mate the saga of the broken machine on her night duty, and the subsequent subterfuge she had to resort to.

"Bloody hell!" June said aghast, "Let's hope you get away with it, but knowing old bugger-lugs I wouldn't bank on it." she said with serious warning.

"Oh cheers! A great comfort you are." Basher said with alarm.

"I'm just pointing out that we both know what a sneaky sod he can be. I wouldn't put anything past him. So just be on your guard, that's all."

Bashers agitation began to show as she rounded on her mate.

"I'll tell you this much June, the bastard will begin to wish he had never mentioned the poxy dirty kitchen to me. I'll teach him!"

June wished her mate good luck, and told her to keep her posted if anything transpired. Then glancing at the clock Basher pointed out that it was time to get going.

Basher had only been on duty around half an hour when Warrant Officer Pratt entered the office. In silence he pulled up a spare chair and sat down next to her. Her heart began to thump in her chest, she tried desperately to keep her cool as he began speaking very slowly choosing his words. "Tell me Berry... did you receive any transmissions at ten minutes past three this morning?"

Bashers mind scrambled, this was undoubtedly a trick question, and by his obvious arrogance he either suspected something had gone wrong, or worse, he might even know the truth and was making Bashing suffer. There was nothing else for it, except to call his bluff and make a calculated guess.

"Yes there was." Basher responded defiantly. He glared at her, his small piggy eyes burnt into her very being. Then in silence he picked up the phone and asked to be put through to Four Group Signals Section.

Bashers heart continued to thump as she heard him ask the same question of the sergeant on duty. It seemed to take a year whilst she checked... Suddenly he put the phone down and turned to Basher who by now wanted to vomit... "It would appear you must have been dreaming, there were no signals at that time, so what's the story... were you asleep?"

"No I wasn't!" she screamed at him. "If you really want to know I spent hours cleaning the poxy kitchen, as that appeared to be first on your list of priorities, but I waited until the transmissions had ceased."

Something stopped Basher from telling him the full story. However he was infuriated by her explanation, and in a burst of obvious temper he yelled "You are on a technical charge for neglect of duty!" and with that he stormed out.

Basher shook from head to foot because she was aware that this was a much more serious charge than for example, being absent with out leave, or even June's drunken charges. She waited for ten minutes to be certain he was well clear of the section before picking up the phone and explained to her mate next door, what had transpired.

Two days later she found herself lined up between two guards feeling like a criminal waiting for the order to enter, and hear the charge read out.

The WAAF officer spent a few moments studying the charge papers after they had been read out. Then with a grave face she looked directly as Basher and said "This is a most serious matter Berry. What have you to say for yourself?"

Basher explained in some detail that despite being absent from her section for more than two weeks at Group Headquarters, on her return she had been accused of making the section kitchen a mess. She pointed out that Warrant Officer Pratt had for reasons best know to himself, been victimising her for some considerable time. Rather than cause a fuss, during her night shift when her transmissions had quietened down, she had spent several hours cleaning the kitchen. She went on to explain that she could hear the rattle of her machines whilst she was working out of the room, but it wasn't until she had completed her chores that she discovered a machine had in fact broken down. In order to rectify the situation Headquarters was immediately alerted and an urgent enquiry about Form B's being transmitted during this period was made. This was my number one priority, but I was told there were none.

Arrangements were then made for re-transmission of the missing signals.

The officer listened intently to her explanation, and said she was aware of two things. She was a good operator, the very fact she had been sent on loan to Group Headquarters indicated this. Had this not been so, the punishment would have undoubtedly been more severe. She had acted promptly once she could see that there was a problem with the machine. But the officer made Basher forfeit three days pay, because she explained that she should not have left her section, or the machines unattended. She made it clear she was going to have a word with Warrant Officer Pratt about this matter.

Basher returned to her section feeling pleased with herself. Her plan had paid off. She called in to see June to briefly explained the outcome. June swung her chair around to face her mate.

"Well, that's not too bad is it? It could have been worse. I bet old Pratt face will think twice before he blames us again in a hurry" she said grinning.

CHAPTER 7

The train pulled in at New Street station Birmingham around three the following Friday afternoon.   Having made enquiries Basher quickly found the YMCA. She paid her fee at the desk and was allocated a bed.

The huge dormitory housed at least fifty beds. The organisation had made it as comfortable as they could, in this disused warehouse.   It was clearly a temporary wartime measure. In an attempt to get away from the military style barrack rooms, they had placed a dressing table complete with mirror, between each bed, and set up partitions so as to make the twin bedrooms as private as possible. Basher found an empty bed in the corner. A WAAF was sleeping in the one opposite. Basher threw her bag on to her bed, took off her cap and undid the buttons of her jacket.

She had disturbed the young woman opposite, for she looked up and said cheerfully, "Hallo kid, what's your name?"

With introductions quickly over, Basher found her new companion very friendly, and had introduced herself as Sheila. They decided to go to the canteen to have a yarn over a cup of tea. Basher found herself telling this stranger about her problem.   The turmoil of what to do about her situation was heightened by the fact that she was on the brink of meeting up with Ron, and he would need some answers.

Having spilled out the outline of her predicament Basher went on to explain "My fiancé is a nice enough bloke I suppose. He has a physical handicap sure, but it's made up for in other ways. He's introduced me to some of the more finer things in life like good music, but on the other hand he isn't prepared to share my interests. This new guy and I have everything in common, so I feel it only fair that I should end my engagement. The very fact I'm here at all, puts the depths of my feelings for Paul in doubt" Basher explained.

"Who exactly are you trying to convince, me or you?" her companion asked.

The two girls conversed for at least an hour. Basher suddenly checked her watch. "My god! Look at the time, if I don't hurry I'll be late."

On arrival back at the dormitory Sheila also began to get ready. Basher suddenly realised that the entire conversation had been about her problem. She had no idea why Sheila was here. Where she was stationed or very little about her except she seemed a nice friendly kind of girl.

"Are you meeting someone too?" Basher finally asked as she combed her hair.

"Yes. I too am on the brink of an engagement myself. I met this guy at the base where I'm stationed. We work together. A right character this one and no mistake" she said smiling. "But I love him to bits and woe betide anyone who stands in my way" she added.

Basher grinned at the enthusiasm of her new found friend. "Has anyone tried yet?" she asked.

"Wouldn't give them the chance. I'd hang on for dear

life. He probably thinks I'm a bit clingy, but I can't help it. Nobody but nobody will take him from me, and that's a promise" she said with some feeling.

"What's his name? He sounds real nice."

"Ron" her friend replied.

"What a coincidence that's the name of my bloke" Basher said naively. "Has he a surname?" she asked, now beginning to feel slightly uneasy.

"Broughton" her chum responded as she applied her lipstick and totally unaware of Basher's alarm. Who now froze as she glared at the back of her companion almost afraid of continuing the conversation. Then trying hard to keep control, for it was apparent that Basher's new found airman wasn't all she thought him to be. It seemed he was playing a double game here, and had made a double arrangement. One of them was about to be hurt and badly let down. Sheila innocently explained the time and place she had arranged to meet Ron.

It was then the position became clear to Basher. He clearly intended to meet her, because her date was the earlier of the two. It quickly became abundantly clear that her friend of only two hours, was to be let down.

Basher sat down heavily on her bed, there was no way out of this, she would simply have to explain the circumstances to Sheila.

Sheila began to sob as Basher explained the time and place of her arrangement, adding that he had booked her place at the YMCA. Basher had mixed feelings of anger, betrayal and deep sorrow.

The man she thought to be so kind, caring and genuine was to all intents and purposes playing the field, and treading on people's emotions while he was at it.

Sheila finally wiped her eyes and said she had a plan. "You go off and meet him. Just leave the rest to me" she said confidently.

Ron was waiting at the rendezvous. The moment he saw Basher he ran toward her and grabbed her into his arms, almost hugging the life out of her.

"You'll never know how much I've missed you Blossom" he whispered in her ear as he snuggled close to her, his entire body shaking, "Darling girl I really do love you."

Basher's whole being wanted to respond to him, and wanted desperately to believe him. But warning bells were clanging loudly in her head shouting *BEWARE!* Her silence didn't seem to faze him either. He took her hand in his, and they strolled down the darkened street. Basher couldn't hide her anger any longer. He had caused so much pain to her new companion, and betrayed her in the bargain. She finally blurted out what she had discovered and demanded an explanation. Ron made no attempt to deny the facts, but he wanted to justify the situation.

"Blossom, she means nothing to me. She has chased me constantly, and to a degree I was flattered. But to tell you she was engaged to be married to me is a figment of her imagination I do assure you. It's you that I want... honest. Look the fact that I booked your accommodation and made yours the first appointment surely that proves the point?"

"No it doesn't!" Basher almost yelled at him. "Why make an appointment with her at all? You are feeding her expectations. She really believes you are in love with her. She has made it clear that nobody else will have you, she is determined."

As she spoke she could hear footsteps very close behind them. Were they the footsteps of Sheila? Had she witnessed their loving meeting? Basher cringed at the thought of what she might have seen and heard.

The debate continued, Ron getting more and more desperate in attempting to convince Basher that she was the one he wanted. At last they entered the massive dance hall.

Ron found a seat for Basher, and then made for the bar. A cheer went up from a group of guys sat at the next table. Basher quickly got the picture. They had turned up to give the new girl friend the once over, and could have possibly been aware of the double date. Basher's face began to burn with embarrassment. Ron quickly returned with some drinks only to find Sheila sat at their table!

"Good evening" she said evenly between clenched teeth. Ron responded coolly and controlled, as he turned on his heel and returned to the bar to buy Sheila a drink.

Her eyes met Basher's. As he was returning she whispered "watch this"

Ron calmly sat down and went to speak. But Sheila rose, picked up her drink and tipped it over Ron shouting... "Take that! How dare you attempt to play with the lives of innocent people. Are you aware she's giving up a perfectly respectable bloke for you? You don't deserve it!"

Then she swept from the room to a resounding cheer from Ron's mates, who had witnessed and clearly enjoyed his public humiliation.

Ron did his best during the rest of the weekend to convince Basher that he really had no interest in Sheila. But the doubts had crept in, and spoilt the anticipation of a future relationship.

The following afternoon Ron tenderly touched Basher's face and begged of her to believe him. They were stood by the open door of the railway carriage that was to take Basher back to her home town for the rest of her leave. He held Basher close to him, then finding her lips kissed her hungrily. Basher's head spun, who was she to believe? Both Ron and Sheila sounded equally as convincing. She desperately wanted to believe Ron. He begged of her not to end their relationship, explaining that at the first opportunity he would make it abundantly clear to Sheila that they had no future together. With all his heart and being he wanted Basher to believe him. He was indeed charming, nobody had made her feel quite so special or as needed, as he did. They clung together in one last desperate kiss, before she boarded her train.

As the train pulled out Ron took a couple of steps back, blowing her a kiss and waving... But then from behind one of the pillars on New Street station Sheila appeared. She took his arm and looked lovingly up at him, then smiling, waved to Basher!

A tumultuous emotion engulfed Basher as tears smarted her eyes. She turned her head toward the window for she did not want fellow passengers to see her grief. What the hell was going on? Did he know she was there? If so, it didn't make any sense. He had confirmed his intention to end their friendship - totally denying that there had ever been a relationship in the first place, and yet he appeared unperturbed by her sudden presence... and so her thoughts rampaged on.

Having arrived home early in the evening it became obvious that Basher's father suspected she had something on her mind. He was very close to his eldest daughter and seemed to know her every mood.

After supper he invited her into the lounge to have a chat. He sprawled out in his easy chair, his long legs crossed over in front of the fire that was now burning brightly in the grate. He was a handsome man in his early forties, with a hint of greying hair at the sides of an otherwise almost black head of thick hair. Like Basher a well built man. He was as Just and Fair as his daughter. A generous father who was not long out of the RAF himself, on medical grounds.

Basher had a very close bond with this man. They both knew when the other was unhappy or had something to say. Because they were of similar character they also both knew that they could never 'beat about the bush.' They were both equally forthright in their approach to the other. Basher had decided that this was not a time to pussyfoot around, so when both were equally comfortable she announced that she had decided to end her engagement. Her father looked visibly shocked, what ever he was expecting, it clearly wasn't this.

Basher went into great depths and honesty about her meeting with Ron. How she felt about him, and what she had discovered just this weekend. But pointed out that the fact she had even contemplated meeting someone else, was an indication that she could not love Paul enough to spend the rest of her life with him, and therefore it would be more honest and fair to end the relationship.

Her father sat thoughtfully rubbing his chin, after a few minutes he began. "You will find throughout life that you will meet up with all kinds of temptations. But if you consider uprooting major relationships as a result, your life will be in chaos girl."

At this point Basher's mother entered the room and by the look on her face, she knew what was being discussed. She did have a habit of listening at doors! Her remarks clarified Basher's suspicion as she waded in "You are the most ungrateful, inconsiderate person I've ever met. You don't know a good man when you see one. You wait my lady, if you consider going off with this dance band Johnny, he'll be off out half the night every night! You wait and see how you feel then. How long do you think that will last?"

Basher fumed as she retorted. "Excuse me mother but you're assuming I'm going to marry this new man. It doesn't even enter the equation. This is about my decision to end my present relationship with Paul because I happen to think it's the right and honest thing to do. I'm not ready for marriage yet, in any event."

Her mother ignored the outburst and treated Basher with the utmost contempt, as she turned to her husband and asked if he wanted his bed time drink.

When he refused, she stomped out of the room banging the door as hard as she could, making her feelings very clear on the matter.

The argument flared for a further two hours between Basher and her father. When he realised that she would not give in, his patience began to disintegrate. "You are the most stubborn, short sighted girl I've ever come across" he stormed in desperation.

"I've had a good tutor haven't I?" Basher retorted. "In any event when are you going to get it into your thick skull that I intend marrying for the love of a man, not for what he can provide."

Her father put his head in his hands and said he thought this was the most unrealistic statement he had ever heard. Paul was a decent man studying to better himself, so that he could provide her with everything she might need for her comfort. He emphasised that this was something he had never been able to do in his life for his family, he didn't have the brains.

Suddenly he screamed at her "Don't you know that love in a garret flies out of the window, the moment poverty strikes?"

A terrible atmosphere pervaded the once close loving family circle, during the course of the following days. Then during the early evening half way through the week Basher answered a knock at the door and there stood Paul!

Her mouth flew open in surprise, "What are you doing here?" she asked

"That's a nice welcome. I was summoned to the inner sanctum actually" he said with a hint of sarcasm.

Basher was shocked by the sudden arrival of her fiancé but intended finding out as much as she could before her father came home. So keeping him in the hall, out of the earshot of her mother she asked "What do you mean you were summoned to the inner sanctum. By whom, and why?"

Paul explained that he had received a telegram from Basher's father asking him to come down, as he had some serious business to discuss. I managed to get a few days off from work, and here I am!

Alerted by voices in the hall her mother suddenly appeared, and in her usual doting manner welcomed Paul, telling him she had just made a fresh pot of tea, and making the deliberate point for Basher's benefit, of saying how tired he must be after such a long journey from Yorkshire.

Basher's father arrived whilst they were all having some tea and biscuits. He took Paul immediately into the lounge. Basher knowing she was not wanted in this discussion, went to her room. As she lay on her bed she considered the high handed way her parents had dealt with this situation, and succeeded in making her feel like a criminal and an outcast in her own home. Her anger began to boil over at the thought of it. What right had they to do this? It was her life, they shouldn't interfere. How dare her father send for Paul behind her back. She could have dealt with him on her own, it was her right. After all this was all because she wanted to do the right thing and be honest!

Her thoughts rampaged, until suddenly she decided that she would not allow them to have their private discussions, it was about her life not theirs.

She went to the bathroom and splashed cold water over her face, then returning to her bedroom sat at her dressing table and combed her hair into place before she marched downstairs.

As she reached the lounge she heard her father saying that he had changed his mind about the ruling he once made, that he would not allow them to marry until the war was over. He reassured Paul that they he had done everything he could to put pressure on his daughter to re-think this thing through...

Then seeing his daughter in the door way he deliberately put his arm around Paul's shoulder and said "Don't worry son, she'll see sense. This is undoubtedly because you've been engaged too long, it's put too much of a strain on the relationship."

Basher fumed. How dare he patronise her in this way. She glared from one to the other. How could her father betray her like this. She shook with temper in every limb and then announced "Well seeing as you both think you have my life stitched up, I'll leave you to it. I'm returning to my camp right now, because I've just about had enough of this. Sorry Paul I would have preferred to have discussed this with you privately, but my father likes playing God" and with that remark she swept out of the room.

CHAPTER 8

It was well past midnight by the time Basher reached Kings Cross station only to discover that there wasn't a train to York until five the following morning. She wandered to the waiting room feeling totally dejected, and every time her thoughts turned to the events of the past hours she boiled inside with anger. To her dismay on arrival at the waiting room found soldiers, sailors and airmen from most nations of the world stretched out on the floor using their kitbags as pillows. The benches were full of bodies laid out in deep sleep. An uncomfortable apprehension swept over her. She wanted to run.

Not feeling at all safe she made her way to the only cafe that was open, and ordered a cup of tea. The amber liquid calmed her down and her anger subsided. Going over the events of the day the one question that kept repeating over and over in her mind, was why was her father so insistent in trying to run her life? Didn't he think her capable of making her own decisions? she pondered. Through the ferocious debates he kept pointing out that he had struggled to bring up his family, and he wanted better for his own children. Basher could understand this to a point, but surely he must be aware that he can't run the lives of others. If their choice was someone with a limited income, which ultimately meant a material struggle, then perhaps this is meant as a learning process for them. After all was this not what her mother chose?

So deeply involved was she in her thoughts, that she was unaware of a soldier who had seated himself at her table.

"Penny for them love?" he commented.

Basher glared at the soldier before replying, "My thoughts are not for sale."

"Ah... have we been jilted then?" the soldier persisted as he swayed in his seat.

Oh my god! Basher thought to herself, he's drunk. The last thing she needed was a drunken companion for the next three hours. She decided she would get away as politely as she could.

"I've not been jilted, just missed my train that's all." she replied rather coldly.

Suddenly the soldier threw up all over the floor. Basher grabbed her bags and fled. She considered that perhaps the waiting room would be safer after all.   Climbing over bodies that lay on the floor, she finally found an end of seat that was vacant. Placing her bags beside her on the floor, she squeezed into the tiny space as gently as she could.

Stiffening with nervous tension she gazed around the male dominated darkened waiting room. The only light that shone was from the station itself. Despite her tension the urge to sleep overtook her. Her head nodded forward, but each time she came back to consciousness she was filled with the fear of missing her train, added to that, she considered the possibility constantly as to what might happen if one of her sleeping companions woke up. Time stretched before her as a huge empty void.

Finally after what seemed like hours there was an

announcement "The train now standing on platform one is for Newcastle, stopping at all stations to Sheffield, Leeds and York."

Gathering her things she quickly stepped over the bodies who were still in deep sleep, and made for platform one.

Once inside the train she snuggled down and was fast asleep before it left the station.

Then on hearing a platform announcement she woke with a start. Rubbing her eyes she tried to focus as she gazed out of the window. Had they not left London yet? she considered. There was something familiar about this particular station. Where were they?

Then another announcement was heard "The train now standing on platform one is for Newcastle, hurry along please."

"Gees" she yelled... "this is it.... York!"

Grabbing her things she just managed to get out of the train as the guard blew his whistle. After that surge of energy she wearily left the station.

The clock that hung outside, told her it had just gone eleven. Now what do I do? she asked herself. It's too early to return to camp, my leave doesn't finish until tomorrow night. One thing for certain she reminded herself, you can't hang around here. Maybe if I take a bus to town an idea may grab me en route.

But by the time the bus reached the Market Square she still had no idea what to do. Perhaps if I have a wash and brush up, it might liven me up, she decided. It didn't take long to find the public toilets. By the time she emerged the Minster clock was chiming midday. Feeling much fresher and more alert, she decided it was time to visit the notorious Betty's restaurant for some tea and toast.

Betty's, unlike Toch H or the Red Shield club was a little more refined and a famous rendezvous for aircrew from all over the world.

Because of it's respectable ambience the restaurant treated its customers with dignity and warmth. Tea was served in silver pots. The toast and biscuits were served complete with doilies.

Basher found an empty table for four, and took up one of the seats. She ordered tea and toast. The pretty waitress looked trim in her black dress and brilliant white dainty apron that tied around her waist, and an equally brilliant white starched cap that was perched on her head.

Three aircrew entered the restaurant at that moment and took the remaining seats at her table. She felt a little self conscious sat alone. The airmen ordered, then a sergeant airgunner glanced at Basher remarking. "You look like I feel."

Basher explained about her plight of missing her train and having to sit all night on Kings Cross station.

"Oh dear, not pleasant" remarked the airgunner.

"I've had better nights, particularly when a drunken soldier attempted to chat me up in a cafe before throwing up everywhere!"

"Dear god! What an ordeal. So are you on your way back to your base then, and where would that be?" he asked.

"Breighton." Basher replied.

"Hey we come from there! Not seen you around, where do you work?"

"Signals. I'm responsible for making certain you get your instructions for imminent raids."

"Ah yes... I know where you're at now. We've been on a bender to end all benders. Hence feel rather fragile. When we've had our tea and toast we are heading back to Breighton. Want a lift?"

Basher smiled for the first time since leaving home. This was certainly an offer she couldn't refuse. The alternative was catching a slow train to Bubwith and then walking two miles to the camp, or staying in York for a further twenty-four hours. She had very little money in her pocket, so her mind was well and truly made up.

"Thanks a lot, I'd appreciate that." she said.

On arrival at Breighton RAF station Basher was never more pleased to see those camp gates, she couldn't make her mind up as to whether her wait at Kings Cross station in London was more nerve racking that the drive from York with the three lunatic aircrew, who had 'yahoooed' as they screamed around hairpin bends at a hundred miles an hour!

Having flashed their passes Basher thanked the boys for the lift, picked up her kit and found her hut.

As she threw her kit on her bed, she was greeted by the group of Geordies who lived in the hut "Hi hinney had a good leave?"

"No! ...bloody disastrous" was Basher's response. Not being in the mood for explanations she left the hut and decided to look for her mate June. She poked her head around the door of her friend's hut but discovered it was empty.

Perhaps she was on duty. But as she entered the

switchboard room a lone operator was the only one on duty.

"Isn't June on duty then?" she asked.

The operator explained it was her day off, and she should either be in her hut or in the cookhouse.

But Basher found the cookhouse also empty. The only place she could be was the NAAFI unless... God forbid she'd gone on one of her benders.

Basher searched the NAFFI but there was no sign of her. Then just as she was leaving, June ambled out of the toilets.

"I've been looking everywhere for you!" Basher cried, now relieved at having found her mate.

"What yer doing back here anyway, yer not due until tomorrow night?"

"It's a long sad story. Can you hold on a minute while I collect my bike from the stores?"

With the bike collected the two girls strolled along the perimeter of the runway.

Basher was so relieved to have the opportunity of sharing her anguish with a trusted friend. As she went through the events of the past week in detail, June was seen to open and shut her mouth on several occasions as the plot unfolded.

Finally she burst out with... "So what are you doing about Ron, for a starter?"

"Nothing, he's a two timing sod. I can't get over him swearing on oath that it was she that did the chasing, and emphasising that he was not interested. When all the time there she was, not daring to show her bloody face till she was certain my train was moving out." Basher explained near to tears.

"Hey hold on a minute, something here stinks. How do you know she was there all the time? It sounds to me as if she was determined to get him at any cost, and let's face it, she stood a better chance than you, she works with the guy" June remarked emphatically.

Basher swung on her mate her face red with anger.

"He could have told her to shove off. He seemed just as keen, the way I saw it."

"Listen mate, I'm a bit older and wiser than you. There are women in this world who will go to any length to get their man. You've simply got to learn to do the same." June explained.

"Not likely!" retorted Basher. "If he wants me that badly then no matter what, he can come and get me."

"You are living in cloud cookoo land mate, it doesn't work like that. The male species have enormous ego's and are flattered by attention. If there's a contest they'll play the bloody field. I wouldn't mind betting, that if you put up as strong a fight as this Sheila bird, you could win him back, hands down!"

Basher looked horrified and told her mate in no uncertain terms that she had her pride, and explained that she chases no one. June told her, that in that case, she'd end up a very lonely old woman.

"Did you chase Ted?" Basher asked her friend angrily.

"No I didn't have to" June replied.

"Well then... I rest my case." Basher said quietly.

June threw her arms in the air and said she really didn't understand because Ron seemed so keen.

Basher's tears welled up once again, because that's

what she thought too, and although relieved to be able to discuss the matter with her friend, she found it far more painful that she first realised.

For a while the two girls walked in silence. Then June broke the silence explaining what a wonderful weekend she'd had with Ted. He'd taken her to his home town and introduced her to his family. Basher half heartedly said how pleased she was, but in truth the last thing she wanted to hear was her mate's account of a deliriously happy weekend.

Then after a few more moments of silence, June suddenly blurted out with "I can't get over the interference of your father, that would have pissed me right off."

"Why do you think I'm here twenty four hours before I need to be?" Basher said angrily.

June was keen to change the subject, as it was getting rather heavy. The two girls discussed their next duties and Basher explained that hers was the following night, but June said she was on duty that very night. They both realised that they would have a few nights together at work, and that cheered them both up slightly. June noticed how tired and drained her mate looked.

"You must be bushed after being up all night." she remarked.

"I don't feel so bad right now. I did manage to get some sleep on the train for a few hours. In fact if I hadn't woken when I did, I would have been in Newcastle right now." Basher said grinning.

"Get an early night then mate, and catch up before your next night duty, otherwise yer won't be worth living with!"

Basher didn't feel much like work the following night as she entered her section. Warrant Officer Pratt must have got his message across to the rest of the staff as the kitchen was reasonably clean.

By midnight she had cleared a back log of transmissions. It was then a Form B began coming in. With the doors locked as usual, and the hatch open she watched carefully over the machine as it typed out it's instructions about the forthcoming raid. As she turned around she nearly jumped out of her skin, for peering at her through the hatch were the glazed eyes of the male corporal telephonist who clearly was very drunk.

"Hi Bash... how is yer?" he slurred.

Basher explained that she was fine, but asked where the hell he'd been, to get into such a state?

"Shelebrating" he said nodding his head as if it were about to fall off his shoulders.

"Celebrating what?" Basher asked now amused at the silliness of this corporal.

"I've been made up to Group Captain." he said grinning an inane grin.

"You stupid bugger" Basher retorted.

"I hear you've been a naughty girl in my absence, and got yerself on a technical charge... join the club mate... mine comes up tomorrow."

So this is what this was all about Basher thought. She admitted to being on a charge. Just then the corporal suddenly bent down and momentarily disappeared from view. Then let forth singing in operatic style, making up the words as he went along and using the overprinted signal that had got Basher into so much trouble two weeks earlier. With full throttle he began "Her tiny hand was frozen... as she cleaned up the kitchen... oh yes... oh yes... the aircrew should have been beating the hell out of gerry... but the signals kitchen was much more important... oh... yeeeees" he sang.

Basher laughed till she cried she hadn't heard anything so hilarious in a long time. Then aroused by the hilarity June appeared.

"Where the hell did you get that from?" Basher asked the corporal.

"Ah... he said as he swayed from side to side, and trying to rub the side of his nose at the same time.

"I thought I'd destroyed it" Basher said with some concern.

"Not very well, by all accounts." June observed.

"Give it to me" Basher said wanting to ensure that all the evidence of her misdeed be totally destroyed. She grabbed the long ream of paper from the drunken corporal and stuffed it into the belly stove to burn.

"Come on mate, get off to yer bed, or yer won't be fit for yer charge in the morning" June suggested as she shoved him through the door.

When the two girls were at last alone Basher enquired as to what he was to be charged with. June for once went all serious, explaining that his was a very serious charge as he had smashed up a vehicle that he was driving whilst he was drunk.

"I'll tell yer what mate, he's for the high jump and no mistake.

"The silly sod told me he was being promoted to

Group Captain! No wonder he got drunk he had some need to." Basher remarked as she peered at her mate through the hole in the wall.

"This won't be a fourteen days confined to camp job, more like the glasshouse!" June emphasised.

Basher was suddenly aware of the silence of her room, turning around she realised that her transmission was over.

"Listen have to go, important work to attend to. See you later" she said dismissively to her mate, as she turned her attention to her classified machine.

CHAPTER 9

During the following weeks pandemonium broke out in the signals section. The corporal telephonist was sent to a military prison awaiting court martial, and an epidemic of dysentery went through the section like a tornado, with one staff off after another. The shift system went to pot. Basher found herself not working the same shifts as her mate June.

But by the beginning of the third week things began to settle down. The epidemic passed and Basher and June were both on mornings.

Warrant Officer Pratt marched into the signals section around ten that morning and plonked a bottle of disinfectant under Basher's nose saying "When it's your turn to clean the kitchen, make certain to use this, we don't want another excuse for dysentery to break out"

He then picked up the bottle and marched out. Basher heard him bang it down on the kitchen bench, before issuing the same instructions to the girls who were taking their break.

Basher picked up the pile of signals and placed them on the paper rest before beginning her transmissions. She was concentrating so hard on her work in hand that she was unaware of somebody walking in until she heard a rather familiar voice saying "Good morning Berry."

For the life of her she could not place who it was, neither could she take her eyes from the signal she was transmitting.

Finally she came to the end of her work and turned around...The colour drained from her face because stood before her was none other, than the producer/pilot who went missing presumed killed some months previous. She opened her mouth to speak but nothing would come. She was certain she was seeing a ghost.

The officer aware of the shock he had given her, raised his hand before blurting out "Don't panic... it's really *me!*"

"BBBut how did you get here, what happened to you? Basher asked in confusion.

Perching himself on the edge of her table he attempted to explain. "It's a long story Berry. Let's just say that the French Resistance are pretty wonderful people. So... here I am, fit and well and ready to go again."

"What about the rest of your crew, did they make it too?" Basher enquired

"I honestly don't know. So far I'm the only one to report back here. Anyway the reason I've come to see you is to suggest that we start up another camp concert. Are you and June game?"

Basher grinned a huge grin, "Oh sure! But you'll have to find some new talent won't you?"

"That won't present a big problem, we do have some new aircrew to replace those that we lost, and one of them is a professional singer. I've found another pianist, and then all of the ground staff who made up the original cast" the officer explained.

"Warrant Officer Pratt is going to love you" Basher said getting up and moving toward the switchboard room. "Come on sir, lets go and shock June!"

As they entered June's workplace they found her busy on her switchboard.

"Got a minute mate? ...look who's come to see us."

It was June's turn to lose colour. "Christ... where have you come from? ...the grave?" she asked as she laughed nervously.

"Not quite" the officer replied.

"He wants to set up the camp concert again" Basher informed her mate.

"Great!" was June's response. "Can't wait to see old bugger-lugs face when he discovers this little lot!"

The officer made for the door, explaining he has loads of other people to chase up. Reassuring them he would be in touch at the earliest to give details of the next rehearsal.

"What a turn up for the book!" Basher yelled at her mate as soon as the officer had gone.

"Too right" June said rubbing her hands gleefully. "Just leave old pratt face to me... I can't wait to inform him that rehearsals are about to resume."

At lunch time both girls left together for the cookhouse. "Have you got your script" Basher asked June as they settled down with their lunch.

"Do you know, I almost destroyed it the day I cleared out my locker, but decided to keep it, if only for a souvenir."

"Thank god for that!" Basher said relieved. "Mine's put away somewhere. Will have to have a hunt for it when we get back to the hut."

With their shift over both girls cycled back to Basher's hut. The contents of her locker were suddenly strewn over the bed as Basher frantically searched for her script, but it was nowhere to be seen!

June crept out leaving Basher to her frenzied search, hoping that hers was where she *thought* she had left it.

Suddenly she barged back into Bashers hut waving the piece of paper.

"Here, I've found mine!" she yelled, but stopped dead when she noted the mess and Basher's distraught face.

"Oh... no... don't tell me... you've lost it!"

"I don't ever remember destroying it" Basher said, as she looked around her desperately.

June's face lit up like a beacon. "Tell you what, why don't you take this copy to work, then when you've got a minute type it out on one of your machines. How's *that* for a bloody good brain wave?"

Basher grinned from 'earhole to breakfast time'. "Hey... you clever bastard, why didn't I think of that? I'll do two copies while I'm at it. It will be easier to read and look more professional." she stated.

Just at that moment one of the Geordie's arrived and threw a small packet on to Basher's bed saying; "Here you are hinny, mail for you."

Basher looked puzzled as she picked up the package. She carefully scrutinised the handwriting with a great intensity.

"Don't just stand there looking like a prize pillock, There's only one way of finding out what's in it and that's to open it!" June remarked, clearly as anxious to know the contents as her friend. Basher grinned at her mate's remarks before ripping open the package. Then to her immense shock a dozen or so wedding invitations tumbled all over the bed. Basher picked one up and with a face like stone began to read the contents... The date, time and place all danced before her eyes... this was an invitation to her *own* wedding!

The room swam before her, and her hand began to shake as she pushed the strewn contents of her locker to one side. She sat down with a heavy thud before declaring to her mate "I just don't believe this... look!" as she threw the invitations across the bed.

Whilst her mate was taking in the incredibility of the situation Basher tore open the envelope containing a letter. She recognised her father's writing. It read;

"After you left the other day, Paul, your mother and I had a serious chat. We thought the best way of resolving your problem was to fix a date for your wedding as quickly as possible. We all agreed that as your airman friend had let you down so badly, there was a possibility that your pride might stand in your way. So we decoded to make it easier for you. As you can see the date and time of your wedding is all set. We have seen the vicar and booked the church. We also have the use of the Salvation Army hall for your reception. Your mother managed to borrow a white wedding dress, which luckily is complete with veil and head dress. Your baby sister Rosemary is to be bridesmaid and her dress is all ready made.

We automatically assumed you would want your sister Mary as your chief bridesmaid and her dress has also been made, she is absolutely over the moon about this. All the invitations have been sent to both sides of the family and I've enclosed a few for your own personal friends Of course if you have a preference for a third bridesmaid that will be acceptable to us, but she will have to provide her own gown as all of our clothing coupons have been used up. We trust that you are as excited about this, as we in the family are. Paul returned a much happier man than when you last saw him. It's so generous of him to forgive you so easily. I hope these arrangements meet with your approval. Much love... Dad x x x x x

Basher's mouth opened and shut with every line that she read.

"You look as if you've seen a ghost. What's going on?" June asked.

"Just read this! Ever had the feeling your life's been taken over?"

June looked at Basher half way through reading the letter and glared at her in astonishment.

"Read on!" Basher yelled.

When the sheer enormity of the situation finally sunk in, June spoke "For the first time in my life I'm speechless. Doesn't your family listen to how you feel and what your wishes are? Are they dumb, stupid or what?" she asked angrily.

Basher's emotions of anger, despair and disbelief were almost engulfing her.

She replied barely above a whisper. "My father has some wonderful characteristics, but his weakness is controlling everyone else's life except his own. His star role is playing God." He clearly didn't believe her when she told him she felt it to be more honest to end her relationship with Paul and that Ron didn't come into the equation. It was something she had worked out for herself. To *want* to meet up with someone new put into question the validity of her depth of love for Paul and therefore she wanted to end the relationship, but her father had missed the point totally.

June flung her arms in the air in desperation begging of her mate not to allow this to happen.

But Basher wept in defeat, yelling "What *can* I do? The invitations have gone out!"

June grabbed her mate by the shoulders and shook her. "I don't care if you were half way up the aisle, if you don't want to marry this guy then *don't* for Christ's sake. You'll live to regret it, you mark my words."

Basher sat down heavily on her bed and wiped her eyes before explaining in some depth to her friend that on her mother's side of the family she had always had to put up with being judged and criticised by most of her mother's sisters. They made it clear they had a low opinion of her, and were sitting in the wings just waiting for her to put a foot wrong. Already they had judged her for letting go of the religion she had been brought up with, which of course was theirs too. So before she started she was a hethen.

"If I were to cancel this wedding they would have a field day, particularly as Paul has a physical handicap. I'll leave you to guess what I would be accused of."

June began pacing the floor. She swung on Basher and yelled "But you aren't marrying your bloody family, or your mother's family come to that!"

"You don't know them. Furthermore I daren't think what Paul's mother would make of it. She'd eat me for breakfast and then spit me out!" Basher yelled back in desperation.

June stopped her pacing, and now stood in front of Basher with feet apart and hands on hips. "You really do surprise me Bash. I thought you were made of tougher stuff than this. I wouldn't allow anyone to rule my life to this extent, it's bloody criminal." she said in frustration.

Basher threw the contents of her locker back in the drawer and the invitations with it. Turning to her mate she suggested the entire issue be dropped for the time being. She couldn't think straight at this stage and needed some time and space to think this all through. June agreed. Shrugging her shoulders she said she felt bushed, and was going to get her head down. Basher suspected that her mate was so angry with the entire situation, and not being able to understand the position she found herself in, that she felt compelled to leave the room.

Basher was glad of the space it had given her, to think through the bombshell that had just been dropped into her lap. Once alone Basher took the contents of her locker drawer out again and began to tidy it up.

Finally taking her father's letter from the envelope she read it through again. Her blood boiled as she confirmed that she most certainly had not been mistaken the first time round. Finding her notepad she sat down to begin her response;

Dear Dad,

I'm still reeling from the shock at the contents of your letter and invitations that I have just received. When will you listen Dad? I wanted to end the relationship with Paul. The fact that Ron let me down was not the point at issue. I discovered that Paul didn't come up to my expectations as a future partner. The very fact that in a most innocent way I responded to Ron, meant as far as I was concerned, my feelings for Paul were in doubt, and that equated to not being ready for marriage. I did raise all of these issues with you at the time, but perhaps seeing it down on paper, and spelling it out to you, it might just sink in.

You have played your role of 'god' just once too often, and consequently backed me into a corner. I can either refuse to go along with your Master Plan and risk the slings and arrows of the entire family on both sides, or I go along with it....

I have searched my soul and learned within the last few moments that I don't have the courage to do the former, therefore you get your own way, let's hope you are happy and proud. I will do my best to make it work. If it doesn't well... I will know who to blame!"

By the time the letter was written, read through and posted, Basher had a thundering headache. She lay on her bed and fell into fitful sleep.

The morning shift was well into its stride as Basher and June took their coffee break together, for the first time in quite a while.

"Heard anymore about the rehearsals?" asked June as she sipped her coffee

"Yes it's tomorrow night. By the way have you seen Sir about it yet?"

"Haven't seen him in days." June replied.

"He's been on leave." the corporal butted in, "I think he was due back last night... ah... talk of the devil..." she said as Warrant Officer Pratt strolled into the section.

"You seem to have a nose for the coffee pot" the corporal said to him.

"That's what becomes of being so observant" he responded rubbing his hands.

"Being crafty more like!"

He glanced around the assembled staff, ignored the corporal's last remark, dipped into the biscuit tin and said "Any problems corporal?"

"No, not really, nothing I couldn't handle at least. The place doesn't come to a shuddering halt in your absence, you know. Anyway had a good leave?"

"Wonderful! plenty of hard graft down on the farm. My father has got several Land Army girls working for him so it eases the burden. Damned hard workers they are too, put this lot to shame, I can tell you."

June and Basher exchanged glances. What a bloody cheek Basher thought, never misses an opportunity to have a go at us.

The corporal threw back her head and laughed before daring to suggest to him "By the twinkle in your eye, it looks as though you got you hand in with them... or your leg over, one or the other."

The Warrant Officer went scarlet at this remark then swung on the corporal, "That is most un-professional of you corporal, and not like you to be so coarse. No doubt what comes of working with these two!" he said nodding in the direction of June and Basher.

Basher could see by June's face that she too was boiling over at his catty remarks. So decided to get one in, by bringing up the subject of the rehearsals. Slowly but deliberately she addressed him in the most polite manner, explaining how the pilot/producer had suddenly returned to base and was about to launch into a second attempt at a camp concert. Smiling as she pointed out that the rehearsals were taking place the following night, and making it abundantly clear that the officer had approached them both personally as he particularly wanted them in his show.

"He did what!?" The Warrant Officer replied, unable to believe his ears.

"He escaped the Germans and came back with the help of the French Resistance." June told him.

Warrant Officer Pratt's face turned from red to purple as he glared from Basher to June.

"I thought it was too bloody good to be true. I hardly have time to catch breathe from a wonderful leave to have this lot thrown at me. This means yet another upheaval of the shift system. How many times a week does he propose to hold these rehearsals?"

Basher intervened at this point, trying hard to hide her delight at having him by the 'short and curlies'.

"I would imagine at least twice a week, because he has to start from scratch and find a new cast." The boss drained his cup, turned on his heel and marched out, clearly not pleased with what he had just heard.

June turned her back on the assembled staff and stared out of the window. Then when she was certain that Basher was well within earshot, she said out of the corner of her mouth.

"I really enjoyed that. I knew it would upset the apple cart. He's so up himself, that one day he'll meet himself coming back!"

CHAPTER 10

A group of around forty people were sat in the first few rows of the camp theatre as June and Basher entered. They were late because their working substitutes had turned up at a quarter to seven instead of a quarter past six. Both girls seriously suspected this to be the handiwork of the boss.

"Ah, here comes the last two! Thought you might have had second thoughts" the producer announced.

"Sorry sir but we've only just been relieved from our duty." June explained apologetically. The producer assured them not to worry.

He explained to the rest of the cast that these two were known as the cockney twins, and were in the original show. Then looking at them enquiringly he asked "By the way are you related at all? Because the similarity is quite astounding." Basher assured him they were just mates.

Then turning his attention to the new members of cast he explained how they were to open the show.   June turned to Basher and pointed out that the cross eyed man was still with them.

"Don't bloody start" Basher said nudging her mate. The producer was now leaning across the rows of people and handing out song sheets. Then addressing the two girls he said "I'm aware that you both know this, but there are many here who don't. We will now begin from scratch and learn the opening number." he added addressing the full cast.

"Is this show to be the same as the original then?" Basher asked.

"Yes more or less, but with one or two additions. For the benefit of those who were in the original show, I have now auditioned the new cast and the choice as you can see is now made."

"The pianist is Flying Officer Edward's." He rose from the piano and bowed.

"Then we have Sergeant Taffy Jones, who has a magnificent Welsh voice, and Flight Lieutenant Saunders is our Australian cousin who does a pretty mean drag act."

Wolf whistles rang around the theatre at this announcement.

"So come on everybody settle down. Lets have the intro Terry." the producer requested of the pianist.

"WE ARE BIRDS OF A FEATHER, 78 IS OUR NAME..." they all sang.

As the opening number finished one of the newcomers asked "What does it mean '78 is our name? Because it doesn't even rhyme."

The producer glared at the new cast member before he addressed the entire cast "There always has to be one! ...I wrote this song and it's not suppose to rhyme. In case it has escaped your notice he began sarcastically, we are 78 squadron RAF Breighton... yes? Now you understand where the 78 comes in?

Right now, one more time please, then we line up on stage and I'll teach you the dance routine that goes with it."

Whispers from the newcomers in the cast could be

heard saying "He's got to be joking"!

The producer ignored the sly remarks and lined them up in true chorus girl style. The introductory music began and the opening number was sung with great gusto with legs kicking in the air in unison

The producer seemed reasonably pleased with their first effort. Then came the turn of the Welsh singer... *"I'll be seeing you in all the old familiar places.."*.

They all clapped enthusiastically and June made a rare comment about his wonderful voice. Basher said she could listen to him all night

It was now the turn of the drag queen. Basher wondered whether he would be any better than the original two. He certainly looked uneasy, fidgeted for a while then turned to the producer.

"I feel so bloody bare without me props mate" But the producer was adamant that he would have to improvise until the dress rehearsal. His cultured voice sounded such a contrast to the broad Australian airgunner. Settling down once again, his voice rose several octaves higher as he began his patter, and this big burly Aussie was transformed "Hi possums... fancy seeing yous here. Remember the last time we met?

It was at the Cross, and for the benefit of the pommies present we don't mean Kings Cross here in London, do we possums? Na... we mean the *real* Cross... Kings Cross Sydney, you know... where the likes of you and me has our spooky bit of fun!"

The producer jumped up waving his papers and interrupted the Aussie's flow "Hold it... hold it... I don't like this idea of participation with the audience. It's not at all clear to whom you are addressing. Is there anyone you could use as a stooge? I'll show you what I mean. Come up here you cockney twins. Do your act, and he'll get the gist of what I mean."

June and Basher sailed through their act without a script. The producer turned to the Aussie and said "Now do you understand? Your script is magic but it definitely needs a stooge, someone who just stands and agrees with you. Will you think about it and see what you can come up with?"

"Sure mate... no worries." the Australian officer replied.

The boss eyed bloke was up on stage ripping forth into *'We'll run them in, we'll run them in....'* Basher glanced at the theatre clock. It was just gone eight.

"We've still a hell of a lot to get through." she remarked to her mate grinning from ear to ear.

"Yep we won't get back to our section tonight that's for sure. And you can take that grin off yer face, I know what yer laughing at."

"I can't help it. He still has the ability to crack me up."

Then suddenly the tannoy blared "Will all aircrew report to the briefing room please."

The aircrew in the cast ran for the exit. June looked aghast "Oh my Christ not again! Don't tell me, every time we get this concert going we are in danger of losing the cast."

Both girls were aware that the producer was still with them. "Aren't you included in the briefing sir? Basher asked.

"No not yet. I'm grounded for the time being."

June remarked that at least we had a producer this time, but he reminded them that a producer was not much use without a full cast. The girls suggested they all look on the bright side this time, perhaps they would get lucky.

The producer told the girls that it was a wrap for the night, as their was no point in continuing without a full cast.

The girls mounted their bikes and June suggested that they should return to the section, as the boss would know about the forthcoming raid, and would assume it to be the end of the rehearsal.

"So... you've decided to join us have you?" Warrant Officer Pratt announced as both girls entered the section.

"We could hardly continue rehearsals with half the cast going off an yet another raid now could we?" Basher announced sarcastically.

He marched up and down with his hands clasped behind his back. Then with a half turn said "Well... it happened before lets pray for a repeat performance. After all there must be a limit to how many idiots there are among aircrew who agree to cavorting about on stage. Bloody perverts if you ask me!"

June stood rooted to the spot, she was livid. Her face flushed and her eyes almost popping out of her head. She had never experienced his wrath in relation to aircrew before. She was obviously livid. Basher held her breath whilst June walked slowing toward her boss. Standing in front of him she squared her shoulders before looking him straight in the eye and blurting out'

"With respect *SIR!* It would seem it is *you* who is the pervert. How you could ever consider thinking, never mind hoping, that those boys wouldn't return from a raid, exceeds even the bounds of perversion... it is bloody evil. You are so wrapped up with your own power and arrogance, that provided your nose isn't put out of joint you don't give a stuff what happens to others. What is worse you actually wish them dead!" And with a look of utter contempt June swept out and marched into her switchboard room.

The Warrant Officer's mouth opened and shut in one movement, but now it was Basher's turn.

"If we were to lower ourselves to your level, we could quite easily inform the producer and cast of the camp show - in particular the aircrew - of your views. Frankly they would make mincemeat of you. These boys don't cavort as you so delicately put it. They make a real contribution to the show itself. There are some magnificent talent on camp. But you wouldn't know talent if it were to hit you in the eye." Basher then turned away and joined June in the switchboard room.

The Boss followed, and with a face the colour of beetroot he began to snivel "Come on girls I was only joking, what's up with you two? Thought you were the jokers of the camp. Come on.... where's your sense of humour gone?"

Both girls knew that the threats they had just dished out were a blow bellow the belt. They had always suspected he was a coward at heart. So rather than prolong the argument they simply glared at him in silence... a silence that could have cut the air with a knife. He ran his finger around the edge of his collar before saying "Look, you may as well go back to your quarters. Everything is under control here. So off you go... see you both in the morning."

The bleak miserable November day did nothing to enthuse Basher to go out on her day off. She hated the winter. The girls at Heslington Hall weren't wrong when they said it could get cold in Yorkshire!

She had risen at eight thirty that morning to go for breakfast. Normally she would lie in on her day off and miss the meal, but today she was starving.

The ground was covered in a light smattering of frost and the wind a bitingly cold one. On her return she huddled around the belly stove to defrost her fingers and toes for they were numb. One of the cooks arrived from her early morning duty.

"Gees it's cold out there. Is it your day off hinny?"

"Sure is, but not a clue what I'm going to do. I was going into York but I'm blowed if I'm going all that way to freeze to death" she said despondently.

The day dragged on endlessly. She had slept until lunch time, then sorted out her laundry parcelled it up and by mid-afternoon had washed her 'smells'.

June barged in and sat down on Basher's bed, "Heard the latest?" she asked.

"Nope... heard nothing." Basher said depressingly.

"Well... it's only a rumour at the moment. But the girls reckon old pratt face has been posted."

Basher's face beamed a huge smile and she brightened up immediately.

"You're joking! Thank god for small mercies. He was

beginning to get right up my nose."

"Wonder who'll replace him?" June queried.

"Let's make sure the bugger's going first."

"How can we find out for certain? June asked as she rubbed her chin.

"My corporal will know. She's dead thick with him. I'll ask her tomorrow cos she'll be on duty the same time as me."

June said she hoped that nobody would have the gall to collect for a going away present because her contribution would be a bottle of rat poison!

Both girls laughed. Basher then suggested they went to the NAFFI as she was fresh out of things to do. June agreed with the suggestion and said it was time that they lived dangerously. As they made their way to the forces canteen the sun had broken through the overcast sky and shone a watery light over the surrounding fields. There was no substance of heat coming from it. The wind had dropped, but the temperatures remained at freezing point.

Patterns were beginning to form on the trees and bushes that surrounded the airfield, and hung like spiders webs glistening in the rays of the sun and beginning to take the form of a true winters scene. As they rode they bikes along the tarmac of the runway their round plump races glowed.

The NAFFI was warm by comparison. Taking off their gloves they put their fingers in their mouths to get the feeling back. By the time they had ordered their tea and buns life was beginning to return in the nether regions of their bodies. But they now suffered the tingling burning sensation as the blood once again flowed freely through them. Settling down into armchairs Basher asked of her mate "What yer doing at Christmas... got any leave?"

"Haven't got a bloody clue" June replied.

"What about Ted, has he got time off ?"

"I doubt it. They've been waiting for ages to move on, but Christ knows when.

"Surely they wouldn't move them out so near to Christmas?"

"Do me a favour there's a war on in case you hadn't noticed? They don't care about things like Christmas. If necessary they'll go Christmas Day." June said.

"What do they call your feller? You never did get around to telling me."

"Ted you mindless bugger, I told you ages ago." June said exasperated with her mate.

"Yes I know that. It's his surname that I meant."

Jean grinned and told her mate that she wouldn't believe her if she told her, but Basher was adamant and told her to try her. So with dead pan face June explained that his name was Love.

"You pillock you're having me on!" Basher yelled.

But June insisted his name was Ted Love. Basher screamed with laughter.

"Now I've bloody heard it all. How yer going to feel being called Mrs Love?"

"Better than Mrs Pratt any day. Anyway he hasn't asked me to marry him yet, and I doubt he ever will."

Basher wanted to know why she should assume such a thing? After all he had taken her to meet his family. But June didn't seem to think it meant anything special. She said Basher would understand more if she knew her man.

The two girls had now gone through two cups of tea and several buns. Just then Basher spotted the corporal. "Hey hold on, I want a word with her" Basher said getting up from her seat. As the corporal made her way to the counter Basher caught up and stopped her.

"Is it true that Warrant Officer Pratt has been posted?"

"Yes... the confirmation came through this morning. He's going overseas somewhere. It was a bit of a rushed job by all accounts" the corporal said. Basher had difficulty in hiding her delight, but continued asking who was going to replace him.

The corporal said that because it was so unexpected there would be no replacement for a time. She assumed she would be in charge.

"Oh that's good. Better get going. Cheers, see you in the morning." Basher said as she belted back to join June to confirm the rumour.

June was as relieved as Basher, but said in some respects she would miss the excitement of the row's they had with him.

"Well you speak for yourself, because I bloody wont. Can't see the back of him fast enough. He was a pain in the arse!" Basher said emphatically.

CHAPTER 11

After their evening meal both girls parted company at their living quarters. Basher settled down to catch up with her mail that was long overdue.

At around seven o clock the hut door burst open and a strange corporal stood on the threshold panting "Are you Troxson?" she asked urgently.

"No, I'm Berry." The corporal looked exasperated and clearly wanted to discharge her responsibility.

"Well Troxson is wanted on the phone, some guy called Ted" the corporal explained falling over her words clearly in a rush to return to the guard room.

"Oh my God! OK leave it with me I'll call next door and see if she's in.

"I've not seen her since supper." Basher explained.

"Any idea where June is? Basher asked her hut mates as she stood on the threshold of her hut.

"Yep... in the bath" one of the girls explained.

"Right... thanks" Basher said. Then realising that Ted would perhaps be calling long distance, she thought that perhaps she should take a message. So rushing to the guard room she picked up the phone and panting like mad she managed to call out... "Hallo…"

"Is that you June?"

"No, June's in the bath. I'm Basher her mate."

"Ah... the other half! Hi! Look Basher this is urgent. Tell June to get a forty-eight hour leave pass, as from tomorrow, as I'm off overseas and have just two days leave. Tell her I've got a special licence and we're getting married!"

"What!" Basher yelled down the phone. "Cheers mate... congratulations! Don't worry I'll tell her Ted. I suggest you ring tomorrow around eleven she should have everything sewn up by then. You can then make your final arrangements." Basher suggested, now as excited as if it were her own romantic proposal she was responding to. Then throwing the phone back on its cradle she ran hell for leather to the ablution block. As she entered she yelled "June! June! You in there?"

"Can't I have a bath in bleedin' peace?" June complained from one of the six cubicles. Basher attempted to follow the voice, but began banging on all the doors urgently, to find which one her mate was in.

"Let me in... it's urgent June!"

As Basher stumbled into the bathroom that June had now unlocked, she sat down on the edge of the bath and grasping the edge tried to control her breathing.

"Christ this must be urgent" June said, "What's the problem, has the pissin' war ended, or what?"

"I hope you're ready for this... Ted rang."

June immediately grabbed the side of the bath her knuckles turning white as she gripped so tightly.

"What's up... he's not gone has he?" she asked frantically.

"Not quite, but he's due to go within the next forty eight hours." Basher explained, as she hung out the most important bit of news.

"That's it... I'm getting compassionate leave Bash.

He's not going till I've seen him" June said as her eyes brimmed over with tears.

"Whoa! Whoa! you certainly will need leave mate, because he told me he has a special licence... you are *GETTING MARRIED!!"*

With one enormous splash June jumped up, wetting Basher in the process. Then realising she was starkers folded her hands in front of her. When she finally caught her breath she yelled "He's done what? ...go through it again Bash only this time slowly." June responded, clearly unable to fully comprehend that she had actually been proposed to by proxy.

Basher once again went through the explanation that Ted had asked her to pass on, ending up with "You're getting married me old mate!"

June's mind appeared to go into confusion mode, as she yelled statements at Basher asking "How, When?" before adding she had nothing to wear, and no money for a reception, never mind a wedding cake!

Basher tried to calm her friend down, by reiterating that Ted was ringing the next day, and suggested that her first priority was to get her leave agreed, before ringing her mother, who Basher felt certain would come to her rescue. Finally she took the hands of her friend congratulated her, and added "What the hell June... as long as you're happy."

June's face flushed with excitement and suddenly as the impact of the last few moments hit her, and despite the fact that she was starkers, she began to sing as she slid slowly back down into the bath. *"When you're knees go knockety knock, it's LOVE, LOVE, LOVE!!"*

She then turned on the hot tap, as she prepared to soak

for a while longer and give herself time to digest this wonderful news.

The following day Basher went to an early lunch and just managed to arrive at June's hut as she was emerging with full kit.

"Thank God I caught you. I couldn't let you go without wishing you all the luck in the world mate."

June grinned but her eyes were brimming with emotional tears.

Both girls walked in silence to the main gate. How Basher envied her friend. She was going to the man she loved so dearly. Although Basher had never met Ted and only spoken briefly on the phone, she knew by the way her mate talked about their relationship that this was without doubt, a perfect union. If only it were me she thought as she kicked stones ahead of her.

The roar of the bus engine could be heard. They had to hurry to the last few yards as the bus to York was just pulling in. Basher hugged her mate and said simply "Be happy" June smiled as she boarded the bus that was to take her on the first part of her journey into her new life.

The weekend stretched before her like an open chasm. What the hell could she do with no work? She missed her mate already for they did everything together, it was like losing a limb. Her thoughts rampaged as she sat down miserably to eat her lunch. It was then she realised she had left her script back in the office and decided to collect it after lunch.

"We're expecting a very busy weekend Bash, any chance of doing some extra shifts?" the corporal asked.

"Not a problem, would be glad to. I'm at a real loose end."

During that afternoon Form B's began arriving thick and fast. As Basher perused them she realised that raids were planned over the entire weekend.

Forest De Nieppe The Flying Bomb storage was earmarked for the 1st, 2nd and 3rd. The first batch of aircraft left that very evening, and as one lot returned another took off. The entire squadron was a beehive of activity as mechanics got to work on returned planes in readiness to turn them around for take off a few hours later. Tannoy systems were constantly calling for aircrew, and teleprinters rattled non-stop. With each raid we lost at least two aircraft. Basher became increasingly concerned about the cast of the show. Having lost one lot she was carefully monitoring which aircraft her camp concert colleagues were in, and began scrutinising every one as they returned.

With this amount of activity and work, the weekend passed very quickly much to Basher's relief.

The camp concert was about to perform very soon, so as the last wave of bombers returned safely that Sunday afternoon, Basher made her way back to her hut, with a feeling of well being and joy that the cast of the show remained intact. She lay on her bed and shut her eyes in sheer exhaustion.

Having been violently shaken, she thought she was dreaming as she came from deep sleep to find her mate June standing by her bed. Basher blinked and then gazed at her mate trying to focus. She was astounded to find it was half nine in the evening. She automatically jumped up and greeted her friend.

"Hallo me old mate, how did it all go?"

June stood in silence the tears welling in her eyes as she whispered "Care to come for a walk?"

"Sure... no problem" Basher said, grabbing her overcoat and pushing her arms into it. They walked in silence for some time. Basher wanted to give her friend some space as she sensed an overwhelming sadness. Soon they were on the runway. They strolled along the path that aircraft usually take. Then June suddenly blurted out "He's gone Bash... left this morning... don't know what I'm going to do without him" she said as she burst into tears.

Basher was shocked to find her friend in such an emotional state. This man must have touched a cord in her that no-one had ever before reached.

Basher put her arm around the shoulder of her mate, reassuring that everything would be all right, that he would come back.

Basher had no idea why she felt so positive about this, when every second of every day men were being mowed down and killed in this dreadful war.

Then in an attempt to cheer her mate up she said "Come on mate I want all the lurid details. How did it all go?"

June blew her nose and wiped her eyes before going into the finer detail of her wedding weekend. She explained that her Mum and family were wonderful. How the hell they managed it all at such short notice, she had no idea. For they had organised a new suit and hat for me.

The wedding took place at nine on the Saturday morning and the entire family turned up. My Mum even organised a wedding breakfast at her place complete with cake! I was speechless I can tell you. Ted had booked a hotel at Windsor. He wanted to get of London because of the raids.

The hotel held a dance that night and guess what? I actually danced with him, me the anti-dancer! It was as if the dance was just for the two of us. They played, what has become our own special tune... *'I'll be seeing you in all the old familiar places'*

June began to cry again as she painfully recalled the most poignant moment of her short honeymoon. The hotel room had a balcony overlooking the Thames so romantic.

The management sported a bottle of sparkling wine from somewhere under somebody's counter, no doubt. At least we could pretend it was champers.

We sat on the balcony sipping our wine and watching the moon dance on the water.

"Wasn't it freezing? Basher asked.

"Probably... but we didn't feel a thing. Just a warm glow came from inside, but very difficult to describe. Anyway Ted put the wireless on, and blow me there it was again... haunting us... he took my hand and we danced cheek to cheek all around the balcony *'I'll be seeing you in every lovely summer's day...'* it was the most romantic moment of my life" June said with tears streaming down her face.

"Never mind," soothed Basher "At least you've had all those lovely memories to keep you going till he comes back."

CHAPTER 12

The night of the Christmas camp show had arrived. The producer had carefully planned this date before the personnel left for their Christmas leave.

The theatre was festooned with paper chains and balloons. A huge Christmas tree stood to the left of the stage with lights twinkling from its branches, whilst a fairy was perched precariously on the top.

The theatre was packed to the rafters. The front row was reserved for the Commanding Officer and his lady, whilst various senior staff officers filled the next the row behind.

The producer was now ready having made certain that the cast were in place on stage in readiness for the opening number.

Then checking that the VIP's were in place his voice boomed out...

"Ladies and Gentlemen... the King!"

Someone from the back shouted "Joe for King!" as the pianist rumbled through the opening bars of the national anthem. Chairs scraped across the floor as the audience rose and stood erect, until the last strains of the anthem died away.

The producer then announced... "Ladies and Gentlemen seventy eight squadron proudly present for your entertainment... *BIRDS OF A FEATHER.*"

The cast were lined up behind closed curtains, their

arms around the waist of the other.

The feather tiaras precariously perched on the heads of the females. Basher was certain hers would fall off at the very least, when she did her high kick. The smart white blouses with black dicky bows with an airforce blue waistcoat with gold button and matching coloured short skirts complete with skimpy black knickers underneath, certainly looked smart and very professional.

"Here we go mate" whispered June. "Give it all you've got!"

"Providing I don't break my rotten legs in the process" Basher managed to reply before the curtain swung open.

The audience erupted into screaming and whistling as the cast cavorted and kicked their legs high to the opening song. The various song and dance acts did their own individual pieces, and got the applause they so richly deserved.

Then came the turn of the two girls. The scenery experts had made a very lavish back drop of a working class street, complete with a brick wall adjoining the back yard. The girls were dressed in aprons that covered the whole of the top of their bodies which could only been seen by the audience, as they both leaned on the wall. June had a grey wig with a bun, while Basher had her own hair in curlers and tied with as scarf. As they got into the flow of their sketch the audience rocked in their seats with laughter. Then suddenly Basher 'dried' as she lost the flow of the script, but quickly began to ad-lib. June cleverly picked it up and responded promptly until she carefully led them both back into the script again, which Basher was then able to recall.

The producer hissed from the wings "Hurry it up you've gone over your allotted time." Finally they brought it to an end with a thunderous applause.

The cast assembled in the large dressing room having removed all the heavy make-up, and were enjoying the refreshments that had been provided. The producer stood on a chair and thanked them all for their tremendous effort at making the show such a success.

Just as he climbed down the Commanding Officer entered. Silence fell, and the company stood rigidly to attention. He momentarily looked uneasy as he glanced at the chair appearing indecisive as whether to clamber up as well. But he finally chose to stand where he was.

"That was a magnificent show. Your producer has done us all proud. If he follows this profession once this ghastly war is over he should do well," he said rather patronisingly. "However, it could not have been done without you boys and girls... good show... you are all very talented and none of you should be short of a job in civvy street when the time comes. So thank you once again."

The producer stood to attention and saluted him as he left the room. June turned to Basher "Hope you feel better for those few words. According to him you should be a budding writer when this lots over. What a berk! A right Hooray Henry if you ask me."

"I agree, a bit of a pillock. He ought to do some research before opening his gob. How patronising telling the producer he should get a job in civvy street, he's already a well known producer in civvy street! Where do they get off these stupid people? Don't know about you but my back's killing me, probably all that high kicking we've done. I'm completely bushed."

"I must admit to feeling a bit stuffed myself. And me hips are painful" June complained as she rubbed them.

Shortly after Christmas the camp began to fill up again as personnel came back from leave. The raids began to gather momentum and soon everyone was back in the business of winning the war in Europe.

Basher gazed at the calendar and realised with a jolt it was little over five months before her own wedding day. The realisation didn't inspire her with any joy, but she vowed that she would do her best and would make the most of it.

"Penny for them?" June said as she popped her head around the door of Basher's office. "Dreaming oh my darling love of thee?" she teased.

"Piss off" Basher said irritably.

"Keep yer bloody hair on... see... I was right... not even in the church doorway, and it's irritating you to death. Come on mate, do yerself a favour, get rid. Bugger the consequences."

Basher didn't need reminding that this could be one of the worst moves in her life. In total frustration she yelled at her mate that she just couldn't back out.

June flung her arms in the air shouting "Alright! You've made you're point, it's your life. But yer me mate and I hate to see yer wasting it. I have such a bad feeling about it. However I also have some good news. I'm pregnant! Which means I can get out of this lot, and be ready for my Ted when the war is over. He's a regular soldier so I will be able to join him where ever he is posted."

Basher forgot her own problems in that moment. Her face lit up as she congratulated June on her good news, and told her how much she would miss her. Then it dawned on her that she would not have her around when it came to talking over the lurid details of her own wedding. June looked sad momentarily and told Basher that a little bird had told her that she was to be posted back to Headquarters! She grimaced as she waited for Basher to explode.

"You've got to be joking! Oh my God! Fancy being there permanently" Basher groaned at the prospect.

"Hey come on... cheer up. I thought you rather liked it when you were there on loan?" June queried.

Basher admitted that she had got used to it. June pointed out that by all accounts it wouldn't be for long before the war is over. Our boys are rampaging through Europe. I reckon it's only a matter of weeks, so you won't have long to do. If you put in for your discharge the moment you get back from your wedding leave, you should get priority being married to a civilian... and that's about the only good thing about it." June remarked not being able to resist a further dig.

Basher agreed that she had been so busy sorting out her own affairs that she hadn't taken that much notice of the news items, but agreed it did sound promising.

June suggested that when they got off duty, they start to sort things out. She would go to the sick bay to have her pregnancy confirmed, and she advised Basher to sort our her wedding leave at the admin office.

The Toch H in the De Grey Rooms in York was alive a few weeks later as Basher sat amongst strangers in the same seat that her and her mate June had occupied some three weeks previously. The bells of York Minister peeled out their victory message as crowds fill the quaint Roman streets and joined in the dancing.

Basher joined in the song... *"With someone like you, a pal good and true..."*

She paused for a moment wondering what her old mate June was doing right at that moment. She had now been left the camp over a week, and as a civilian would be waiting to join her beloved Ted.

Just then the music changed and the strains of.... *'I'll be seeing you in all the old familiar places...'* rang through the canteen. The crowd sang full of emotion, whilst bitter sweet tears welled in Basher's eyes as the nostalgic memories of her mate were recalled. What a pity she wasn't here just for this moment, Basher thought. We could have celebrated the very thing we had worked so hard to achieve. She wanted to tell her that her father's wishes had come true after all, the war was well and truly over before she married.

Basher wiped the nostalgic tears from her eyes as she sat on the veranda in the Newcastle suburb of Australia and said to June.

"Ready for another bottle mate?"

"Why not, it's thirsty work this reminiscing." Basher laughed as she stepped indoors to collect another Chardonnay from the fridge.

As the wine was being poured June said "Don't tell me Simon's dead?"

"No, I managed to remain married to him for nineteen years. We are divorced, and he's re-married now. So it's water under the bridge."

"I never thought it would last that long" June said in all honesty.

"It became a very painful experience and one I wouldn't care to repeat. What about you, what happened to Ted?"

"He died in tragic circumstances" June said, her eyes welling with tears, "I don't want to talk about it. Did you re-marry as well?" she finally asked.

"Mate the sagas that followed that marriage breakdown would take three novels to explain, and put me through the wringer in the process." Basher said.

"I guess we've both had our fair share mate. Now it's time for a new start in a new country. What an unbelievable coincidence that all these years later we meet up again in a different country the other side of the world! Reckon we could find some of those hunky aircrew that were stationed at Breighton?"

Basher threw back her head and laughed. "They're probably as old and decrepit as we are mate"

"That suits me," said June, "But we could have a good laugh and a walk down memory lane, especially if we find the one who caught you with your drawers down in a field having a pee!"